LOCKED IN SILENCE

PELICAN BAY #1

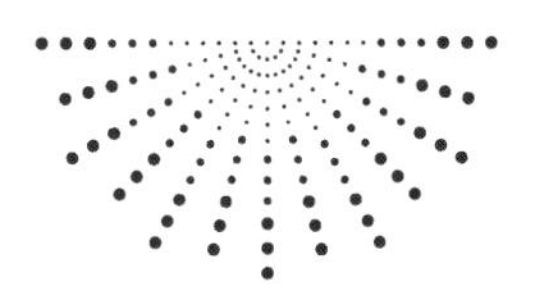

SLOANE KENNEDY

CONTENTS

Published in the United States by Sloane Kennedy

Copyediting by Courtney Bassett

ISBN-13:
978-1976149948

ISBN-10:
1976149940

LOCKED IN SILENCE

Sloane Kennedy

TRADEMARK ACKNOWLEDGEMENTS

The author acknowledges the trademarked status and trademark owners of the following trademarks mentioned in this work of fiction:

Buick
Jeep
Grindr
Google
Stradivarius
Avengers
Marvel Comics
D.C. Comics
Disney World
Etsy
Disney's Cars
Matchbox
Etsy

ACKNOWLEDGMENTS

A big thank you to Lucy Lennox for "special ordering" this book and for the quick and entertaining beta read (and no, I'm not ever letting you off the hook for what happened at the 91% mark)!

Thank you to Claudia and Kylee for the helpful feedback and to Courtney for the thorough proofing job!

As always, thank you to my soul sisters, Claudia, Kylee and Mari for your love and support! (And yes Mari, I am dedicating this book to you because you're so pretty)

PROLOGUE

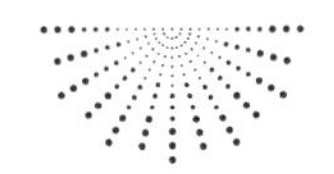

Nolan

God, I hated the cold.

Hell, it wasn't even that cold yet, but October in Minnesota and October in sunny California were two very different animals. Of course, pretty much everything was a different animal when it came to pitting the Land of Ten Thousand Lakes against the Golden State.

"Slow down, Nolan," my mother groused as she leaned across the console and lifted her glasses enough so she could study the speedometer. "You're not in Hollywood anymore," she reminded me as she leaned back and focused on her knitting needles once again.

Don't do it.

Don't do it.

I chanted the words to myself several times and then did it anyway.

"San Francisco," I murmured.

Why, Nolan? Just why?

I shook my head at my inner voice because I didn't have an answer for that.

"What, dear?" my mother asked without looking up.

"I was in San Francisco, Mom." I took my eyes off the road long enough to glance at her. "San Francisco, not Los Angeles."

She didn't answer. She just took her hand off one knitting needle long enough to wave her hand.

Dismissed.

As usual.

I sighed and forced my attention back to the road. I was never going to make it. I'd been home for less than twenty-four hours and I felt like I was going to bust out of my skin.

Home.

Knowing my mother wouldn't notice, I shook my head. Pelican Bay, Minnesota wasn't home for me. It never had been. Yeah, I'd spent my first eighteen years here, but it hadn't ever been home. At best, it was purgatory.

A harsh comparison? Maybe. But after having experienced the freedom that came with living anywhere but Pelican Bay, I supposed I was just a little more than biased about the subject.

My mother clucked her tongue as she glanced at the radio. "Need to be home by four or I'll have to pay Mrs. Kellogg for another hour."

I wasn't sure what to say to that comment. I certainly couldn't tell her what I wanted to. That we wouldn't be late if she wasn't such a control freak when it came to driving. Or that maybe if she hadn't spent an extra twenty minutes complaining to anyone who would listen at the medical device supply company about the price of the walker we'd gone there to purchase, we wouldn't be running behind now.

So, I settled for staying silent since it was really what she wanted, anyway.

My stomach rolled uncomfortably, but I knew it wasn't from anything I'd eaten today.

"Mrs. O'Reilly is coming over tonight to pick up her casserole dish. She doesn't know about...you know," my mother said with another wave of her hand. "*The incident*," she added, lowering her voice.

I forced myself to take a deep breath.

I'd heard that word more times than I could count in the last twenty-four hours and it made me want to scream every time.

"She thinks you're just home for a visit. No need for her to know about...*the incident*."

I bit into my lip to keep my mouth shut this time.

"I'll be going to Edith's for bridge, so you make sure to thank her and tell her I'll call her tomorrow."

I didn't answer, and she clearly wasn't expecting a response because she began humming to herself.

Fifteen more minutes.

I just had to get through fifteen more minutes and then we'd be home – no, not home. That word didn't fit. The house – we'd be at the house. Fifteen minutes and we'd be at the house and I could have a few minutes to myself.

I let my eyes scan the quiet road around us. Dusk was already threatening to fall, signaling the start of what would be a long, brutal winter. A winter I had no clue how I was going to get through.

Tall trees lined the winding road, so it wasn't until I rounded a curve that I saw it. The small lump in the middle of the road. I shifted the steering wheel so the tires wouldn't roll over the body of the poor raccoon that hadn't been quick enough while attempting to cross the road. Just as I was about to avert my eyes so I wouldn't have to take in the gruesome sight, I saw another bundle of fur moving, and I instinctively slammed on the brakes and jerked the steering wheel to the right, causing the car to violently swerve.

My mother let out a gasp as the car careened along the shoulder before skidding to a stop.

"Nolan!" she shouted as her purse and knitting needles went flying. "Watch out!"

I ignored her and put the car into park as I tried to catch my breath. Adrenaline surged through my blood. I lifted my hand to adjust the rearview mirror, ignoring my mother as she scolded me with some comment about the terrible driving habits I'd picked up in Hollywood.

My eyes settled on the dead raccoon and I once again saw movement.

I jerked open the car door.

"Nolan, what are you-"

I cut off my mother's words when I shut the door behind me. I quickly scanned for traffic, but the country road was dead to the world. I trotted up to the poor corpse and tried to quell the nausea that went through my belly at the gruesome sight. I'd never been allowed to have pets as a kid, but I'd always had a soft spot for animals. So when my eyes fell on the baby raccoon trying to shrink away from me as it curled against the dead raccoon's body, my heart broke for the poor little thing. I swiveled my head to see if I could see any other raccoons around, but the forest around me was silent. Cold air seeped through the thin material of my jacket, reminding me that I really needed to go shopping for winter clothes soon.

Another bout of nausea hit me, but this time it had nothing to do with the poor dead animal at my feet or its orphaned offspring.

I debated what to do, since there was no way I could leave the baby sitting in the middle of the road or it would end up just like its mother. I quickly stripped off my jacket and used it to carefully scoop up the baby, which hissed at me pathetically a few times and struggled in my hold. I jogged to the shoulder and stepped into the heavy brush before putting the baby down. When I went back to the road, I waited so I could watch the small animal wander off into the woods. I had no clue if the raccoon was old enough to survive on its own, but I figured it would hook up with some other raccoons or something. When the animal didn't move, I turned to walk back to the car, assuming my presence was probably making it nervous. But when I glanced over my shoulder, I saw the little animal scurry across the road and right back to its mother's body.

I let out a huff and debated what to do. I knew it was just nature's way, but I couldn't leave the animal there to die. I hurried back to the raccoons and again bundled the baby in my jacket. This time it didn't make as much of a fuss, so I took that as a sign from above that I was doing the right thing. I hurried back to the car.

"Nolan," my mother chided as she worked to reorganize her purse. "Was that really necessary?"

I kept the bundled-up raccoon on my lap and got my seatbelt buckled. "Sorry," I murmured. "I couldn't just leave it there."

"Leave what there?" she asked. Her eyes bugged out when she saw the baby raccoon. "Nolan, get that filthy thing out of my car!"

I wasn't someone who often went against my parents' orders, even at the ripe old age of twenty-eight, but there wasn't even an ounce of hesitation when I said, "No."

I'd been forced to return to a living hell, but I'd be damned if I was going to consign the poor creature to a certain death. It was a small battle, but I was fighting a big-ass war and I needed this win. I'd save the little thing if it damn well killed me.

Okay, yeah, I was being overly dramatic, but I needed this.

"I want that thing out-"

"Is old Doc Cleary still in business?" I asked.

"What?"

"Doc Cleary," I said. "The vet over on Mulberry Street. People used to always bring him baby birds and stuff, right?"

My mother looked at me like I'd grown a second head. "Yes," she finally answered. "But he's in Florida visiting his daughter this week."

"Damn."

"Nolan, language!"

I barely managed not to roll my eyes as I pulled up the browser on my phone.

"What are you doing? Mrs. Kellogg is going to charge-"

"For another hour. I know, Mom. I'll pay for it, okay?"

"Don't take that tone with me, young man," she snapped. "People might talk to their mothers in Hollywood like that…"

I tuned out the rest of her words. It was scary how easily I was able to fall back into that particular habit.

It didn't take long to find what I was looking for. It turned out there was a wildlife rescue center just outside town. I tried calling, but the call went to voicemail. The raccoon had gone really quiet on my lap, which had me worried, so I hung up the phone. I'd just have to risk that someone would be at the center, so I put the car in gear and got us back on the road.

My mother was still ranting at me, but it wasn't until I pulled off the main road we were on that she finally fell silent. After a few beats, she picked up her knitting and I swore I heard her mutter something about Californians disrespecting their mothers under her breath.

I ignored her and followed the instructions my phone was giving me on how to get to the center. The GPS app had me turning onto a desolate dirt road that had low-hanging trees lining it. The sound of the branches scraping gently over the roof of the car was creepy, and I noticed my mother had finally looked up from her knitting.

"Where are we going?" she finally asked. Her eyes fell on a small wooden sign that said *Lake Hills County Wildlife Rescue and Sanctuary*. "We shouldn't be here," she murmured. "He doesn't like visitors."

"Who?" I asked. "You know the people who run this place?"

"Edna Moreland dropped a bird off here once and he threatened her. She told the cops and they came out here to question him, but he got off with just a warning. Like he did that night…"

My mother's voice dropped off.

"What night? Who?"

But she didn't answer me, so I focused on avoiding the ruts in the road. We reached a gate that, luckily, was open. There was another sign displaying the name of the sanctuary on the wooden fence that held the gate in place. I drove through the gate and the trees began to get thinner and thinner until we reached a large clearing. There was a large farmhouse sitting on a slight rise in the far corner of the property. Several outbuildings, along with dozens and dozens of different kinds of pens, were scattered over a large swath of the clearing. The dirt road switched over to gravel, which I followed to one of the smaller outbuildings that had yet another sign with the center's logo and name on it. I put the car in park and glanced at my mother. Her eyes were wide and she was clutching her knitting needles.

I didn't even bother to ask if she was coming with me. And I didn't bother telling her I'd be right back. My mother had a tendency not to really hear me, anyway.

I held my jacket to my chest as I got out of the car. I heard the locks on the car engage right after I shut the door. I wish I'd been smart enough to grab the keys, since I wouldn't put it past my mother to crawl over the console and drive off without me at the first sign of danger.

Maternal instincts were something my mother didn't really have in spades.

I glanced down at the raccoon. Its eyes were closed, but it was still breathing. "Hang in there, buddy," I murmured as I scanned the property. I could hear dogs barking and a variety of other sounds, but I didn't see anyone. I hurried to the door of the small white building I'd parked in front of, but a quick tug confirmed my fear.

Locked.

Fuck.

I glanced around again. "Hello?" I called out.

Nothing.

I debated between trying the house and checking around some of the pens and finally decided to go with the pens, since I could hear dogs barking excitedly. I shot my mother a quick look and motioned with my head which direction I was going, but her eyes were swinging wildly around.

Looking for my would-be murderer, no doubt.

Hell, the car likely *would* be gone by the time I returned.

I walked around the building and followed a dirt path past a large paddock that housed a couple of horses and a donkey. Some goats and chickens were also roaming around the pasture, but when my eyes fell on an animal that most certainly didn't belong with the little group of farm animals, I came to an abrupt stop.

A zebra.

An actual zebra.

Where the hell did you get a zebra from in Minnesota?

Remembering the poor little charge in my arms, I quickened my pace. As interesting as this place was, I didn't have time to explore.

But I still couldn't stop myself from checking each pen I walked past.

That was why I didn't see it until I was practically on top of it.

Not to mention the damn thing didn't make a sound.

It was the sudden shock of white in my periphery that had me coming to a rough halt.

It was a wolf.

A fucking wolf.

A fucking wolf that *wasn't* in a pen.

I swallowed hard and felt my muscles lock up tight at the sight of the animal standing less than fifteen feet from me. Its lush coat was stark white and I couldn't help but think how that coat would look covered in my blood.

"Oh, God," I whispered as the animal's dark eyes settled on me and stayed there. I cuddled the raccoon closer to my chest as if that could somehow protect it from the wolf's jaws.

Hell, who was I kidding? The animal would likely come after me first.

I took a few steps back, ever so slowly, but the wolf automatically stepped forward, so I stopped. I broke out into a cold sweat as fear engulfed me. I wanted so badly to run, but my instincts told me that was the last thing I should do. I could scream, but would anyone hear me?

I wanted to laugh at the irony of it all. I'd been silently screaming my whole life and no one had ever heard. Now that I was prepared to do it for real, it likely wouldn't change the outcome.

I was just about to open my mouth when I heard a loud snapping sound. The wolf suddenly turned around and I watched it trot several feet away. I lifted my eyes to follow the animal's path and settled my gaze on a tall figure standing near a small building. He was bundled up in tan coveralls that were covered in dirt and stains and there was some kind of scarf wrapped around his neck. A baseball cap covered his head.

The man snapped his fingers again and the wolf dropped to the ground. Its eyes stayed on me, but it didn't move.

The man and I stared at each other. He was a big guy...easily several inches taller than my own five-ten frame. The coveralls hid his figure and from the distance, I couldn't really make out his facial features.

"Um, hi, I...I need some help," I stammered when the man didn't say anything. A shiver snaked up my spine as he stared at me. It reminded me of the way the wolf had stared at me.

"I found this baby raccoon on the road," I murmured as I forced myself to take a few steps forward, though part of me still wanted to run the other way. Why the hell did it feel like the wolf was the less dangerous of the pair?

The man began moving when I said raccoon, and I froze in place as he approached me.

Yep, he was definitely a big guy. But I knew what was under the coveralls wasn't a portly figure. Don't ask me how I knew, I just did. I still couldn't see the guy's face because of the cap. I managed to stay still as he neared me and he lifted his big hands toward me. Logically, I knew he was just reaching for the raccoon, but I was still on edge so I automatically stepped back. I looked up just in time to see the man lift his gaze to mine and I saw his jaw harden.

There was something familiar about him and I desperately wanted to push the cap off his head so I could really see his face. But the sensation of the man's fingers grazing mine distracted me.

A lot of shit happened all at once in that moment as the man took the raccoon from me.

His touch sent a shock of electricity through me that had air whooshing out of my lungs.

Heat seeped into my skin where his fingers touched mine.

And he hesitated right in the middle of taking the small animal from me and lifted his head enough so I could finally take him in.

"Dallas," I breathed in disbelief as recognition hit me hard and fast as soon as I saw his eyes. Deep, dark, gray-blue eyes that reminded me of the waters of San Francisco Bay on a rare, stormy day.

He flinched as his gaze held mine for the briefest of moments.

"You're Dallas Kent," I murmured as I released my hold on the raccoon. The man didn't confirm or deny my statement. He didn't do anything at all except cuddle the baby, which was still wrapped up in my jacket, to his chest.

And then he turned his back on me and walked away, a slight limp marring his gait.

He didn't say a thing…not one single word.

Just like in fucking high school.

I watched as he walked into the building, the wolf silently following him. It occurred to me that I should go after him so I could make sure the baby raccoon was going to make it, but I found myself turning away instead.

And then I did what I'd done ten years ago when I'd left Pelican Bay to start my perfect new life, which had ended up being anything but.

I ran.

CHAPTER ONE

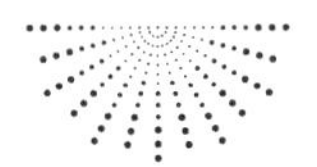

Nolan

This can't be right.

I shook my head in disbelief as I stared at the numbers in front of me…the red numbers.

"This can't be right," I said out loud this time, to no one in particular. The din of the television blaring from the living room began to add to my headache, but I resisted the urge to get up and go turn it down again.

"Nrngh!"

I sighed at my father's garbled shout and rose to my feet. Anticipating what he wanted, I went to the refrigerator and grabbed a beer and the plastic container of macaroni salad my mother had prepared earlier in the day. I took both to the living room and walked around my father's worn leather recliner, nearly tripping over the walker that was lying on the floor. I set the beer and the container on the table on the left side of the recliner so my father could reach it and then leaned down to pick up the walker.

My father let out a grunt and I looked up to see him look pointedly at the TV and then me. I moved out of the way and then dropped down onto the couch and studied the man I no longer recognized.

I'd been a surprise for my parents, who'd both been in their forties when I'd been conceived, and I'd often wondered if that fact had played any kind of role in the relationship I had with them. But there'd never been anyone to ask, since all my grandparents had been dead by then and there'd been no extended family around. I wasn't sure, but I'd kind of figured both my parents had been content with their solitary existence, having just each other to rely on.

A reality I'd intruded upon.

It was a fact I'd eventually come to accept over the years, despite the fact that it meant facing a truth I'd been denying for so long.

Some people just weren't meant to have kids.

I watched as my father's gnarled hand reached out for the can of beer. He held it against his chest while he opened it one-handed, his other hand lying useless on the armrest. Though I knew it wasn't actually useless, just weak. In that sense, my father had been lucky because the stroke had left him with weakened limbs and not full-on paralysis.

He struggled for a moment, but I didn't dare take the can and open it for him since I'd made that mistake once already. I'd learned my lesson yesterday when he'd thrown the open beer across the room, which, because of his weakened state, hadn't sailed more than a few feet from the recliner. He'd grunted what I could only assume had been curse words at me, and then he'd tried to chuck the remote at me while I'd been cleaning up the spilled beer. It too had fallen short, but while my father's verbal skills were impaired, my mother's most certainly weren't, and I'd gotten an earful about the new stain on her carpet. The fact that he'd even cursed at me was proof of the stroke that had changed him in so many ways. My father was and always had been a gruff man, but he'd never taken the Lord's name in vain or used any kind of off-color language.

My parents were throwbacks to that generation where the husband was the man of the house and the wife was the little woman whose sole purpose was to care for the home and the children. It was a role my mother had followed to the letter, though she'd apparently interpreted the care for the children part a bit differently than most. Somewhere along the way I'd become more like an extension of the house rather than a separate entity. My mother had always made sure I had neat, clean clothes and that I minded my manners, but things like hugs and emotional support had been a foreign concept to her.

And still were.

I stood and stepped away from my father before saying, "The physical therapist will be here in the morning."

He growled deep in his throat but didn't look at me. I didn't bother mentioning that I'd managed to find him a speech therapist too, but that we'd have to go to her for the appointments. I'd let my mother break that one to him since even in his altered state, he tended to give in to her requests.

I returned to the kitchen and dropped down into the chair. I pulled up my bank account information and scanned the numbers, hoping like hell I'd somehow gotten a couple of numbers switched around last time I'd checked the balance and there'd magically be more money in the account today than there had been yesterday.

Or that Trey had grown a conscience and put back even a fraction of the money he'd taken from me.

But there most definitely hadn't been an increase in the balance. Nope, it was down by several hundred dollars since I'd had to pay for Dad's walker. I shifted back to the spreadsheet and shook my head.

It wouldn't even be enough.

I felt tears sting my eyes as the reality of my situation crashed down on me. When the side door abruptly opened, I quickly wiped at my face to make sure a tear hadn't managed to escape unnoticed.

My mother shuffled in with a grocery bag slung over her arm. She cast me a brief glance as she settled the bag on the counter and then went to put her purse on a side table.

Everything in its place.

"There are more bags in my trunk," she said as she reached up to straighten the little pillbox hat on her head. I would never understand her need to be dressed in her Sunday finest every day of the week.

"Mom," I said as I leaned forward and settled my hand on the stack of bills I'd been sorting through all morning. "We need to talk about this."

"Groceries, Nolan," she commanded, her voice stern and unwavering. "I'm making a roast for your father tonight. Don't want it to spoil."

Frustration consumed me as I studied her. I wanted to tell her the goddamn groceries could wait the few minutes it took for my entire future to go up in flames, but I quelled the instinct and climbed to my feet. She was heading to the living room, and just before I reached the door, I heard her greet my father brightly and tell him she was making his favorite dinner tonight. I went to the car and got the bags and returned to the house. My mind was racing with any possible alternatives I could come up with to deal with the situation at hand, but there was nothing.

Not one goddamned thing.

As my mother puttered around the kitchen, unloading the groceries and getting the ever-so-important perfect roast going, I stared at the computer and willed the numbers to change...anything to make them smaller. It was a good twenty minutes before she put the roast in the oven and had wiped down all the counters. It was only after she removed her apron and hung it on the hook next to the refrigerator that she turned her attention to me. "Now, what is it?" she asked. "I've promised Edith I'd help her get ready for the church bake sale this weekend. I'll need you to watch your father tonight."

"Did you know you're behind on the mortgage by four months?" I asked. "The credit cards and home equity loan, too?"

My mother sighed and eased herself into the chair on the other side of the table. She waved her hand impatiently. "Your father handles all that. If that's true, I'm sure there's a reason for it."

"I can't really ask him what that reason is, can I?" I asked.

"You watch your tone with me, young man," she said, her eyes narrowing. "It may be okay to speak to your elders that way in Hollywood-"

"You're going to lose the house," I cut in, my frustration getting the better of me. I lifted up the stack of bills. "Electricity, phone, cable...all that shit's gone in less than a month."

"Nolan, language!"

I ignored her and leaned forward. "There's nothing left. Do you understand me? Your savings, retirement – it's all gone."

"Your father knows what he's doing..."

"My father can't string two words together right now," I responded as I dropped the bills to the table and pinched the bridge of my nose to ward off the pounding in my head. "You can't sell the house because you owe more than it's worth. And neither car is worth anything."

"Well, then, we'll go to the bank and talk to Mr. Wilson...explain the situation to him. He'll understand," my mother said with a smile.

"It doesn't work like that anymore, Mom," I said tiredly, but she'd already risen to her feet and dismissed me.

"I need to go change. I promised Edith-"

"To help her with the bake sale, I know."

She shook her head at me and I didn't need to hear the words to know what she was thinking.

As she left the kitchen, I stared at the computer again. Even if I paid all the overdue bills, there wouldn't be enough money left to pay off the credit cards. And there sure as hell wouldn't be enough to get me out of Pelican Bay anytime soon.

How the hell had I thought this would be easy?

Had I really told myself it would take a week or two at most to help my mom get my dad back on his feet and then I'd head to anywhere that wasn't Pelican Bay?

A dark thought entered my mind and admittedly, it was hard to shake. It would be so easy just to get up and walk out that door. To pretend I'd never gotten the call from my mother telling me I had a duty to come home and help her take care of my father.

But as quickly as the thought entered my mind, I pushed it away, because as strained as the relationship was with my parents, they were still just that. My parents. They might not have been the most emotionally giving people in the world when I'd been growing up, but they'd kept me clothed and fed. There was no rule that said you had to love your kids too.

I'd give as good as I'd gotten. Maybe they didn't deserve it, but I knew myself well enough to know that if I wanted to start my own life fresh, I'd have to deal with this first. Only then could I put Pelican Bay and everything that had happened in the ten years since I'd left behind me and start anew.

With that thought in mind, I pulled the computer closer and reached for the first bill.

"N*olan, is this thing working? Remember that you need to be home by seven to sit with your father while I go to evening services."*

The message continued, but I didn't bother listening since my battery was nearly dead. I felt numb inside as I got my parents' old Buick started and on the road to begin the long trek back to Pelican Bay. There was no way I was going to make it home by seven, since it was already six-thirty and I had over an hour's drive ahead of me.

Mom and church were just going to need to spend some time apart tonight.

I tried to will away my bad attitude, but I couldn't even find a scrap of optimism left to get me there.

Not surprising, considering the shitty week I'd had. The morning after I'd paid all of my parents' most crucial bills, I'd done what I'd been avoiding since I'd gotten back to Pelican Bay and had ventured into town. And "town" was exactly what Pelican Bay was. The insular community of just over a thousand people sat along the edge of one of the larger lakes in northern Minnesota, which meant it was a pretty decent draw for tourists.

And the residents of Pelican Bay took full advantage of that fact, even if they did tend to grumble about it a bit.

But one problem with being a town that relied heavily on the buckets of cash that tourists dropped was that you had to rely on the tourist seasons. For Pelican Bay, summer was the busy season, with winter ice fishing offering a little bit of a boost to the economy during the cold months. And while October was cold, it wasn't quite cold enough for the ice fishermen to make their way north just yet.

Which meant the local businesses were surviving off the meager summer earnings, as well as the little bit of income they received from year-round residents. That meant the jobs just weren't there, and if someone happened to be hiring, the competition was stiff. Not that that had even mattered in my case.

I'd had high hopes when I'd gone into the local grocery store when I'd discovered they were looking for a cashier. But the second I'd handed over my completed application to the owner, he'd looked over his glasses at me and then read my name off the form.

"You're Nolan Grainger?"

I'd nodded. "I am."

"You live over on Waterview road?"

"Um, yes sir, I do," I'd responded.

He'd tapped the application on the edge of the counter. "You're the one who ran off to that hoity-toity school, aren't you?" he'd asked.

"Uh, I went to Juilliard," I'd responded. "To study music."

"Right," the man had said. "I don't think we've got anything you'd be a good fit for," he'd declared as he'd handed the application back to me.

Desperation had caused me to swallow my pride and I'd said, "Can I ask why? I'm a quick learner and I'll work really hard. I'm flexible…I can work full or part-time, weekends…whatever."

The man had sighed and taken off his glasses. "People in California might be okay with what you done out there, but we've got values here. I knew what you were like when you used to sit in aisle seven all day."

I hadn't been able to keep from looking at the aisle in question. Aisle seven was where they'd kept the small assortment of books for sale. When I'd been a teenager, I'd had a particular fascination with romance novels (still did, actually) but when I'd used my allowance to buy one, my parents had lost it. Not only because I'd been reading what they'd unabashedly called smut, but also because it was something boys just didn't do. So, I'd sinned twice. My allowance had been immediately revoked, as had my library card, so I hadn't been able to get my fix that way. Since I hadn't been willing to give up my stories of unconditional love, scorching passion, and perfect fairytale endings, I'd resorted to telling my parents I was out playing with friends when, in reality, I'd been hunkered down in aisle seven with the latest and greatest romance novel by my favorite author. I'd taken the extra steps to put the book inside the pages of a nature magazine so shoppers wouldn't see what I was actually reading and report it back to my parents.

Apparently, I hadn't been fooling anyone.

But I knew what Mr. Scarborough was really talking about. I was just surprised he hadn't used the term "the incident" like my mother was prone to do. Since I doubted she'd been the one to tell him, I could only suspect she'd made the mistake of telling one of the ladies in her social circle, probably so she could get some sympathy for the actions of her wayward son, and that woman had spread the news around town.

I'd been proven right when the only other two places in town that were hiring had turned me away with similar comments. Desperation had driven me to try the next town over and then the next one after that. I'd spent the better part of the week driving to every town within an hour's drive of Pelican Bay, and while none of them had turned me away simply because I was Nolan Grainger, the rejections had stung all the same.

It turned out that a classically trained Juilliard violinist who'd played in concerts all over the world wasn't as qualified to run the cash register at Carl's Fuel Mart or wait tables at Delia's Dine 'n Dash as one might think. My ego had taken a blow when Carl himself had informed me he thought the nice young man from the local high school who'd interviewed just before me would be a better fit for the position.

The hopelessness of my situation sank in as darkness began to settle over the horizon. I could keep trying to drive farther and farther out, but the cost of gas would start to cut into any salary I might make. Still, it was better than nothing. My mother would pitch a fit that I wouldn't be around as much to help her take care of my father, but I was tired of placating her about the situation. I'd tried more times than I could count this past week to make her realize how dire the circumstances really were, but she'd steadfastly insisted that my father would fix things once he was better.

Problem was, there'd be nothing left to fix.

You could call Trey.

Bile curled in my belly as the thought permeated my brain. I was desperate, but not *that* desperate. The vindictive son of a bitch had ruined my career. No fucking way was I going crawling back to him, though I knew that was exactly what he wanted.

I tried to think of even one friend I could lean on for help or even just to vent my frustrations to, but there was no one. I'd figured out too late that my friends had been Trey's friends first.

I sighed as I flipped on the car's headlights. The job hunt would resume tomorrow. I'd find something and I'd get my parents back on their feet and then I'd get the hell out of Dodge.

That was my last thought before the car suddenly shuddered and the steering wheel vibrated under my hands. I looked down at the dash just in time to see the gauges and lights go dark as the engine cut out, and I quickly pulled the wheel to the right so the car wouldn't stop right there in the middle of the road. Once on the shoulder, I tried getting the car started several times, but it wouldn't even turn over. I automatically reached for my phone, but sometime in the last thirty minutes the battery had finally given up and died completely.

I was stuck.

In the middle of nowhere.

"Fuck," I muttered.

I sat in silence for a good ten minutes as I contemplated what to do. The temperature in the car began to drop pretty quickly as the heat faded. It wasn't brutally cold yet outside, but as the sun fell from the sky, the temperatures had started to dip into the upper twenties. I got out of the car and looked around but couldn't see any lights anywhere, which meant there likely weren't any homes nearby. The road I was on connected Pelican Bay to its neighboring town of Greenville, but in between was just a whole bunch of nothing. I debated what to do and figured my safest bet was to stay with the car. I checked the back seat for any kind of blanket, but there was nothing. Popping the trunk from inside the car, I got out and went to check it too. There wasn't enough light to see by, so I had to feel around with my hand. I wanted to laugh at the fact that there was absolutely nothing in the trunk. Not even a stray wrapper or plastic grocery bag.

"Perfect," I whispered as I slammed the trunk closed.

I'd just started to head toward the front of the car when headlights lit up the road in front of me. In California, the sight would have had me nervous, but in Minnesota, there was only one thing those headlights could mean.

Rescue.

I put out my hand in a slight wave as I waited for the car to slow down, but to my surprise – and annoyance – it flew past, not slowing down in the least. All I could make out of the vehicle was that it was a large pickup truck.

"Ass," I breathed as I shook my head. So much for not having to sleep in the damn car tonight.

I was reaching for the door handle when headlights illuminated me again, this time from behind. I thanked whatever deity had decided to give me a break tonight, when I realized it was the very same truck that had sped past me before. I watched as it pulled in front of my car. I waited nervously as a tall figure climbed out of the driver's seat and walked slowly toward me.

It was too dark to make out the man's face as he came to a stop a few feet away. He didn't say anything, which just had me more on edge.

"It just stopped," I blurted out to him. *Please don't kill me,* I silently added. *Especially not in Pelican Bay, or they'll fucking bury me here for sure.*

The man jerked his arm toward the hood of the car, but still didn't say anything. When he did it again, I quickly surmised he wanted me to pop the hood. I opened the door and pulled the lever. The man was blocked from view as he lifted the hood. I saw a flash of light and felt a moment of excitement. Light meant the car had electricity, which meant maybe it would start. But as I walked around the front of the car, I realized the man was using the flashlight from his phone to examine the engine.

His gloved hands worked quickly as he fiddled with some wires and then he was motioning to me. He held the light over his hand so I could see him doing a twisting motion and I realized he wanted me to start it.

As I hurried back to the car, I wondered if maybe he was a foreigner and didn't speak English. I turned the key in the ignition, but nothing happened. The man didn't say anything and I wasn't sure what to do, so I stayed where I was. I saw his hand come over the hood so he could tap on it, and I took that to mean that I should try again.

Still nothing.

The hood slammed closed and I got out of the car. The man didn't move and he didn't speak as I approached him.

"Do you know what's wrong with it?" I finally asked, since I wasn't completely sure he didn't speak English.

There was enough light from the flashlight on the phone to see him nod his head. But he didn't say anything.

Okay, so he could understand English but not speak it? I guess that wasn't unheard of.

The man swept his arm toward the pickup truck. I hesitated as I glanced at it. Realistically, he didn't need to get me into the truck if he wanted to rob me or off me – he could do that right here, right now. So why was I hesitating?

"I should wait here," I said. "I'm sure a police officer will be by soon," I added, hoping he'd get the hint.

The man shook his head and pointed to the truck again.

"Thank you, but I'm okay," I said. I knew I was being unreasonable, but every PSA I'd seen as a kid about not getting into a stranger's car came back to haunt me.

So much for my Minnesota roots – I'd clearly become a suspicious Californian without even realizing it.

The man was getting agitated as he tried two more times to get me to go to the pickup truck. When I refused for the second time, he seemed to stiffen and then he threw up his hands dismissively. I expected that to be the end of it, but I was caught off guard when he suddenly turned on his heel and strode toward me. I backed up until my body hit the hood of the car. I told myself I needed to fight or at least run, but I was frozen in place.

But he didn't try to grab me.

Not even close.

No, he merely shrugged off his jacket and handed it to me. I stood there in disbelief, the man's jacket in hand as he made a twisting motion with his finger.

He was giving me his jacket?

I was so surprised that I didn't move quickly enough to suit him, and he grabbed the jacket and shook it out and then wrapped it around me before I could even react. He was stepping back before I even realized what had happened.

Then he was walking back to his truck.

The heat from his jacket washed over me as the heavy material weighed down my shoulders. I caught a whiff of some kind of after-shave or cologne along with a muskier scent that I couldn't quite pinpoint. Whatever it was, the combination of smells wasn't at all unpleasant.

I expected the man to get in his truck and drive away, but instead, he paused at the driver's side door, then looked at me. I couldn't see his face, of course, but I felt that look in my bones, and a shiver of awareness ran up my spine. I felt trapped there in his stare, which was pure insanity because I still hadn't seen his face or heard his voice.

What the hell was wrong with me?

I couldn't say how long we hung there for, but when he began walking toward me again, I wasn't afraid.

Yeah, complete and utter insanity.

He stopped a couple of feet from me and then dug out his phone. I watched in surprise as he began punching something into it, but instead of putting the phone to his ear like he was going to make a call, he handed it to me.

I took it and read the screen.

I had to read the note he'd typed out twice before I understood what I was seeing.

It's me, Dallas.

I looked up in surprise and watched as he grabbed the phone, turned the flashlight on and then held the light up so I could see his face. "Dallas," I said in disbelief.

Jesus Christ, my savior was Dallas *fucking* Kent? Why the hell hadn't he just said so and saved us both all the drama? I was about to ask him that very question when he suddenly raised his hand and reached for the fabric wrapped around his throat. I couldn't stifle my gasp as the material fell away to reveal a jumbled mass of scars all over his throat. Realization and horror dawned at the same exact time.

He hadn't spoken to me because he couldn't.

Dallas Kent, Pelican Bay's golden boy and my secret high school crush, was mute.

CHAPTER TWO

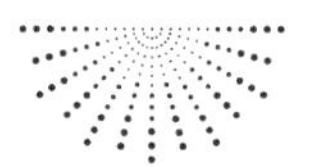

Dallas

I resisted the urge to check the bandana around my neck and put the truck in gear, not sparing my unwelcome guest a glance.

Nolan Grainger.

It just figured he'd be the one I'd run into tonight. I mean, I hadn't been able to stop thinking about him since I'd seen him a mere week ago, so why *wouldn't* Fate decide to throw him into the mix tonight of all nights?

God, I fucking hated Fate. She was an ugly, cruel bitch that had been toying with me for years.

The cab was completely dark except for the lights coming from the dashboard, so it wasn't enough for Nolan to see me, but I still saw him glancing my way every few seconds. I gave into the urge and reached up to make sure the bandana was still in place just in case there *was* enough light from the dashboard, and then promptly cursed myself for the move.

What was I trying to hide? He'd already seen my fucking neck.

Since I couldn't tell him to knock it the fuck off, I shot him a dark look and hoped he'd get the message.

He did.

But for less than two minutes, and then he was doing it again.

"Um, thank you," he stuttered. "For helping me, I mean."

Silence, and then, "I really wasn't looking forward to spending the night out here."

I could practically hear the agitation rolling off him in waves. He was doing what most people did around me…though blessedly, there weren't that many people I had to deal with anymore.

"I don't know what happened. The car was fine earlier."

I kept my eyes on the road as he rattled on about how he'd filled the car with gas and that it hadn't been acting weird and on and on like that. I tried shooting him another look in the hopes he'd get the message that just because I couldn't speak, didn't mean he had to talk twice as much, but he was looking straight ahead.

I returned my eyes to the road. Luckily it was only a thirty-minute drive to Pelican Bay, and I was sure he'd run out of things to say in the next few minutes when he realized I wasn't going to answer him.

It was something else people did. Since it took their minds a while to catch up to the fact that I really couldn't speak, they habitually said things to me that required some kind of response. Then they'd catch themselves and fall silent or apologize, wait a minute or two, and then the pattern would repeat itself.

Unless they were from Pelican Bay.

Then it was a whole different game.

People from Pelican Bay didn't speak to me.

At all.

They spoke *about* me because they seemed to think I'd lost my hearing in addition to my voice, but they never spoke directly to me unless it was absolutely necessary.

Which it rarely was, since I almost never went to Pelican Bay anymore and the people almost never came to me.

The exception was when one of them was brave enough to venture out to the center with an injured bird or orphaned nest of baby rabbits that needed help. That didn't happen often since most people went to Doc Cleary and he brought me my new charges.

Fortunately, Doc Cleary wasn't a talker, even when he was interacting with someone who could respond to him. So when he showed up at the center, he rattled off what kind of animal he'd brought me, what he'd treated it with if it was an ailment he could handle, and then he left.

It was an ideal relationship.

On cue, Nolan said, "I didn't take you away from any plans tonight, did I?"

He realized his mistake pretty quickly, and even though I couldn't see him, I had a feeling his pale skin had pinkened with color. I cursed myself for the fact that I *couldn't* see that.

"Sorry," he mumbled. "I just...I hope this didn't mess up your night," he murmured awkwardly.

It had most certainly messed up my night, but even if I'd been able to tell him so, I wouldn't have. It's not like I wanted to tell the man I'd been on my way for an anonymous hookup with a guy three towns over who I'd met on Grindr.

Well, "met" wasn't the right term. I'd seen his post about his open-door policy tonight and had decided to take advantage, since I normally had to drive to a larger city to find a random guy to fuck.

One who didn't give a shit if I didn't talk dirty to him or engage in any kind of foreplay.

And while the idea of being one guy among many to fuck some random stranger who got off on being used like he was nothing more than a human receptacle for the basest of bodily needs left me feeling cold inside, it wasn't like I had a ton of options.

Beggars couldn't be choosers, after all.

As repulsive as it was, guys like that were only interested in my dick and didn't care about my voice – or lack thereof – or my scarred body.

So, even if it was something I'd never dreamed of doing when I'd been younger, it was a disgustingly perfect fit.

But I couldn't tell Nolan Grainger that.

I couldn't tell him anything.

Silence filled the cabin for several minutes and I was sure Nolan had finally figured out that talking to me wasn't necessary, or welcome, when he said, "How's the baby raccoon?"

I shook my head in irritation.

"It didn't make it?" Nolan said softly, his voice thick with some unnamed emotion.

I looked at him and ground my jaw. He'd clearly taken my response to *how* he'd asked the question as affirmation that the baby hadn't made it. I tapped my fingers on the steering wheel for a minute and then reached down to turn the dial on the interior lights until the cabin lit up.

I tried to figure out how to clear up the confusion without having to pull over and type it out on my phone when I glanced at Nolan. My breath caught as I saw him discreetly wipe at his eyes. His eyes shifted briefly to me and he laughed, but there was no humor in it.

"Sorry," he said. "I know it's stupid," he added. "I just...I needed a win, I guess."

He turned his face away from me to stare out the window. I turned my attention back to the road.

I didn't care.

What difference did it make if I cleared it up for him? It was more trouble than it was worth.

I was about to turn off the interior lights when I shot him one more look.

His elbow was resting against the door and he appeared to be toying with his mouth in some kind of self-soothing move. Guilt went through me and I left the lights on. I reached across the seat and brushed his hand with mine.

And regretted it almost instantly.

Electricity, raw and powerful, surged up my arm and shot straight to my dick.

Fuck.

And it wasn't even the first time it had happened.

Nope, first time had been when I'd taken the baby raccoon from him a week ago. I'd passed the sensation off as a fluke, but sure as shit, it was very, very real.

Nolan let out a little breathy sound, but quickly masked it as he turned to look at me.

I struggled to ignore the tightness in my pants and focused on how to tell him what I wanted to say. I finally settled for holding my arm against my chest like I was cradling a human baby.

"The baby raccoon?" Nolan asked.

I nodded and then held my fingers together in the universal "OK" symbol.

"It's okay?" he asked, his mouth tugging into a soft smile.

I nodded.

"It's really okay?" he repeated, though it didn't seem like he was expecting an answer. I gave it to him anyway and nodded, just because I liked seeing his distress fade away and his expression light up with pure joy.

He sat there for a moment and stared out the windshield before he turned to me and said, "Thank you."

I wasn't sure what he was thanking me for exactly, but I nodded anyway and tried to ignore the pleasurable sensation that flooded my belly.

A sensation that wasn't about the current hard-on I was sporting.

For Nolan Grainger.

Cute, spindly little Nolan Grainger who'd always had his nose buried in a book at school. Quiet, weird, too-pretty Nolan Grainger who'd been the butt of cruel taunts, practical jokes, and ugly locker room talk that I'd never participated in, but that I'd never put a stop to, either.

Because I'd been too much of a coward to risk anyone realizing I had one pretty big thing in common with "Nerdy Nolan" and "Grungy Grainger."

Shame washed over me and I quickly shut off the interior lights, pitching the cab once again into darkness.

Fortunately for me, Nolan seemed to figure out what a waste a one-sided conversation was, so he fell silent. I couldn't help but keep glancing at him every few minutes as I tried to catalogue all the differences between present-day Nolan and the shy, awkward Nolan of ten years ago.

Unlike Nolan, I hadn't been born in Pelican Bay, so my memories of him started at the awkward age of sixteen when I'd entered Pelican Bay High School as a junior. The majority of the small class of students had all known each other their whole lives, so I'd been the dreaded new kid on the block. But I'd been accepted pretty quickly into the fold for reasons I couldn't say I was exactly proud of.

First off, I'd come in as a star athlete, something that, for whatever reason, had been seen as a high-value characteristic. Second, I'd known how to charm everyone...and I mean *everyone*. Students, teachers, hell, even the principal had liked me. Which meant I'd won all sorts of accolades that had made the jaunt through high school that much easier – student council president, prom king, homecoming king, captain of the football team, debate team, baseball team...the list went on and on. On top of the charm and the natural athletic talent, I'd also been graced with good looks, something I'd had little to no control over but had been valued for just the same.

But as much as I'd thrived in high school, I'd eagerly waited for the moment I could put the small town of Pelican Bay in my rearview mirror forever. It wasn't the town itself I'd had an issue with – it was more of what it had represented to me.

Of all the places my parents could have decided to live out their golden years, they'd picked a tiny town in the middle of nowhere. That by itself I could have dealt with, but Jeremiah and Julia Kent hadn't been content to just to settle into obscurity. No, like all the other times in their lives, they'd needed to be the center of attention, even in a nothing town like Pelican Bay. And being the center of attention meant me and my older brother, Maddox, didn't get to just blend in with our surroundings like we'd craved for so long. We didn't get to be just regular high school students trying to navigate the chummy waters of adolescence. Life wasn't allowed to be boring for a Kent.

"Dallas..."

Nolan's voice had me looking over at him and I was surprised to see enough light streaming in through the window that I could see his face. It took me a moment to realize that at some point we'd entered town and were currently driving down Main street where there were enough street lamps to illuminate the cab of the truck every few seconds. I also realized that Nolan was touching me.

Fuck, how had I missed the fact that we'd reached town?

Because you were taking a walk down memory lane, idiot.

Memory lane – yeah, right. Nightmare alley was more like it. I pulled my arm free from Nolan's touch. I was glad I was at least wearing long sleeves, since I already knew what kind of reaction his bare skin on mine would lead to. As it was, my belly was still churning with an unexplained sensation that I could only classify as butterflies.

"You missed the turn," Nolan said. "I live over on Waterview."

I knew exactly where he lived, though I didn't want to dwell on *how* I knew where he lived. But, of course, that was exactly what happened as I took the very next right and made my way over a few blocks to get to his street. I tried to shrug off the memory, but it refused to be ignored…

"Okay, give it here," Jimmy said with a laugh.

I glanced over at Jimmy Cornell as he took the bag from Doug Parsons who was sitting in the back seat. "Go right here," Jimmy said to me.

"Where are we going?" I asked as I steered the Jeep onto a quiet road lined with the same boring little Cape Cod style houses that Pelican Bay seemed to pride itself on. No surprise that my parents had gone a whole other way and built a massive Victorian style home on a bluff by the water that had made the surrounding cottages look like shacks in comparison.

"You'll see," Jimmy said with an air of mischief in his voice. He flopped down in the seat and began rifling through the plastic bag.

"I thought we were going to the baseball field to hit a few," I reminded him. Jimmy and Doug weren't the most reliable of guys when it came to getting in some extra batting time outside of normal practice, but Doug had a couple of decent pitches in him that at least made putting up with their childish antics worthwhile. I didn't recognize the neighborhood we were in and wondered if we were planning on picking up someone else to join us.

"Is this where Manny lives?" I asked, using Tim Mandrake's well-known nickname.

"He's over a couple of streets," Jimmy said. "Open your sunroof. Hurry up, he'll be rounding the corner any second now."

"Who?" I asked as I did what he said.

But Jimmy ignored me and unbuckled his seatbelt and climbed onto his seat so he could stick his body out the sunroof. He braced one foot on the console between the front seats. "What the hell, Jimmy?" I asked. Doug was practically hanging out the back window.

"Now!" Jimmy yelled. My eyes were on the intersection we were just starting to enter, so I didn't notice him right away.

And by the time I did, it was too late.

Too-small-for-his-age Nolan Grainger let out a few soft cries as he was pelted with one egg after another. His violin case went flying as he tried to cover his face, and his backpack hit the sidewalk. The book he'd had his nose buried in was immediately covered in sticky yellow yolks.

"Jimmy, what the fuck?" I shouted as I instinctively hit the brakes.

Which didn't help the situation because it made it easier for Doug and Jimmy to hit Nolan with the last of the eggs.

Jimmy was laughing his ass off when he dropped down into the seat. "Go, go!" he yelled at me.

I didn't go, of course, because I was too busy watching Nolan as he dropped his arms and tried to wipe at his face. Even from where I sat in the car, my window open, I could hear him crying.

"Fucking go, Dallas!" Doug yelled from the back seat. The car suddenly lurched forward, and I realized Jimmy had reached over to jam his foot down on top of my own on the gas pedal. I barely managed to swerve the steering wheel in time so the car didn't go up onto the curb on the opposite side of the street.

"Get off!" I snapped at Jimmy as I shoved him hard. He and Doug collapsed into a fit of laughter as I got the car moving. My brain was screaming at me to turn around and make sure Nolan was okay, but coward that I was, I didn't.

I couldn't.

Because Dallas Kent couldn't stick up for Nolan Grainger.

Not in his world.

Not in mine.

Not in any.

So, I numbly drove until I pulled the Jeep into a spot by the baseball field at school. As Jimmy and Doug climbed out of the car and high-fived each other, I sent Nolan Grainger a silent apology, and then I got out and followed my friends onto the baseball diamond. It was an apology I'd never have the guts to speak out loud.

"Turn here," Nolan said softly. I did as he said, even as I stifled the urge to pull the car over so I could get out and throw up the meager dinner I'd eaten just before I'd left my house to go meet my anonymous hookup. "It's the last one on the left."

I pulled into the driveway, since I figured Nolan would probably go through the side door rather than the front one. A light over the garage came on, flooding the inside of the cab with light. I knew I should look over at Nolan and send him some kind of benign farewell message with a nod of my head or something, but I couldn't do it.

Even if I could have spoken, what the hell was I supposed to say to him?

Sorry I was such a prick back then, but if it makes you feel better, I'm paying for it now.

"Um, thanks for the ride. I really appreciate it."

Don't fucking thank me, Nolan. Don't ever fucking thank me for anything because I'm a cowardly piece of shit.

I nodded, but didn't look at him. There was absolute silence for a moment before I heard him finally open the door. The second it closed I was putting the car in reverse and before I even put my car in drive to head back to the center, I did something I hadn't done in a really long time.

I begged Fate and God and anyone else who would listen to make it so I never saw Nolan Grainger again.

CHAPTER THREE

Nolan

"Nolan, it's eight. Time to get up," my mother announced from somewhere behind me. I was lying on my side facing the window. I'd actually been awake for several hours, but I didn't tell her that. The only reason to tell her would have been if I'd thought she'd be curious about what had kept me up all night.

I also didn't bother telling her I was a grown-ass man and could decide when I wanted to get up, since there was no point in staying in bed feeling sorry for myself anyway. Self-pity wouldn't pay the bills. Nor would revisiting the past where Dallas Kent had been equal parts tormentor and secret fantasy.

I waited until I heard the door close and then climbed out of bed. I hurried through a shower and got dressed, then grabbed Dallas's coat from where I'd draped it over the back of my desk chair the night before.

My father was, unsurprisingly, parked in front of the TV.

Predictably, he didn't acknowledge me when I walked through the living room. There was a plate of half-eaten food sitting on the table next to his chair. "Are you finished?" I asked as I motioned to the plate.

He harrumphed at me, so I took that as an affirmative and took the plate with me into the kitchen. My mother was humming quietly to herself as she cleaned the countertops. "Eggs, dear?" she asked absently.

I didn't bother reminding her for the umpteenth time that I wasn't a breakfast person, preferring just a cup of coffee to get me going in the morning.

"No, thank you. I need to get going."

"I need you to stay and watch your father this morning," my mother said as she began rinsing out the sponge she'd been using to clean with.

"I can't."

"Nolan," my mother groused, clucking her tongue. "I don't think it's too much to ask for you to spend some time with your father while I run my errands."

It was on the tip of my tongue to tell her that babysitting my father was not the same thing as bonding with him. "Your car broke down last night on Highway 12. I need to arrange to have it towed."

My mother turned, her expression pinched. "What did you do to the car?"

I sighed inwardly as I went to get a mug and filled it with coffee. "I didn't do anything to it. It broke down last night. I told you that when I got home, remember?"

Her eyes narrowed and she shook her head in irritation. "No, you didn't. You came in and went straight to your room. Didn't even apologize for making me miss evening services."

I welcomed the burn of the coffee as it singed my tongue. "I need to deal with your car, and then I need to drive over to Ashburn to see if anyone's hiring."

"Ashburn? That's over an hour away. What am I supposed to do without my car for two hours?"

"I won't be driving your car since it will likely be in the shop. I'm taking Dad's car."

My father's car was a thirty-year-old hatchback sedan that had a manual transmission, which my mother had no clue how to drive. I had no idea why they'd kept the rattrap so long, since my parents usually shared the car that was only twenty years old, but I was glad for that fact today. What I wasn't glad about was that I'd have to use what little room I had left on my singular credit card to pay for repairs to the Buick.

"So, what, I'm just supposed to sit here all day?"

I barely managed not to ask her if she wanted to switch places and she could get her ass out there to find a job.

"What happened to Dallas Kent?" I suddenly blurted as my eyes drifted to his coat, which I'd laid over the back of one of the kitchen chairs.

My mother made a low sound in her throat and shook her head. "Nothing he didn't deserve," she said. "Those poor parents of his," she added, and then she was making the sign of the cross against her chest.

"What happened to them?" I asked.

"That boy killed them," she said, her voice dropping to a whisper as if we were in a crowd of people she didn't want to overhear her gossiping.

After all, gossip was so uncouth.

"His parents are dead?" I asked in surprise.

My mother nodded and went to fetch her knitting bag from a side table. She returned and dropped down into a chair. Apparently, knitting and gossiping went hand in hand because she didn't continue until her hands were moving the knitting needles in a practiced rhythm I didn't quite get.

"His mama died instantly, but his daddy suffered for years."

"How so?" I asked. "What happened?"

"It was the night of the Fourth of July picnic...after the fireworks. He was driving them home when he ran the car off the road. Folks say they saw him drinking."

"Did he come home for the holiday or something?" I asked. Dallas Kent had been on the fast track to get out of Pelican Bay. He'd earned a full-ride scholarship in baseball to Vanderbilt University. I'd overheard the high school's baseball coach telling my father once that baseball scholarships were insanely difficult to get to any school, so the fact that Dallas had gotten one, and a full-ride one at that, had been nothing short of a miracle.

Not that it had really mattered, since his parents had been loaded.

But I suspected it had been more about the prestige than anything else. Especially since everyone had known Dallas's goal in life had been to make it to the Major Leagues.

My mother's eyes lifted to meet mine briefly. "He never left, dear. It happened the summer after you all graduated."

I swallowed hard. Dallas hadn't gotten out? He'd been stuck here for ten long years? How was that even possible? And drinking? I couldn't believe that, because Dallas had been the kind of guy whose sole focus in life had been baseball, and he'd been careful about taking care of himself.

But of course, I'd never really known him...just drooled over him from afar. It was reasonable to say I'd painted this perfect, but unrealistic, picture of him in my head.

"What happened?" I prodded, since my mother had fallen silent.

"Well, they found the car at the bottom of the ravine leading up to their house. All three of them had been thrown from it," she said. "Poor Mrs. Kent didn't make it out of that ravine," she added.

"And his father?"

"A shame, what happened to him," she said with a cluck of her tongue. "Spent the rest of his life in a wheelchair. Died two years later from a blood clot or something...Edith says it was probably a complication from the accident."

My mother's best friend had been a nurse before retiring, so I didn't doubt she was full of opinions about the whole thing, especially since she was as bad of a gossip as my mother.

"And Dallas?" I asked.

"All the pain that boy caused and he was the only one to survive."

I bristled at her words. "Just because he was driving didn't mean he deserved to die," I bit out.

"Now don't go puttin' words into my mouth," she returned. "I'm just saying he should've known better. Those Kents were good people. Raised those boys right."

I knew she was talking about Dallas and his older brother, Maddox.

"How did he lose his voice?"

My mother didn't ask how I knew about Dallas's condition. "Edith heard from a nurse friend that a piece of the car went through his throat. Nearly killed him. Doctors saved him, though. He was in the hospital for months. Didn't even wake up until long after they'd buried his mama." My mother shook her head. "His daddy begged the cops to go easy on him. Said Dallas was paying enough for what he done. The Good Lord will judge that boy," she added.

"Did he go to jail?" I asked.

She shook her head. "Sheriff Tulley had a new deputy that summer. He forgot to ask the doctors to get proof that Dallas had been drinking. His daddy confirmed he was, but wouldn't say how much. Edith figured he was trying to protect his boy."

I wanted to point out that if that were true, he wouldn't have told anyone his son had been drinking in the first place. But I wisely kept my mouth shut.

"Reverend Pickney says Dallas got what he deserved anyhow, so people didn't put up much of a fuss."

I straightened at that. "What does that even mean?"

She looked at me over her glasses and shrugged her shoulders, but didn't respond.

"So, what? Dallas *deserved* to lose his voice and God knows what else? That it was God's punishment for the *accident*?"

Another shrug of her shoulders.

God, no wonder I hated fucking Pelican Bay so much.

"What about his brother?"

I knew that Maddox Kent had been accepted to West Point four years before Dallas and I had graduated.

"He came home long enough to take care of his daddy while Dallas was in the hospital. He left again just as soon as that boy got out. Edith went over there once to check on Mr. Kent and heard Maddox yelling at Dallas – she says Maddox told his brother he was the one who should've died, not their mama."

Revulsion curled through me as I considered her words.

Even if the rumor that Dallas had been drinking was true, it didn't mean he'd deserved the harsh treatment he'd gotten. Not from the town, and most certainly not from his brother.

"How did he end up running the wildlife center?" I asked.

My mother shook her head. "No idea. We thought he'd left town after his daddy died, but he just sold the house and bought the old McClaren farm and made it that" – she waved her fingers – "place." She paused before saying, "Still managed to get his half of his mama and daddy's money, I guess. Edith's daughter works for a lawyer down in the Twin Cities…says Maddox sued his brother for all of the money but lost. Guess Dallas took his share and did whatever he wanted with it. He should've given it to charity or something." Another shake of her head.

I stared at the woman across from me in disbelief. I knew she had a tendency to be cold with me, but her complete lack of compassion made something deep inside of me twist painfully. God, I really just needed to get her and my father back on their feet and get the hell out.

"I need to go," I said as I climbed to my feet. My mother said something to me, but I didn't even hear it as I grabbed Dallas's jacket and my father's car keys and left the house.

CHAPTER FOUR

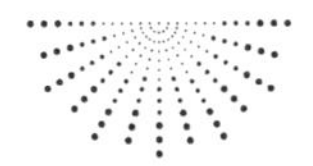

Dallas

I was in the middle of repairing the outer fence for the bear habitat when Loki nudged my arm and then stepped back, his golden eyes watching me expectantly. I'd long ago learned what it was the wolf hybrid was saying to me, though he rarely made a sound, which I attributed to his wolf side rather than his dog side. Only on the rarest occasions did Loki growl or bark. The growling was always a bad sign, but the barking was actually a good thing because it meant he was feeling playful.

I climbed to my feet and Loki immediately trotted toward the driveway. I heard the sound of car tires crunching over gravel a minute later. I immediately tensed up because it wasn't often that I got visitors and Doc Cleary hadn't called to say he was bringing me a new charge. It was probably just someone who'd found an animal in need, though they likely wouldn't be from Pelican Bay, since most everyone in town had learned to go through Doc Cleary.

Except Nolan.

I cursed the fact that my subconscious had managed to work the man's name into my tired brain yet again. I hadn't managed to go more than a few minutes without thinking about him and wondering what he was doing back in Pelican Bay. I hadn't ever really talked to Nolan in school, but there'd been a big announcement right before the spring concert that the small high school orchestra had put on that Nolan had been accepted into Juilliard right out of high school. The announcement had been met with a smattering of applause and a couple of guys yelling out the various cruel nicknames they'd bestowed on Nolan. Nolan had steadfastly ignored everyone and just focused on the music stand in front of him as he'd gotten ready to play.

The principal had hushed everyone and the orchestra had started playing some kind of classical piece right after that, but it wasn't until Nolan had played part of the song by himself that I'd straightened in my seat and let my eyes drink their fill of him. The lights had been low enough in the small amphitheater that I'd been able to get away with staring at him as he'd played his violin like it was an extension of his body. When he'd finished, I'd expected the room to erupt in applause because surely, they'd heard what I'd heard. But there'd been little response and I'd wanted to rail at everyone and ask them how they couldn't hear what I'd heard. How they couldn't see what I'd seen.

Nolan fucking came alive when he played.

A week after the concert, my own scholarship to Vanderbilt had been announced and the entire class had gone crazy. School officials had actually cut an entire period short by half an hour just so they could gather the entire school together to share the news. They may as well have announced that I'd won a spot on the next Space Shuttle expedition. And through it all, Nolan Grainger had sat quietly on one of the first-row bleachers – by himself – and politely clapped.

And I'd felt like the biggest fucking fraud on the planet.

I forced away thoughts of Nolan and headed the direction Loki had gone in. As soon as I rounded the corner toward the driveway, I ran right into the object of my unwelcome obsession.

And by run into, I actually did just that because Nolan had been looking over his shoulder, presumably at Loki who was just feet behind him. Nolan let out an oomph as his chest slammed into mine, and I instinctively grabbed his upper arms to keep him from falling as he stumbled backward.

"Shit, sorry!" Nolan said as he righted himself. I noticed he had a bundle of fabric pressed up against his chest that he was hugging tightly. I wondered if he'd managed to find another critter of some kind.

"Are you all right?" he asked. I wanted to laugh at that since I was a good four inches taller than Nolan and I probably outweighed him by at least thirty pounds.

I nodded and then realized I was still holding onto him. I instantly let go of him and stepped back. I pointed to him in the hopes that he would get what I meant by the gesture.

"Yeah, I'm okay," he said with a nod, surprising me that he'd figured out what I'd wanted to know. "Just...can you tell your dog... wolf...dog...whatever, to stop looking at me like I'm a pork chop or something?"

If I could have laughed, I would have.

Nolan's eyes kept shifting back to Loki, and I used his distraction to study him. He hadn't changed too much since I'd last seen him at our graduation ceremony ten years ago. He was taller, of course, but he really hadn't filled out much. His hair was still the same dirty blond color, though it looked a bit longer then it'd been in school. He'd barely been above the five-foot mark when I'd first moved to Pelican Bay. That, combined with his scrawny body, had made him look like a twelve-year-old kid until he'd finally hit a little bit of a growth spurt a year later. It hadn't been much, granted, but I'd felt like less of a letch for admiring the sleek lines of his lithe body during gym class after he'd shot up to a whopping five-four. It had taken him another year to grow a few more inches and the last ten years had added a couple more, so he just barely came up to my shoulder now. He'd filled out a little, but he was still lean. Though his body reminded me more of a swimmer's than anything else.

Nolan finally turned around, giving me a chance to take in the exact color of his eyes since we were standing so close.

I'd always thought them blue like mine, but, in fact, they were a mix of blue and green, and I absently wondered if one color tended to come out when he was experiencing a certain emotion.

Like fear.

Joy.

Passion.

I cursed myself because as soon as I thought of what passion would look like on Nolan Grainger, I imagined those long limbs of his wrapped around me as I drove into him.

Fuck, I needed to get back on track. I reached for my phone so I could ask him what he was doing here, but quickly realized I'd left it in the house to charge, since I'd forgotten to plug it in overnight.

Damn, this was going to be a pain in the ass.

I sucked at communicating even when I had the means to do it.

I pointed to the fabric Nolan was holding protectively against his chest and lifted my brows.

"Oh, um, no, I didn't find another one," he quickly said, again amazing me that he'd figured out what I was asking on the first attempt.

"It's your jacket," he murmured as he carefully unbundled the fabric and ran his fingers over the material as if to smooth out the wrinkles. His fingers were long and lean, but I could see the strength in them. God, what would they feel like stroking over my body like that?

Jesus, Kent, get a grip.

I took the jacket from him and nodded.

"You're welcome," he said with a nervous smile.

I pointed to the jacket and then to him. It took him a minute but then he said, "You have my jacket?"

I nodded and then motioned to the small office door. He followed me, though he kept glancing over his shoulder occasionally.

Still worried about Loki, presumably.

I went to the coat rack where I'd hung Nolan's jacket a few days earlier. I'd expected him to return right away for it, but when he hadn't, I'd figured he'd left town and forgotten it. The fact that he was still here had me wondering how long he was actually in town for.

I handed him his jacket and then put mine on the rack, but not before catching a whiff of the scent that clung to the material.

Nolan's scent.

I had to resist the overwhelming urge to shrug off the jacket I was currently wearing and put the one Nolan had returned on instead.

Yeah, I was fucked.

Nolan needed to go.

Like now.

I turned around to show him out of the office and saw him standing frozen in place as Loki sniffed his shoes.

"He's not going to pee on me or something, is he?" he asked, his voice hoarse.

I chuckled, even though there was no sound to accompany it. And it felt fucking weird. My only saving grace was that Nolan hadn't heard the strange rumble in my chest.

I snapped my fingers and Loki immediately dropped to his haunches. I twisted my fingers and the animal stuck out a paw in greeting.

Nolan let out a wisp of air as he marginally relaxed, and then he was looking over his shoulder at me. "He won't bite?" he asked.

I shook my head. I couldn't fault Nolan for his line of thinking since Loki looked more like a wolf than anything else, and his silence often put people on edge. And while he still had the blood of a wild animal running through him and that needed to be respected, I'd had Loki since he was a pup, so he'd spent more of his life experiencing the world as a dog.

Nolan still seemed hesitant to touch the animal, so I grabbed his hand and forced it down to Loki's paw. Nolan stiffened, but then he was returning the doggy handshake. He smiled when Loki licked his hand.

"He's beautiful," Nolan murmured. "You rescued him?" he asked when he turned back to me. My eyes fell to the bags beneath his eyes, and I wondered how long he'd been having trouble sleeping. I didn't remember seeing the smudges a week ago when he'd dropped the baby raccoon off.

I nodded again and put my hands close together, leaving about a foot between them.

"When he was a puppy?" Nolan asked as his eyes fell to my hands. When I nodded he said, "What happened to him?" And right after that he seemed to realize his mistake because he dropped his eyes and said, "Sorry."

It would have been better if I'd just ignored the question and sent him on his way, but something had me leaning down and motioning to Loki with a small jerk of my fingers. The animal instantly got up and came to me. He sat down and snuck a lick along my cheek. I took his right paw in my hand and gently pinched my fingers around it. My hand looked like a large claw surrounding the paw.

"He hurt his paw?" Nolan asked. I nodded and again showed him the claw around the animal's foot. "In a trap?" I gave Nolan the okay sign with my fingers and then motioned him down so he could see better. I spread Loki's paw wide so Nolan could see for himself that two toes were missing. A frown twisted his features as we both straightened, and I used two fingers to mimic a walking motion and then shook my head.

Nolan nodded in understanding. "He was hurt and couldn't walk." To Loki he said, "Poor baby," and then ran his fingers over the animal's head. He smiled when Loki licked his wrist.

Nolan's gaze returned to me and the smile fell from his pretty mouth as his eyes held mine. My body instantly responded. Nolan swallowed hard and then his tongue was coming out to wet his lips. I groaned and Nolan snapped his head up at the sound. I half expected him to accuse me of lying about not being able to talk or something, he was staring at me so hard.

"Sorry," he said, quickly dropping his eyes. "Google said you can still make certain sounds because you're forcing air out of your body but I..."

His voice dropped off suddenly as he realized what he'd said.

I, myself, was stunned.

He'd googled my condition?

Why?

"Shit, I mean...Oh God, I'm sorry, Dallas. I wasn't trying to pry into your business but I was curious last night and...fuck."

I smiled because there was just no getting over how cute he was when he got all flustered. His skin had flushed a pretty shade of pink and I was half-tempted to reach out and touch it just to see how warm it was.

Yeah, I really did need to get him out of here.

Since his eyes were downcast, I tapped his arm and then flashed him the okay sign. He nodded but didn't say anything. I didn't like how dejected he looked. But I ignored the compelling need to touch him again and went to the door to open it, hoping he'd get the message.

He did.

I followed him outside and watched as he headed toward his car. It wasn't the same car he'd been driving the night before, so I could only assume that one was in the shop. I watched as Nolan searched his pocket for his keys. He cast me a glance and nodded his head briefly. "Thanks again for last night." He didn't wait for me to respond as he went around to the driver's side of the car. His eyes were downcast as he reached for the door handle, but once he wrapped his fingers around it, he just hung there.

I waited for him to move or, at the very least, say something, but it was like he was locked in place. I was about to tap on the hood of his car to get his attention when I saw his shoulders start to shake. Despair tore through me as I realized what was happening.

And how wholly unequipped I was to handle it.

"Dallas?" Nolan whispered. He didn't look up as he dashed at his eyes.

At the tears I knew were there, but that I couldn't see because he refused to look up at me.

"Can I…can I see the baby raccoon?" Nolan asked, his voice barely there.

Something inside of me twisted painfully at the all-too-familiar scene of the Nolan Grainger who'd haunted my dreams in school.

And not in the good way.

As badly as I wanted to send him on his way, I couldn't. It was like I was back in my Jeep watching Nolan wipe those fucking eggs off his body as he softly cried.

But there hadn't been anyone to hear him.

Except me.

And I'd been a goddamned coward.

I tapped on the hood of Nolan's car to get his attention, since he hadn't lifted his gaze after asking about the raccoon. He wiped at his eyes a bit more before he finally raised them. His pain-filled expression was like a sucker punch to the gut.

I nodded my head and then motioned with my fingers for him to follow me. When he finally did, I noticed Loki nudging his hand as he walked, and I wanted to hug the animal for sensing how vulnerable Nolan was feeling. Nolan smiled at Loki's attention and I heard him suck in a deep breath.

I led Nolan to a small building behind the office and opened the door for him. I motioned him through first and barely refrained from grabbing him when his body brushed mine.

Once inside the room, Nolan stood nervously in the middle. I used the room to house the orphaned babies in my charge and while it was often jam-packed in the springtime, the raccoon was, thankfully, my only resident. I handed Nolan a pair of heavy gloves that would minimize his human scent getting on the youngster as well as protecting his fingers on the off-chance the baby tried to bite him. I grabbed a pair of gloves for myself and then got the baby raccoon out of the small cage. There was some initial awkwardness as I handed the baby over to Nolan, but once we got it figured out and the little animal huddled against his chest, Nolan let out a small smile that eased some of the pressure in my chest.

"Oh my God," Nolan murmured as he studied the baby who'd settled in his hold a bit. In the week I'd had the baby, I'd been feeding it in the hopes of getting some weight on it, so it wasn't completely terrified by the contact now. "Are you going to let it go again when it's older?" Nolan asked.

I was about to tell him yes but then paused. I moved to the large whiteboard I'd hung on one wall so I could keep track of each patient's feeding schedule. Grabbing the marker, I quickly wrote, *Have a mother raccoon with a baby. Going to see if she accepts him.*

A big smile lit up Nolan's entire face. "You are? So he'd get a new family?"

I was so caught up in how happy Nolan looked that it took me a second to nod in response. I knew that smile of his had to have done something to me because before I knew it I was writing, *Was going to try it later today but can do it now. Want to watch?*

Nolan nodded vigorously. "I'd love to."

I nodded and then went for the door.

"Dallas, don't you want to take him?" Nolan asked from behind me.

I shook my head and motioned at him. He got the message. As he neared me, I put out my hand to stop him. Nolan tensed as I reached for the zipper on the bottom of his jacket.

"Right," he said, letting out a breath as I began zipping up the jacket. "Don't want the baby to get cold."

But as soon as he realized that with the way he was holding his arms, the raccoon wouldn't benefit from the closed jacket, he tensed again and his eyes found mine. My fingers were still on the zipper as I held him with my gaze. Yeah, I didn't really have an explanation either for why I'd been worried about him getting too cold.

I was leaning toward him before I realized what I was even doing.

I jerked back at the same time Nolan did and I had to grab his arm when he stumbled. Once he was steady on his feet, he tried to hand me the baby raccoon. "Um, here, you should take him. I might fall."

If he'd just been babbling nervously, I would have passed his reaction off as a side effect of what I'd been about to do. But no, he was freaking out. Like he really thought he'd fall and hurt the baby.

I put my hands on his lower arms to push them back against his body and hold them there. Fortunately, the raccoon wasn't reacting overly much to the commotion.

"No, Dallas, seriously, I might drop him. I'm a klutz and I don't want to hurt him."

Since I didn't want to release him to go back to the whiteboard, I just held him there until he calmed. He fell silent and took several deep breaths, which seemed to ease some of his tension. When he finally looked up at me, he nodded, but said nothing.

I was tempted to reach out and touch his face just because I hated how pinched his features were.

But I refrained and motioned with my arm for him to head outside. I followed and then led him past a couple of pens to the building where I kept the animals that were nearing the end of their stay with me. Despite all the pens we were walking past, Nolan kept his eyes on the ground, and I couldn't help but think he was focused on not losing his footing.

Once we stepped inside the building, he relaxed and finally began to look around. I knew what he was seeing. I'd worked hard on designing the entire center to meet the needs of my guests, but I was extremely proud of this building in particular. I'd worked with a zoologist to create pens that would be most conducive to acclimating an animal back to the wild. So instead of them being stuck in cages as they recovered the strength they needed to survive in the wild, they had small habitats that were most like their natural ones. The building we were in housed the habitats for the smaller animals.

Nolan's eyes were wide as we walked past several habitats that included rabbits and various other small mammals, birds, and even some reptiles. While I had a couple of raccoons that were being rehabilitated, I'd kept the mother and her baby in a smaller, separate habitat. Since I'd been planning to see if the mother would accept the orphaned raccoon, I'd limited her and her baby to a small section of the habitat that I could easily access to remove the orphan if the mother showed any sign of hostility toward it.

I tugged on my own gloves and then carefully took the baby from Nolan. I motioned for him to flip the latch on the smaller door at the base of the larger door. I sent up a silent prayer and gently eased the baby into the enclosure. The mother hissed at me and backed into a corner, her baby hidden behind her. I closed the door and took Nolan's arm and had him step back with me so we'd be out of the mother's direct line of sight but could still see her.

I'd expected Nolan to put some space between us, but he didn't, and I could feel his body occasionally brush mine whenever he shifted on his feet to try and get a better look. It took the mother raccoon a good five minutes to finally move so she could investigate the bundle of fur in the center of the sectioned-off part of the habitat. I studied her behavior as she neared the baby, but nearly took my eyes off the scene in front of me when I felt Nolan's fingers wrap around my wrist. I'd missed it, but at some point, like me, he'd taken off the gloves. Heat and energy surged up my arm at the contact and I wanted desperately to look at him. I highly suspected he was fearing for the baby raccoon, and I wished there was some way I could reassure him I wouldn't let any harm come to the animal.

Since I couldn't tell him so, I did the only thing I could and used my free hand to cover the fingers that were clinging to my wrist. I could sense Nolan's eyes on me, but I kept my gaze on the mother raccoon who'd started sniffing at the baby. She hissed at it several times, but the baby wisely didn't move. It took a good ten minutes of investigating before the mother raccoon began nuzzling at the baby. When the orphan moved for the first time, the mother didn't react other than to step back a little. A few seconds later she returned to nosing at the baby.

Nolan and I stood there for another twenty minutes as we watched the mother accept the baby.

And he held onto me the whole time.

When the two babies curled against the mother so they could

nurse, Nolan let out a rough breath. "It's okay, right?" he asked. "She's accepted him."

I nodded at him and he rewarded me with a huge smile. It wasn't until that moment that he finally seemed to realize he was still holding onto me. He dropped my wrist like he'd been burned.

"Sorry," he mumbled as he took several steps away from me. "I was just...sorry."

We watched the mom and her babies for a few more minutes before I led Nolan back toward his car. I was both glad and disappointed that I was finally getting him out of here.

For his part, Nolan was once again quiet, and I wondered about his earlier breakdown. As we neared the building where I kept the orphaned babies, I was half-tempted to pull Nolan back into the room so I could make use of the whiteboard. But I stopped myself because it didn't really matter. I needed Nolan gone.

He was way too much of a temptation.

And not just in the I-want-to-pin-you-to-the-wall-and-fuck-your-brains-out kind of way.

Nolan's eyes darted around us as we made our way back to the driveway. Just before we rounded the corner, he stopped and looked at me. "Dallas, do you-"

That was as far as he got before he shook his head and began walking again.

Five steps later he stopped and turned so he was suddenly facing me. "Do you...do you by any chance need any help around here?"

The question caught me off guard.

"I mean, it's a big place and I didn't see any other cars out front or any people and maybe that means you do all this by yourself or maybe it means they're just not here but if they aren't maybe it means you need help and I could help if you need help."

He stopped the verbal diarrhea only long enough to suck in some air. Anxiety was practically wafting off him as he jammed his hands into his jacket pockets.

"I'm a really quick learner and I'll work hard, Dallas, I swear. I mean, I know I've only ever played the violin, but it doesn't mean I can't learn and I'll accept whatever you're paying and it isn't true what you might have heard about me. I never stole that violin. Trey, he only said that so he could-"

And just like that, his tirade came to an end and his eyes went wide.

"Oh God," he whispered. He turned on his heel and hurried toward his car.

I was still trying to catch up to everything he'd said, but my instincts had me hurrying after him. I reached him just as he was opening his car door. I put my hand on the doorframe to stop him. I ended up pressed against Nolan's back, my body trapping him against the car, my hard cock practically nudging his ass. Luckily, he didn't seem to notice.

"I'm sorry," he said as he shook his head. "I'm sorry, Dallas. Just... I'll go, okay? Just pretend I didn't say any of that."

He was shaking hard, and I could hear the tremor in his voice that hinted he was on the verge of another breakdown.

What the hell had happened to him in the years since he'd left Pelican Bay? Stealing a violin? Desperate for a job? None of it made any sense. He should have had the world at his feet.

"Dallas, please," he whispered, and I wondered if he was still begging me for the job or asking me to let him go.

Or maybe it was something else he needed so desperately.

I leaned into him and carefully wrapped my arms around him before I realized what I was doing. I heard a sob catch in his throat and then his hands were closing over the arm I had pressed against his chest. I was nuzzling the back of his neck before I could stop myself.

But for whatever reason, hiding the fact that I was gay from Nolan just didn't seem to matter right now. Hell, what I was doing wasn't even about sex. I just wanted to...

What?

What was it that I wanted?

I wanted to go back in time and wrap my arms around Nolan long before those assholes could pelt him with eggs. I wanted to protect him from all the cruel jokes and names that had been lobbed at him over the years. I wanted to insulate him as he went out into the real world and learned that the cruelty he'd faced as a child was only the beginning.

Remarkably, Nolan had managed to hold back the tears I sensed were a constant threat. When the tremors in his body seemed to ease, I carefully turned him around, but, predictably, he wouldn't look at me. He wiped at his eyes.

"I'm sorry, I should go."

His voice was still thick with emotion, but there was something else, too. Something I really, really didn't like.

A finality of some kind.

Like he was giving up.

Yeah, that just wasn't going to work for me. Not after I'd watched him fight all those years ago. Even if he'd never won, he'd never backed down from his tormentors. He hadn't pretended to be something he wasn't just to mollify them.

Not like me.

I was still using my body to keep Nolan from moving away from me. I gently grabbed his chin and forced him to look up at me. I put my hand to my ear in the universal sign for a telephone.

"No, you don't need to call someone for me," he murmured. "I'm okay."

I shook my head and did the move again, then pointed to him. It took Nolan a moment to say, "You want my phone?"

I nodded, and he immediately took the phone out and unlocked it before handing it to me.

I opened the notes app and typed my message.

You need a job?

Nolan read the message and then began chewing on his upper lip. I could see he wanted to deny it, but he nodded his head instead. Humiliation flooded his eyes and he looked away and then tried to turn around, presumably to escape me.

I pinned him with my body, since I needed my hands free to type.

I knew it was a mistake – knew it deep in my belly.

But that didn't stop me from typing my message out and it didn't stop me from grabbing Nolan's chin once again to force him to look at me. I held his gaze for a moment before I stepped back and then put his phone in his hand. He studied me briefly, then started to turn, probably so he could get in his car, but stopped when his eyes fell on the phone and the message I'd written that I knew I'd probably come to regret, but couldn't find it in me to care.

When can you start?

CHAPTER FIVE

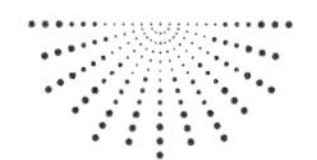

Nolan

"Keep it together, Nolan," I said to myself as I drove through the gates of the center the next morning.

I still couldn't believe it.

Any of it.

Not the way I'd spewed all that shit at Dallas the day before.

Not that he hadn't told me to get the hell off his property.

Not that he'd actually said yes.

Not that he'd pressed his big body against mine as his lips had skimmed the back of my neck.

I knew I'd imagined the last part, but that hadn't stopped me from clinging to the phantom sensation of those warm, firm lips pressed against my skin. Or using it as part of a bigger fantasy as I'd jerked off in the shower this morning. I still bore the slight red mark on my arm where I'd latched onto my skin to keep from screaming out at the sheer pleasure my orgasm had torn from me.

Nothing about the day before had gone as planned.

Well, that wasn't true.

Nothing had gone as expected *after* I'd arrived at the center to return Dallas's jacket. Everything before had gone *exactly* as expected. The towing of my mother's car to the shop had eaten up what little cash I had left. The estimate to fix the car had caused my heart to pound frantically in my chest as I'd handed over my credit card to pay the full amount before the work had been done since Bryce, the owner of the shop, had mentioned he'd need the payment up front since he knew all about me and "the incident."

My trip to Ashburn had ended the same way it had started.

With me feeling more helpless than I'd ever felt in my entire life. I'd been trying to figure out how to tell my mother she and my father were going to lose the house and everything else they owned when I'd spied Dallas's jacket on the passenger seat of the car. I'd told myself Dallas would need the thing back since the temperature this week was supposed to dip below the freezing mark each day, but in truth, I'd just wanted to delay having to go home.

I hadn't missed the irony that had come with that realization.

That I'd rather be in the company of the man who'd made me miserable in so many ways in high school than spend any more time in the company of my parents or cooped up in my childhood room.

It wasn't that Dallas had actually been the one to torment me in the two years we were in school together – it was because he'd always seemed to be around to witness my humiliation. I'd accepted from an early age that, despite what grown-ups told you, bullies didn't forget about you if you ignored them. It had never really made sense to someone as invisible as me that I'd still been the target of endless persecution. Even long before I'd been deemed "faggy," it'd been the same handful of boys who'd hated me on sight for whatever folly I'd committed against them. It had begun in kindergarten when I'd been excluded from the rough games the boys had played and the girls had just looked at me like they hadn't really known what to do with me. Accepting that I didn't fit and I never would should have been the end of it, but my persecutors hadn't gotten the message, because the practical jokes and name-calling had followed me until the very day I'd left

Pelican Bay. My only saving grace had been that I'd never fought back in any kind of way, so I'd never been subjected to the beatdowns I'd been threatened with.

I'd become oddly complacent with the abuse over the years, but things had changed when Dallas Kent had arrived in Pelican Bay. I'd already suspected I was gay at that point, but the strapping, gorgeous sixteen-year-old baseball star had sealed the deal for me. And suddenly all the humiliation had been amplified because Dallas had, more often than not, been there to see it.

In the deepest, darkest part of my soul I'd kind of hated Dallas Kent.

It was an admission I wasn't particularly proud of. It wasn't that I'd expected Dallas to actually ride in on his white horse and save me – though in truth, I'd fantasized about that way too often to be considered healthy. No, my anger at Dallas had been because it had made the torment go from being just a fact of life to an endless prison of humiliation. Before Dallas had come along, I'd been able to at least dismiss the cruel taunts and painful practical jokes, because it had been easier to pretend I hadn't cared what my tormentors and their friends thought. But when the boy I'd put on a pedestal had witnessed it all, I'd started to wonder if maybe I really was all those names I'd been called. I'd begun to question why I hadn't tried harder to fit in when I'd been younger – maybe doing so would have meant Dallas wouldn't have looked at me with pity all the time.

Well, he was definitely going to be looking at me with pity now, considering everything I'd said yesterday.

I'd even told him about "the incident." Maybe not the whole story, but I sure as hell hadn't missed the shock in his eyes as soon as I'd admitted that I'd been accused of theft.

Although theft really didn't cover the fact that a million-dollar Stradivarius violin in my possession had gone missing.

The mere thought of what had happened three months earlier had me shoving the memory away.

However I'd gotten here, I didn't care. If I was lucky, Dallas would stick me to work somewhere I wouldn't have to interact with him or any of his other staff, and I could just keep my head down and earn enough money to get my parents back in the black and my butt out of Pelican Bay.

The parking area was empty as I pulled in, making me wonder if Dallas even had any other employees. I made a mental note to ask if I needed to park my car somewhere else, since that could be the reason I wasn't seeing any other cars. Within a few seconds of getting out of the car, the wolf-dog trotted around the building like he had the day before. But this time I didn't completely panic at the sight of the animal. He still made me nervous, but if I was going to prove to Dallas that I could handle this job, I needed to man up around the wolf... dog...wolf. Damn, I really needed to ask Dallas what exactly the animal was. It most certainly looked like a wolf, but from everything I'd seen on nature programs about the majestic creatures, I knew they couldn't ever be considered pets. Which had me guessing the animal was at least part dog, because I doubted Dallas would risk endangering people who came to the center by letting a wolf run around unattended.

After letting the wolf-dog sniff my hand, I risked running my fingers over his head. He didn't thump his tail like a regular dog would, but he did lick my wrist.

Dallas had told me to arrive by eight in the morning, and even though I was early, I still wanted to make a good impression and show my new boss I was taking this job seriously. So I gave the animal a final pat and then went to see if Dallas was in the office, since he hadn't appeared when his pet had. A glance through the glass portion of the door showed the office was empty, so I followed the wolf-dog who'd wandered back the way he'd come, figuring he'd lead me to Dallas.

I found him face to face with a bear.

And not the kind of bear that you'd find in pretty much every gay club in existence.

No, this bear was covered in a thick layer of fur instead of hair, and its dark eyes were on Dallas, who was standing on the opposite side of the heavy fencing that separated the pair. There was a second fence surrounding the entire pen, so Dallas was actually standing between the two sets of fencing. The bear was sitting on its haunches, its huge paw pressed against the fence as Dallas fed the animal something through the links.

Even though I knew the animal couldn't get to Dallas, I still felt a sliver of fear for him. Dallas was a big guy, but the bear was just huge. I didn't know anything about bears, but my gut was telling me it was a grizzly bear.

I didn't dare move even a muscle as I watched the two of them. The sight was both frightening and beautiful at the same time. Knowing that they were natural-born enemies, yet they'd found this moment of peace between them...

Something tightened in my throat, and for the first time I really thought about where I was.

It was at that moment that Dallas chose to turn around. His eyes met mine, and even with the distance between us, it felt like he was touching me.

He's not gay, you idiot. Get your damn head out of the clouds.

I sent Dallas an awkward nod and then tore my eyes free and began looking around. After dinner the night before, I'd checked out the website for the wildlife center. I'd told myself it was simply research for my new job, but secretly I'd hoped to find some kind of explanation for how someone like Dallas Kent had ended up running a wildlife sanctuary and rehabilitation center. I'd secretly observed Dallas enough when I'd been a kid to know he'd never seemed overly interested in animals. It had been baseball, baseball, and baseball for the star athlete.

The website had been a disappointment, since it had only consisted of a single page with the center's contact information and instructions to leave a message on the office's voicemail. There was also a note to call Dr. Cleary in Pelican Bay in case of an emergency. It was a harsh reminder how difficult it must have made things for Dallas to not be able to talk. He wouldn't have even been able to return a call to someone.

Funny how none of that had been much of an issue the day before when I'd stopped by to return the jacket and had gotten to taste one small victory when Dallas had put the baby raccoon in with its new family.

Predictably, even thinking of that moment had me remembering how I'd grabbed onto Dallas's wrist. I needed to be more careful, or Dallas was going to kick my ass for sure. I hadn't really hidden my sexuality when I'd been a kid – there just hadn't been anyone to tell. Based on the names I'd been called back then, most people had figured it out, anyway. But that didn't mean I wanted to be obvious about it, and I had enough sense not to let someone like Dallas catch me ogling him. He may not have ever outwardly attacked me as a kid, but it wasn't unheard of for straight guys to go off the rails when they thought a gay guy was hitting on them. Something as innocent as a handshake could be interpreted wrong.

It was that thought that had me keeping my eyes to myself as Dallas left the bear enclosure and headed my way. It wasn't until he was standing in front of me that I nodded my head. "Morning," I murmured.

Dallas sent me a nod and then motioned around us. He pulled his phone out a moment later and typed out *Tour?*

I nodded and fell into step next to him.

The property was huge, and with Dallas typing out messages about each pen, it was a slow process of making our way around the place. But I was glad when he took the time to explain things to me, because I was learning much of what I would have expected to find on the website.

The center was a mix between a rehabilitation facility and a sanctuary. Dallas indicated his goal was always first and foremost to rehabilitate an animal so it could be returned to the wild, but in some cases, that just wasn't possible. He used the bear he'd been interacting with as an example.

He indicated the animal's name was Gentry and explained how he'd received the bear after authorities had discovered Gentry and several other bears as part of an attraction at a roadside zoo. Gentry had been kept for years in a cage that had barely allowed the bear enough room to turn around in. He'd been malnourished, covered in scars from the abuse he'd suffered at his former owner's hands and near death when Dallas had gotten him. Sanctuaries all over the country had volunteered to take the rest of the bears in, but they'd all been in captivity too long to be released back into the wild. Dallas went on to explain that while Gentry was used to humans, it was important to never forget that he was still a wild animal at heart. My respect for Dallas climbed several notches when he told me that he never got into the cage with Gentry, no matter how gentle the bear acted. I suspected many people wouldn't have had that same level of restraint.

Although the center was geared toward wildlife, I saw many domesticated animals as well, including dogs, cats, and a variety of farm animals. I was more than a bit relieved when Dallas indicated it would be these animals that I'd be working with for starters.

The tour took longer than it probably should have, since I couldn't stop asking questions about each animal's story as we went along and Dallas was forced to type out his responses on his phone. Despite the awkwardness of it all, I could tell Dallas was extremely proud of what he'd built for his animals and I enjoyed watching him interact with each one. Like Gentry, there were several animals that had no chance of surviving in the wild and would spend the rest of their days at the center. He explained that the majority of the domesticated animals were up for adoption, but finding them homes was a challenge.

There was a hint of something besides disappointment in his eyes when he said that last part, but he didn't expound on the comment, so I left it alone.

After the tour, he led me to his office. My nerves began to kick in, because despite his openness on the tour, there was a certain distance he'd kept between us. I knew it was likely just me overreacting, since it was admittedly hard to gauge the reactions of someone who couldn't talk, but I couldn't shake the feeling that, despite offering me the job, he wasn't happy to have me around.

I was half-tempted to tell him the feeling was mutual, since I hadn't been able to escape the humiliation I'd been feeling ever since

I'd driven away from the center the day before. By the time I'd arrived home, my pride had insisted at least ten times that I turn around and return to the center to tell Dallas I couldn't accept the job.

I'd even composed an email that I'd planned to send to him via his website, but every time I'd tried to hit the send button, my eyes had fallen on the pile of unpaid bills sitting on my nightstand. When I'd told my mother this morning that I'd finally found a job, she'd told me that was nice to hear, and then she'd told me I needed to be home by three to watch my father so she could go with Edith to the hairdresser's.

I'd left the house without saying anything.

She'd figure it out soon enough at three. At least she'd have more fodder to share with Edith about her good-for-nothing, ungrateful, Hollywood-crazed son.

A light tapping sound had me dragging my eyes from where I'd been staring at a wall full of framed photos of various animals. I recognized Gentry in one of them.

I turned my attention to Dallas who'd been rifling through his desk for the paperwork I needed to fill out.

I still couldn't believe the guy I'd been crushing on for two long, miserable years (and maybe still a little now) was my boss. All the work I'd done to escape the shame and humiliation I ever felt around Dallas Kent and his friends, and none of it had made a difference.

I was right back where I started.

Only, I wouldn't be able to pretend to ignore the man when he came to the realization that he'd made a terrible mistake in hiring me. Not only did I know nothing about animals, I had next to no experience doing any kind of manual labor.

God, this was so very, very bad.

I ignored the urge to confess to Dallas that I was a fraud and took the paper he handed me. I scanned it and realized it was a pay period schedule. My eyes automatically fell to the bottom of the page where the hourly rate was listed.

And barely managed not to cry.

It was too much.

Way too much.

I should have been relieved to know I'd be making so much more than minimum wage, but all I felt was embarrassment. There was no way in hell a position cleaning up after and feeding animals paid so much.

I could feel my skin heating as I handed the paper back across the desk. "It's too much," I said. I hated that my voice carried notes of both humiliation and anger in it.

Dallas held up his hand and shook his head.

I wanted to laugh at the irony of it all. The salary was pittance compared to what I'd been making just a few short months ago as the First Chair violinist in the San Francisco Orchestra. I'd even made considerably more my first year after finishing Juilliard. But if I'd learned anything over the last two weeks of job hunting, it was that being able to play Bach's *Chaconne from Partita in d minor* to a roomful of San Francisco's elite wasn't worth the sheet music the notes were written on in a town like Pelican Bay. And it sure as hell wouldn't come in handy when I was cleaning up dog shit or scooping litter boxes.

"It's too much," I repeated softly, though I didn't try to hand the paper back to Dallas again. I swallowed around the lump in my throat and tried to count down the minutes it would take for all this to be over. At least once I was out there cleaning up shit or filling water bowls or whatever, the animals wouldn't pass judgement on me.

When Dallas tapped his fingers on the desk again, I forced my eyes up because that was my job now. I expected him to hand me the forms I needed to complete, but instead he was studying me like a bug under a magnifying glass. I forced myself not to look away, though it was really fucking hard. It wasn't until I straightened my spine in some kind of silent act of defiance that I saw Dallas's mouth twitch into something that almost looked like a smile.

He finally slid the papers across the desk and then held out a pen. But just as I went to reach for it, he put his finger up to stop me and then jotted down something on the forms he'd pushed toward me. Once he was done, he climbed to his feet and came around the desk. Since I was still sitting, I had to crane my neck to look up at him.

He handed me the pen, but when I took it, he held onto it for a second. Even though we weren't touching, I still felt the current of electricity between us. Dallas released his hold on the pen and then motioned to the door and then to me. I nodded in understanding. He wanted me to come outside when I was finished.

I waited until he left the office to read the note he'd left me. A shiver ran down my spine, and not entirely in a bad way.

Don't worry, Nolan. I'm going to get every penny out of you.

Any innuendo I'd chosen to read into Dallas's words was gone by lunch time, and by day's end I was silently cursing my parents, Trey, the animals, and basically anything in my orbit that converted oxygen to carbon dioxide for the hell spawn that was Dallas Kent.

Okay, so yeah, I was overreacting a bit. But having one's limbs turn into one large raw exposed nerve did that to a guy.

On the positive side – and there really was only the one positive – any guilt I'd felt about the large wage Dallas was paying me fell by the wayside pretty quickly.

Along with my sanity.

And my patience.

My sense of pride.

My love of hygiene.

The problem had started from the second I'd stepped outside that office door, and I definitely was blaming Dallas for that one.

Because he'd lulled me into a false sense of security by having me start in the kitten room.

I mean, how could anyone go wrong in a room full of kittens?

I'd practically been in seventh heaven as I'd easily cleaned out the three litter boxes that the seven kittens shared, changed their water, and filled the food dish. The hardest part of the task had been watching where I stepped, since the excited bundles of fur had followed me all over the large space. Since Dallas had given me permission to do so, I'd spent a good ten minutes just cuddling the babies and plying them with love. And while I'd felt a little dejected as I'd waved my goodbyes to the warm little bundles of joy, I'd actually been excited about meeting their adult counterparts in the next room over.

And that's where it had all gone downhill.

The adult cats had definitely come with a lot more attitude, but I'd managed to escape the room with just a minor scratch across the top of my hand after I'd made the mistake of trying to move what I could only guess had been a geriatric cat out of the way so I could clean the litter boxes. I definitely hadn't felt any guilt about saying my goodbyes to the adult cats.

The dogs had been next, and they'd been crazy with excitement from the second I'd walked into the area they were housed in until long after I'd left. There'd been no actual kennels for the fifteen dogs of all sizes, just little cottages set up in a row over nearly an acre of land. The dogs had all come running as soon as I'd entered the enclosure and, like the kittens, the mob had followed me everywhere. Only problem was, they'd made it a lot harder to see where I was walking, so I'd stepped in multiple doggy landmines.

The same landmines the dogs had stepped into right before they'd jumped on me, spreading the filth all around. And while all the dogs had been friendly, a particularly hyper German Shepherd had torn the sleeve of my shirt when I'd had the audacity to pick up the tennis ball it had kept dropping in my path.

My muscles had been quietly protesting the abuse by lunch time, but despite the stinging hand, torn clothing, and pungent scent of dog shit literally following me everywhere, I'd still felt somewhat in control.

And more than a little proud that I'd survived a whole three hours on my own. Dallas had come to check on me several times, but had stayed only long enough to answer questions and lay out my next task for me.

I'd both been grateful for his minimal intervention and a little annoyed, too.

By the time I'd finished with the hooved residents in my charge, I'd been cursing Dallas to hell and back. Not only was the work backbreaking, the warning Dallas had given me about the single non-farm animal in the enclosure – the zebra that had somehow ended up with the innocuous moniker of Jerry – had been wholly inadequate.

Dallas had described the black and white monstrosity as "ornery" but not dangerous. And while the "not dangerous" part had been accurate, the "ornery" part had been way off the mark.

The animal was a menace.

Jerry had seemed friendly enough at first as he'd come to check me out as I'd cleaned the stalls that opened into the large paddock the animals shared, but I'd quickly figured out it was all a ploy to lull me into a false sense of security.

It had started when Jerry had inadvertently knocked over the pitchfork I'd had leaning against the wall. I'd jokingly admonished the animal and urged him out of the stall. The second I'd had my back turned, Jerry had been back to sniff through the wheelbarrow full of shit.

The wheelbarrow that had ended up overturned seconds later.

It had been followed by the full water bucket I'd momentarily set on the floor of the stall getting tipped over, forcing me to clean up the wet shavings for the second time.

The second I'd gotten the stall perfectly clean, Jerry had taken a dump *and* a piss in it. I'd once again shooed him off, re-cleaned, and then moved to the next stall.

Where the process had started all over again.

It wasn't until almost three hours later as I'd been cleaning the last stall that Dallas had shown up, spied Jerry in the stall with me, and then promptly asked me why I hadn't closed the outer stall doors leading to the paddock to keep Jerry out.

If I'd been holding the pitchfork in my hand, I'd have probably stabbed Dallas in the foot with it. As it was, I'd managed a polite smile, thanked him for pointing that out as an option *three hours after the fact* and proceeded to the paddock to scrub the water trough and refill it.

The water trough Jerry knocked me into when it was still half full of icy cold water.

Which was the reason I was in my current predicament.

Standing half-naked in Dallas's bathroom, a towel wrapped around my waist as I waited for the man to appear with the promised clothes.

As if he'd had some kind of crystal ball, Dallas had shown up within seconds of Jerry pushing me into the trough. With my humiliation complete, I'd cursed Jerry and my new boss and had stomped toward the small barn so I could finish my last assignment of the day, feeding the animals. My goal had been to save the few remaining scraps of my pride by getting the hell out of there and going home to cry in my shower and then crawl between the clean sheets of my bed.

Dallas, of course, had had other plans.

He'd stuck around to help me feed the animals, and when I'd bid him farewell and headed toward my car, he'd snagged my arm in a tight grip and practically dragged me toward the blue farmhouse on the southwest corner of the property. With darkness falling, I'd been too cold and tired to protest much. I'd barely even gotten a look at the inside of the warm house before Dallas had led me to a bathroom on the second floor and pointed to the shower and then my clothes. I'd gotten the gist of his demand and had been too damn uncomfortable to even consider arguing.

Of course, I hadn't been expecting him to steal my clothes while I'd been in the shower.

The shower with the tempered glass walls.

I studied myself in the mirror as I took in the things Dallas would have been able to see if he'd chosen to look hard enough as he'd been collecting my clothes.

My scrawny body.

Limbs that were too long and gangly.

Pale skin.

I shook my head. "What the hell are you doing?" I asked my reflection.

I jumped at the knock on the door and then carefully opened it a crack. Dallas was holding a bundle of clothes for me, which he promptly handed my way. He kept his eyes averted and as soon as I took the clothes, he pointed down and then disappeared, leaving me to wonder if that was his way of telling me to come downstairs when I was done.

The fact that he'd worked so hard *not* to look at me should have had me feeling relieved, since it meant he wouldn't have likely paid me any attention while I'd been in the shower. But all I felt was humiliation of a different kind.

"You're ridiculous," I muttered to my reflection once again as I placed the clothes on the vanity. The clothes Dallas had given me included a pair of sweatpants that thankfully had a drawstring and a soft, white T-shirt. Both items of clothing were way too big on me, but they were dry and didn't reek of dog shit and ornery zebra, so I was happy.

The fact that I was wearing Dallas's clothes wasn't lost on me, but I tried not to think too much about it. Especially not the part where I was currently going commando in a pair of pants that Dallas could have quite possibly been commando in at one time or another.

Once I was dressed, I forced myself to leave the safety of the bathroom. I needed to get my clothes and get the hell out of there. My body ached, my pride was in tatters, and I was so physically exhausted that I was afraid if I sat down even for a minute, I'd never get up again. As it was, I'd probably end up sleeping in my car in the driveway once I got home, because I doubted my protesting muscles would work long enough to get me out of the car and into the house.

As I made my way toward the stairs, I caught sight of several closed doors along the hall, presumably bedrooms. The only open door was for the bedroom at the end of the hallway, and all I could see was a large bed with a brown comforter on it. As tempting as it would have been to sneak a peek at Dallas's bedroom, I ignored the urge and hurried down the stairs. I slowed my step after noticing the pictures on the wall. There weren't many of them, and while most were of more animals, including several of Dallas's wolf-dog as a puppy, one picture in particular caught my attention. It was of Dallas and his older brother, Maddox. Maddox was wearing some kind of formal military uniform and he had his arm around Dallas. I knew Dallas had to be around eighteen at the time the picture was taken, which had me guessing it was for Maddox's graduation from West Point. I remembered my mother's story about how Maddox had told Dallas he should have been the one who'd died in the accident. I couldn't correlate the hatred that it would take to make that kind of statement with the picture I was looking at.

A creaking sound from downstairs had me hurrying past the picture. My bare feet padded along the cold hardwood floors as I made my way toward the sound of water running. I found Dallas in the kitchen. His back was to me and I could see he was filling a pot with water.

I cleared my throat and felt my stomach jump when he looked over his shoulder at me.

God, he really was beautiful.

Outside, he'd been wearing the same coveralls I'd seen him wearing the day I'd brought the baby raccoon to him – an outfit that made sense now, considering how filthy I'd gotten working around the animals – but now he was wearing a pair of jeans and a soft-looking knit sweater that hugged his broad upper body. It looked like he'd made use of a shower too, because his hair was damp. But I was surprised to see he was still wearing the ratty-looking bandana around his neck. After a moment of contemplation, I realized why it was there and felt a stir of pity for him that he felt the need to hide his scars.

"Um, I'll just grab my clothes and go," I said as I scanned the kitchen. It was surprisingly modern considering how old the farmhouse had appeared from the outside.

Dallas turned, full pot in hand, and motioned with his chin toward the kitchen island, which had a couple of stools on one side.

"No, I shouldn't," I said. "I need to get home."

Dallas put the pot on the stove and got it going, then scratched something out on a pad of paper sitting on the island. He pushed it in my direction before returning to the stove.

Your clothes and shoes were a mess. They're in the washing machine. Cooking spaghetti. Stay.

That last word had my insides dancing with butterflies.

"Um, I don't want to be any trouble," I said as my eyes automatically drifted to Dallas's ass as he moved around the kitchen. Despite the pronounced limp that seemed worse now than it had earlier in the day, he still moved gracefully as he pulled more cookware from the cabinet next to the stove.

Dallas turned around again and pointed to the note.

To that one word on the note.

Stay.

His eyes held mine this time, and I found myself nodding. I'd never hear the end of it from my mother, but I found myself moving to sit on one of the stools anyway.

I watched Dallas work. The forced silence should have been awkward, but there was a strange comfort in it instead.

Dallas moved to the refrigerator and then opened it. He began holding up drink choices for me. "Beer," I said when he was done. "Thank you."

He twisted off the cap and handed it to me, then grabbed one for himself.

A snicking sound caught my attention, and I looked to my left to see the wolf-dog coming in through a large doggie door in the kitchen door. He trotted first to Dallas to press his nose against Dallas's leg, which earned the large animal a friendly pat, and then he came to me and sat down, his yellow eyes somber.

"Is he all wolf?" I found myself asking as I let my fingers trail over the animal's head. A glance up showed that Dallas was watching me.

He shook his head and then took another sip of his beer. Despite the bandana, I could still see some of the muscles in his throat working as he swallowed. But when Dallas caught me watching him, his eyes darkened and his jaw tightened and I realized why.

He thought I'd been staring at the bandana and thinking about the scars beneath.

As he turned away, I started to correct his thinking, but realized if I told him the truth, he'd kick my ass for sure. But as soon as I saw the tension begin to leech into his movements, I forced myself off the chair and went around the island. As I stood behind him, I sucked in a breath for courage and then grabbed his arm.

He was stiff as a board as he turned to face me, and I could see the anger glittering in his eyes. Then I did something I knew could very well end up either outing me or earning me a beatdown.

Likely both.

I reached up to remove the bandana.

CHAPTER SIX

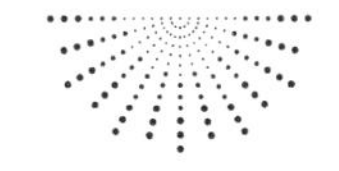

Dallas

I clenched my fists so I wouldn't be tempted to shove Nolan away.

Or grab him and pull him closer.

I knew what he was planning as soon as he lifted his hands, but it wasn't until his fingers touched the cloth of the bandana that I grabbed both his wrists. He let out a soft gasp of air, but didn't struggle in my hold at all.

Nor did he say anything.

No, we stood there like that, both waiting for the other to make the next move.

I was waiting for Nolan to tug his hands free and step back.

Nolan was...hell, I didn't know what the hell Nolan was doing. What I did know was that he wasn't doing anything I'd expected. He hadn't from the moment he'd pulled into the driveway this morning.

As soon as Nolan had driven away the day before after I'd offered him the job and he'd quietly accepted, I'd cursed myself for my stupidity. Not only did I not need the help, I didn't want it, either. The center might be a sanctuary for all the animals who lived there, but it was my sanctuary, too, and inviting someone to invade my world went against every instinct I had. But every time I'd been tempted to try and figure out a way to contact Nolan to tell him the deal was off, I'd remembered his broken voice as he'd swallowed his pride and asked if I needed any help.

Since getting rid of Nolan before he'd even started hadn't been an option, I'd decided to do what I'd been doing from the moment I'd woken up in the hospital, a tube down my mangled throat to help me breathe.

I'd acclimated.

Just because Nolan was working for me didn't mean things had to change. It wasn't like we'd be bonding over lunch breaks or anything. All I had to do was keep Nolan busy enough that our paths would rarely cross. And eventually he'd tire of the physically demanding work or my silence – or both – and he'd find himself something else.

That had been the plan, anyway – ignoring him.

But ignoring Nolan was like trying to ignore the ever-present pain in my hip...the harder I worked to pretend it wasn't there, the more I noticed it.

Such had been the case with Nolan.

I'd ended up spending more time checking on my new employee than I had getting my own work done. I'd purposely given Nolan the easiest jobs, but I'd still been worried he'd push himself too hard, especially after his distress over the salary issue. Not to mention the fact that Nolan was so slight that a stiff wind could have blown him over.

So once he'd started doing the outside work, I'd watched from a distance.

And discovered a Nolan Grainger I hadn't expected.

I'd figured he had to be pretty determined to have made it into a school like Juilliard, but I hadn't been prepared for the unbreakable spirit I'd seen front and center as he'd tackled physical exhaustion and conditions that could only be considered grueling to someone whose life had revolved around a violin and music stand.

Then Jerry had been added to the mix and I'd seen something in Nolan that was very rare indeed.

A good heart.

Because despite all the havoc Jerry had wreaked on Nolan, the man had never once lashed out at the zebra in annoyance or frustration. Yes, he'd most definitely been frustrated, but I hadn't once seen him take it out on the innocent animal. In fact, he'd been kind to the hooved hooligan. I'd seen him petting the zebra on more than one occasion, even after having been forced to clean up additional messes, and he'd spent quite a bit of time talking to all the animals in the livestock area.

I'd been certain I was going lose Nolan to his exhaustion once Jerry had knocked him into the water trough, so I'd made a plan then and there not to let him leave in that condition.

Though I wasn't sure why, since that was exactly what I wanted.

At least, it was what I *should* want.

Especially now, as I saw the same determination in Nolan's eyes as he stood his ground in front of me.

Bigger men than Nolan had backed down when I'd confronted them, but despite the fear I could feel wafting off Nolan's body, he didn't move.

Not to get away.

Not to continue with what he'd been about to do.

And he didn't speak.

I didn't like that.

Nolan Grainger had a lot to say, and I was finding that I liked listening to him. So for him to be watching me with gentle resolve but not back it up with words was unnerving in a way. It would be easy enough just to force him back a few steps, but I didn't want to do that.

So we were at an impasse.

One that I knew I'd have to get us past.

It killed me to do it, but I carefully released Nolan's wrists.

And didn't move beyond that.

Nolan took in a slight breath and then dropped his eyes to the bandana. His fingers were warm against my skin as he let them trace the edge of the fabric. In truth, I hated the damn thing. The damage to my throat already made the muscles in my neck feel tight, and the bandana just added to that. I only took it out of the pocket of my coveralls and made use of it when someone came to the center.

Nolan's fingers only lingered on my skin for a few seconds before his hands moved to the back of my neck where the knot was. The move had him stepping closer to me and I could smell soap, shampoo, and man. It would be so easy just to lift my hands and pull him all the way in. He'd fit my body so perfectly.

Nolan struggled with the knot and I knew it would just be easier for me to reach up and undo it myself, but I was reluctant to do so.

And not because I didn't want him to see my neck. I'd already accepted he would.

No, I didn't want to help him because then there wouldn't have been a reason to step closer to him and lean my head down so that my nose was practically buried against his neck. Mere inches separated our bodies as Nolan fiddled with the bandana. When it finally came loose, we both hung there a moment in the quiet of the kitchen before Nolan gently unlooped the bandana from around my neck.

Just before he pulled it completely away from my skin, he softly said, "It doesn't bother me, okay?"

I managed a slight nod. I wanted to believe him, but then why had he been staring at my neck like he had?

I forced myself to straighten. Nolan stepped back and put the bandana on the island. His eyes went to my neck briefly, but didn't linger. "Can I help?" he asked as he motioned to the stove.

I shook my head.

He nodded and returned to the island and sat down. My eyes locked on his mouth as it wrapped around the opening of the beer bottle.

Fuck, I was so far gone around this man already...

I forced myself to turn around and finish getting dinner done. I caught my hand straying to my neck several times, but every time I looked at Nolan, he wasn't staring, so I began to relax. The buzz of the washing machine had me stepping away from the stove, but Nolan put his hand up.

"I'll get it," he said.

I pointed to a door around the corner from the kitchen. Nolan returned within a couple of minutes and resumed the conversation we'd gotten sidetracked from. "I forgot to ask you his name yesterday," Nolan said as he petted Loki's head.

I went to the pad of paper and wrote down Loki's name.

"Loki," Nolan said with a smile. "Good name. I know everyone thinks Thor is hot, but Loki is way hotter."

As soon as the words left Nolan's lips, he slapped a hand over his mouth and his skin went an adorable shade of pink. I was about to smile at his embarrassment when a look of horror passed over his features and he practically fell off the stool in his haste to stand.

"Shit, I'm sorry," he said. "I didn't mean to say that!"

He looked down at Loki as if he was somehow expecting the animal to help him. "God, okay, yeah, I'm...shit," he stammered before he lifted his eyes. "You might have already figured it out in high school but maybe you didn't, I don't know, but I'm...I'm gay," he blurted. "Maybe I should have told you when you offered me the job, because even though it would make you the biggest dick in the world for not hiring me because I'm gay, I guess that would be your choice-"

I didn't think it was possible that he could get any redder, but he did right after he inadvertently called me a dick. But instead of shutting himself up, his rambling got worse.

"And that thing with your throat, yeah, I was staring because of the way you were swallowing and stuff and it was hot, but I'm allowed to look at a guy and think he's hot – it doesn't mean I'm going to hit on him...you! Jesus!"

Nolan's eyes were wide as he stared at me.

"Please don't kick my ass."

An unbidden smile traveled the length of my lips and I reached for the pad of paper, wrote him a message, and then turned my attention back to the stove but watched him out of the corner of my eye.

I didn't name him after the guy from the Avengers. Loki means "trickster" in Norse legend which fit him because he used to always manage to get out of his pen and follow me around the property while I was working.

"Well, damn," Nolan said softly after he finished reading the message. "Any chance we can just pretend the last thirty seconds didn't happen?"

No chance in hell, but I didn't tell him that. I merely nodded and wrote him another message. I wasn't ballsy enough to admit he and I had much more in common than he thought, but I definitely wanted to put him at ease.

Before we go back in time, am I at least hotter than the guy who plays Loki?

Nolan visibly relaxed and a smile played across his pretty mouth. "In deference to my future husband, Tom Hiddleston, no comment."

Nolan sat back down, and I was keenly aware of him watching me as I finished getting dinner ready. But the self-consciousness that he was just focused on my limp or on my throat wasn't there this time around. I'd always noticed Nolan sending me secret glances when we'd been kids, but to know that he might be attracted to me now was a heady experience. It almost had me wishing I could test the theory further, but the reminder that I wasn't worthy of a guy like Nolan returned swift and sharp. Even if I'd had a sound body and the ability to talk to him beyond some chicken scratch on a notepad or simplistic texts on my phone, I had nothing to offer a guy like Nolan. He might have been back in Pelican Bay because of whatever circumstances had forced him home for the time being, but I wasn't foolish enough to believe he'd stay.

If he'd been any other guy, I wouldn't have hesitated to pursue a mutually beneficial physical relationship. But my gut was telling me Nolan was the kind of guy who didn't do no-strings hookups. And since I'd fucked with Nolan's head enough when he'd been a kid, I wasn't about to do it again.

When I settled a big plate of spaghetti in front of Nolan twenty minutes later, color tinged his cheeks when his stomach let out a loud growl. I smiled and handed him a fork and he immediately dug in. It wasn't until he'd inhaled half the plate of pasta that he slowed down enough to actually savor the food.

"Thank you," he said softly, his eyes meeting mine. I'd sat kitty-corner to him, so I was able to see the expressions play over his face as he spoke. "For everything," he added.

I nodded, and any doubt I had about Nolan working at the center evaporated.

It wouldn't make up for what I'd done to him as a kid, but if I could take even a little bit of that brokenness away from him that I'd spied yesterday, it was worth it. I would just keep my distance from him while he was here.

I reached for the pad of paper and wrote, *So, you're coming back tomorrow? Jerry didn't scare you off?*

Nolan read the message and then looked up at me. He smiled and said, "No, *Jerry* didn't scare me off. I'll be back."

His words shouldn't have sent a scurry of warmth skittering through me.

We didn't talk throughout the rest of the meal.

A fact that I should have been happy about, but that, instead, left me feeling like I'd lost out on something. As I began collecting the dishes, Nolan went to the laundry room to change back into his clothes. He returned with my carefully folded sweats and shirt. After placing them on the island, he said, "Thank you for dinner. I'll see you tomorrow."

I reached out to grab his arm as he walked past me.

I held up my finger to indicate he should wait, then went to turn off the faucet. When he saw me reach for my jacket on the hook near the door he said, "No, it's okay, you don't need to walk me out."

I shook my head at him and luckily, he didn't argue with me. I snagged my gloves and stamped my feet into my work boots before going to the door and opening it for him. It was pitch dark by the time we walked outside, a sure sign that winter was bearing down on us at a lightning fast clip. It would make the work all the harder at the center, and I made a mental note to find more jobs that would keep Nolan inside the heated buildings.

Assuming he even stayed that long.

It didn't take long to walk back to the driveway where Nolan's car was parked. I'd installed motion detector lights along the side of the building that housed my office, so the parking lot and Nolan's car lit up under the bright light as soon as we rounded the corner. I eyed Nolan's shitty car, which was different from the one that had broken down on him. I just hoped that the car was more reliable than it looked since the temperature had fallen considerably as the sun had gone down.

"See you tomorrow," Nolan said as he huddled inside his jacket and searched his pockets for his keys. I'd taken them out of his jeans before tossing his clothes in the wash and had left them on top of the washing machine, so I was hopeful he'd seen them when he'd been getting dressed. The jangle of keys a moment later answered my question. But the sight of Nolan's bare, reddened hands as he fumbled to unlock the car door had me striding forward.

He stifled a soft gasp when I grabbed his hands and pointed to them, then motioned to my own glove-covered hand.

"Um, yeah, I haven't had a chance to go shopping for winter clothes yet."

If he hadn't dropped his eyes, I would have believed his excuse about not having time. But when he tried to pull away from me, I knew there was more there.

And I had a pretty good idea what it was.

I held onto him and then stripped my own gloves off.

"Dallas, no-" Nolan began, but I cut him off with a grunt. I didn't purposely make the sound often, but it did what I'd intended and caught Nolan off guard. I worked my gloves onto his chilled hands.

"Thank you," he murmured. "I'll bring them back tomorrow."

I shook my head and then pulled out my phone and began typing.

Keep them, I have another pair.

Before he could argue, I took the phone back and then reached into my pocket for my wallet. The second I began pulling cash out, Nolan began shaking his head. He refused the money I thrust at him.

Take it, I typed. *Consider it an advance on your salary and buy yourself some clothes.*

"No," Nolan said, his voice firm and unbending as he read the note. "No," he repeated, his eyes connecting with mine. "I'm fine."

Frustration coursed through me and I quickly typed out, *Then at least get a new coat. You know yours won't keep you warm enough now that the weather's changing.*

He shook his head again, but I grabbed his chin and held him still for several beats before typing another message.

Do it for me, Nolan. Or I'll worry about you.

It was a low blow, playing the guilt card, but it was the absolute truth. He held my gaze for a moment before I saw his eyes soften and he nodded. I handed him the cash.

"It's a loan," he said insistently.

I nodded.

"Thank you," he said after a moment. I was glad his voice sounded so even. I really didn't want him to leave here in the same broken-down condition he'd been in the day before.

"See you tomorrow."

I nodded again and stepped back. Nolan climbed into the car. Worry niggled my insides every time he started the car and it sputtered before dying. By the fourth try I was about to tell him I'd give him a ride, but the car turned over. Nolan waved at me through the window and then put the car in gear and backed out of the parking lot. Once his taillights disappeared down the driveway, I snapped my fingers at Loki as I began trotting back to the house...and my truck.

I told myself that my need to follow him to make sure he made it home was just the normal actions of a boss worried about a valued employee, but I knew it was horseshit.

Just this one time, then I'll get us back to where we should be. Employer and employee. For as long as he's here.

Sadly, I didn't need the power of speech to call myself a liar.

It wasn't the one time.

It was every damn night for the two weeks that followed.

Even when he got the other car back, I still couldn't stop myself from following him, especially as the temperatures continued to drop. For early November, it wasn't anything out of the ordinary, but since Nolan still hadn't bought himself some warmer clothes, I'd found it harder to let go of my concern that he wasn't staying warm enough.

He'd done as I'd asked and gotten himself a winter coat, but it hadn't taken a genius to tell that he'd bought it from a thrift store, because it had been too large for him and wore the telltale signs that it'd had a previous owner. I wouldn't have had an issue with that fact if he'd at least taken the rest of the money and spent it on some boots or something. But instead, he'd returned a large chunk of it to me, though not directly. He'd left it sitting on my office desk, so I hadn't even noticed it until the very next day. When I'd tried to argue with him about it, he'd shut me down and insisted he was fine until payday.

Payday had come and gone and he was still wearing the same worn tennis shoes and threadbare shirts. My only hope was that he'd at least splurged on some thermal underwear to put on beneath the clothes.

I'd managed to keep my distance from Nolan, but hell if it hadn't been one of the hardest things I'd had to do, especially in those moments when his vulnerability would show through.

And there were quite a few of those moments.

I hadn't asked, but I suspected things weren't going well for Nolan at home. I'd seen Nolan's parents a few times in church when I'd been a kid, but I'd never really met them or seen how they'd interacted with Nolan. I'd gotten the impression of stiff, unbending people who were more invested in their church than their child, because I'd seen them every Sunday without fail, but I'd never once seen them at school for any of the performances Nolan had given, either as a solo musician or as part of the small school orchestra.

Despite the stress that Nolan seemed to continue to be under, he'd continued to work hard, and when I'd tried to shift his responsibilities so that he was spending more time in the heated buildings, he'd called me on it. For someone who was supposed to be meek and timid, the man had no issue with standing up to me. Afterward, color would heat up his skin and he'd seem surprised by his own actions, but he never backed down.

He was definitely out to prove something.

It was a need I was all too familiar with.

So I'd backed off and left him alone, though I still found myself checking on him several times a day, despite my own heavy workload.

Like now.

The little bit of snow that had fallen that morning crunched beneath my boots as I made my way to the enclosure where most of the livestock lived. Loki was trotting next to me, but I wasn't surprised when he took off toward the barn. He'd gotten quite attached to Nolan and was starting to split his time between shadowing me and following Nolan around as he did his work. Fortunately, the other animals had grown used to Loki's presence over the years, so there weren't any issues with the wolf hybrid being around them and causing them to panic as their natural instincts to avoid predators kicked in.

As I neared the barn, I used the many trees lining the path to hide my presence from Nolan, since I didn't want to explain why I was checking on him as often as I was. It was a creeper move, but it was what it was. I'd long ago accepted that.

It took me a moment to locate Nolan. I'd expected him to be cleaning out the stalls, but to my surprise, he was sitting on the edge of the water trough. Standing in front of him was Jerry. All the other animals had wisely sought out the warmth of the barn. I thought at first that it was some kind of weird stare-off as the pair watched one another. But as Jerry's ears flicked back and forth, the truth hit me.

Nolan was talking to Jerry.

And the damn zebra was actually listening to him.

The one-sided conversation went on for several minutes, and while I'd been amused at first, I recognized the subtle changes in Nolan's body language and at one point, he dashed at his eyes. His frosty breath came in puffs the more he talked, and I hated that I was too far away to hear him. When he'd seemingly finished telling his story, he hung his head, and I bit back the urge to go to him.

Jerry ended up beating me to it.

At first, I was afraid the animal was going to knock Nolan backward into the trough, and I cursed the fact that I couldn't call out to Nolan or make any kind of sound he'd hear. But to my surprise, Jerry merely dropped his head and pushed his muzzle against Nolan's chest.

And damned if Nolan didn't wrap his arms around Jerry's neck.

So yeah, I was jealous of my normally crabby zebra.

I was so much more than just a creeper.

I left Nolan to Jerry's care and hurried to finish up my chores. I'd planned to keep my distance from Nolan, but the need to know what was bothering him overruled my common sense. I'd already written my invitation to dinner on my phone when I saw Nolan heading up the path from the livestock barn. I easily caught up with him as he neared the driveway. I tapped on the siding of the building next to us. Nolan slowed and eventually turned. I hated how gaunt and pale he looked.

I was working him too hard.

My invitation to dinner forgotten, I started a new message and handed my phone to him.

What's wrong?

His brow lifted slightly and he handed the phone back to me. "Is there anything else you need me to do before I leave, Mr. Kent?"

I frowned at that.

Why are you calling me that?

"Is that a no then, sir?" he asked tiredly.

Irritation went through me, and all thoughts of easing Nolan into a conversation about what was going on with him evaporated.

Tomorrow I'm going to show you how to clean the habitats in the small animal building. I'll take over the livestock.

"No," Nolan said calmly as he handed me the phone.

Disbelief went through me. No? That was it?

"Is there anything else, sir?"

I tapped on the phone screen at the message he'd already read.

"If you need me to clean the small animal habitats tomorrow *in addition to* my normal duties, that's fine," Nolan said stiffly.

I was typing my next message reminding him who the boss was when he turned on his heel and walked away from me. I tapped on the side of the building again. Nolan stopped and spun around.

Then he was practically in my face. The motion detector light above us showed the brittle anger in his eyes as he jammed his finger into my chest as he spoke.

"You said I was going to earn every penny of that money! Don't you dare take that from me, Dallas Kent! Don't you fucking dare!" he snapped.

I was too stunned to respond.

"You want to fire me, that's fine. Do it! But you don't get to ignore me for two weeks straight and then play the hero. I don't need you to coddle me!"

I expected him to storm off, but he crossed his arms and looked pointedly at my phone. Despite the fact that he was pissed at me, he was showing me enough respect to let me say my piece, since I couldn't just call out the words to him.

I shook my head.

What was I supposed to say?

I *had* ignored him and I *was* trying to play the hero by protecting him. *I* wanted to feel better about the situation. I'd wanted to protect little Nolan Grainger from a world that was too hard for him.

Only, he wasn't little Nolan Grainger anymore.

He'd proven that by working his ass off for two long weeks without any kind of complaint. And he'd done a good job. In addition to being kind to his charges, he'd taken pride in the quality of his work. The stalls were spotless, the water practically sparkled in clean buckets, and everyone had been getting their proper feed, supplements, and medications.

Nolan turned his back on me and headed to his car. I told myself not to follow him, but the instinct was too strong. I couldn't make sense of it. In my mind, I knew he could take care of himself – hell, he'd been doing it for ten years now.

So why couldn't I stop?

Why couldn't I not spy on him day after day to make sure he was staying warm and not wearing himself out?

Why was I obsessing over what was happening in his personal life that left him looking dejected day in and day out?

Why did the fact that he'd figured out I was purposely ignoring him hurt so damn much?

Why, even after everything he'd just said to me, could I not stop myself from hurrying to my truck so I could follow him to make sure he got home okay?

Once I reached the house, I snapped my fingers at Loki, who responded to the command and ran into the house through the doggie door. Since I was wearing jeans and a sweater under my coveralls, I quickly tore them off and tossed them into the back seat as I climbed into the front seat. My truck roared to life and I turned up the heat as I put it into gear. When I'd built the center, I'd wanted to keep the entrance to the center itself separate from the house, so I'd built a second driveway about a hundred yards west of the center's driveway.

So the last thing I expected to see when I was halfway down my driveway was another car sitting in the middle of the road with the headlights off.

It took just seconds to realize whose car it was.

And to recognize the slim body of the man leaning against the hood of the car, arms crossed.

Oh yeah, he was pissed. My headlights flashing across his pinched features were proof of that.

I put the truck in park and warily got out. I'd already seen more of pissed-off Nolan tonight than I'd wanted. It was an emotion I didn't like on him, especially knowing I was the cause.

"Going somewhere?" Nolan said snidely at my approach.

I didn't bother pulling out my phone to type him a message, because what could I say? He clearly knew what I'd been up to. I absently wondered how long he'd known I'd been following him.

"What is this all about, Dallas?" he asked, his voice going quiet.

Too quiet.

"Are you seeking redemption or something?"

I shook my head, though I wasn't sure why, since I knew what he meant. It was a conversation that was long overdue.

Nolan straightened, but didn't move toward me. Despite the fact that he wasn't yelling, the anger was still rolling off him in waves.

"Is that it?" he asked. "You still see me as that weak, pathetic sixteen-year-old kid who let those guys do all that shit to him?"

I shook my head emphatically and dug around in my pocket frantically for my phone. I had to tell him I never saw him that way. That I never would.

Despair went through me as I realized I'd tossed the phone in the truck's cup holder.

"You know what, Dallas? You can fucking go to hell. I'm not that kid anymore! You want to feel guilty for standing by and doing nothing back then, that's on you. I'm not a fucking charity case."

I could hear his voice catching and knew, despite his anger, he was on the verge of tears. Helplessness went through me with every word and I was just turning back to dash to my truck for the damn phone when he said, "Keep your damn pity. I don't want or need it. I quit."

Panic went through me at his words. Nolan was striding around the hood of his car and I knew if I took the time to get my phone, I'd lose him.

And I couldn't lose him.

Not like this.

I reached him in two strides and grabbed his arm. I frantically pointed to my truck and then my ear, hoping he'd understand I needed my phone so I could talk to him, but he was too pissed to even notice the hand gestures. I began dragging him behind me toward my truck in the hopes he'd figure out what I wanted, but he fought my hold.

"Let go!" he bit out. "I'm done talking to you!"

I ignored him and dragged him to the hood of the vehicle. I pinned him against it and tried once again to tell him I just needed to get my phone.

"I know you want to get your phone!" he snapped. "I don't care! Nothing you say changes things. Don't you get that? Do you really think I didn't see you?" He was huffing from his struggles, but thankfully, he'd calmed enough that I was no longer worried I'd inadvertently hurt him while trying to keep him from leaving.

"You were checking on me every goddamned hour, Dallas! I worked my ass off to show you I could do the job and you *still* kept waiting for me to screw up! Well, you got what you wanted. Are you happy?"

I shook my head in confusion, because I was still stuck on the fact that he'd thought I'd been checking up on him because I'd been waiting for him to fuck up.

"I'm quitting! It's what you wanted, right? You regretted hiring me out of pity, but you felt too guilty to fire me. But I didn't screw up! I did the job and I did it great. If you'd just gotten off your high horse long enough to see that-"

If I'd been able to talk, I would have told him to shut up before I sealed my mouth over his, but as it was, silencing him with a kiss was all I could do to stem the ugly tide of words that spilled from his lips.

Nolan gasped as I crushed our mouths together, but instead of pushing me away in a fit of anger or surprise, he stilled for all of two seconds and then he was kissing me back.

I'd meant the kiss to be a means to silence him long enough so I could figure out how to get him to listen to me. But the second his sweet flavor hit my tongue, I was a goner. Bringing my hands up to clasp his face, I held him still for an onslaught of kisses. His hands wrapped around my wrists, but he didn't try to stop me. In fact, he returned every kiss I laid on him and eagerly opened to me when my tongue slid over the seam of his lips.

I'd dreamed of what kissing Nolan would feel like for a long time. First back in high school, then again these past ten years whenever I saw someone who reminded me of the too-skinny kid with big, bright eyes and soft smile, and again in the weeks since he'd shown up at the center with an orphaned raccoon in the folds of his jacket.

But not one of those dreams even held a candle to what it was really like to kiss him.

In my head, I'd imagined someone I'd have to coax a passionate response out of, but the real Nolan's hungry kisses were giving me a run for my money. If anything, everything he did, every brush of his mouth over mine, every touch of his seeking tongue served to drive *me* higher. The kiss that I'd meant to use as a time-out quickly became something else.

I forced myself to pull back before things got out of hand. But one look at Nolan's plump, wet lips and expressive eyes, and I knew there were no words I could type on a screen or write on a notepad to make him understand why I'd done what I'd done.

Why I never had and never would see him as that lonely, weird, insecure kid that everyone else had pegged him as.

I pinned Nolan's eyes with my own as I let one of my hands slide down his neck, over his shoulder and down until I reached his side. I asked him the question I'd never thought I'd have the chance to and waited for his response.

He was pulling in deep breaths of air, enough that his chest brushed against mine every other second. It seemed to take forever for him to answer me, but when he did, it was unmistakable.

And he didn't have to speak it out loud.

One simple nod and that was all it took. I dropped my mouth back to his. I let the hand I had on his neck slide to cup the back of his head, and the other I wrapped around his waist. Our second kiss started off sweeter and more searching, but it flared white-hot very quickly. Nolan's long arms wrapped around my neck and he reached up onto his tiptoes so he could make up for the height difference between us. I solved the problem by grabbing the backs of his thighs and lifting him. I took a single step forward and pressed him back against the grill of my truck.

He let out a little moan of surprise and then his legs were wrapping around me. The move put him a little higher than me and he took full advantage. His fingers clasped my face as he took complete control of my mouth. I let my hands skim over his ass and reveled in the feeling of his erection pressing against my belly.

My lust spiked exponentially with every kiss and every rub of his body against mine.

"Dallas," he whispered between kisses, his voice carrying a note of awe. "Is this really happening?" he asked. I knew he wasn't expecting an answer, but I gave him one anyway when I pulled back so he could see my eyes. The light from the truck's headlights was bright enough that I had no doubt that he could see exactly what I couldn't speak out loud.

Do you want it to happen, Nolan?

CHAPTER SEVEN

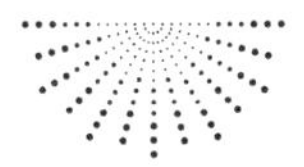

Nolan

I didn't give myself time to think, because I didn't need to.

I'd been dreaming of this moment for weeks now, years if I was being honest with myself. And now that it was here, I didn't want to play it smart and question what it would mean, or think about how it would change things. Hell, I didn't even want to know how it was possible that a man I'd always thought was straight clearly wasn't.

All I wanted was more.

Of his mouth.

His touch.

His strength.

Him.

I didn't care that I was still smarting from the knowledge that he believed me so incapable of taking care of myself that he'd been spying on me at work and following me home for days at least, if not more.

Whatever this was between us right now – it had nothing to do with pity or judgement.

He wanted me.

I didn't need to feel his dick pressing against me to recognize that.

And I didn't need words to tell him what he was waiting to hear. I didn't even have to nod. I saw it the moment he saw my answer.

Because his eyes filled with relief and the softest, sweetest smile stole across his lips.

Lips I couldn't get enough of.

I fitted my mouth over his and greeted his seeking tongue. He carried me around to the driver's side of the truck but bypassed the driver's door for the backseat door. I couldn't stop kissing him long enough to let him open the door, but he managed it anyway. The soft cushion of the bench seat met my back. I finally stopped kissing him long enough for him to climb into the back seat and close the door, then he was on me again. I barely noticed him shoving his coveralls to the floor. The cab of the truck was chilly, but I didn't care because Dallas settled his big, warm body on top of me. I opened my legs so he could fit between them, then I was wrapping myself around him as he practically assaulted my mouth. His work-roughened hands skimmed down my sides as his mouth latched onto my neck. He sucked hard and I automatically smiled. Dallas must have noticed because he paused and looked at me, his eyes going soft. He tilted his head and brought his thumb up to trace my mouth. I understood the unspoken question. He wanted to know what had put the smile there.

"Dallas Kent just gave me a hickey," I murmured. I reached up to stroke his face. "Do you have any idea how many times I wished for that to happen when we were kids?"

I'd expected him to smile, but he didn't. There was an odd sadness to him as he studied me, and I regretted saying anything at all. I pulled him back down for another searing kiss. He let me control it, which was something I wouldn't have expected from a guy like him. We kissed for several long minutes before Dallas began making his way down my body. His big hands pushed my jacket off my shoulders, but he seemed too impatient to work it or my shirt off my body. Instead, he shoved the shirt up and then his mouth latched onto one of my nipples. I let out a hoarse shout and grabbed his head to keep him there, but he easily broke free and sought out the other nipple. His mouth blazed a trail down my chest and over my belly. At some point I'd closed my eyes, but when his hand closed over my cock through my pants, I couldn't *not* look at him.

His eyes met mine as he rubbed my dick teasingly over and over, then he was reaching for the button of my jeans. I bit my lip to keep from telling him to hurry up as he carefully opened my pants. I waited with bated breath for him to pull my dick out of my underwear, but all he did was palm me through the fabric.

"Dallas, please," I begged, even as I arched my back and bucked my hips up to try to get more of his touch. His heavy hand settled on my belly as he held me down, then he dropped his head and began nuzzling me through the fabric. I was writhing with need by the time he finally pulled my underwear aside enough to release my bouncing, leaking cock.

And he gave me absolutely no warning before sucking it into his mouth and to the back of his throat.

"Fuck, yes!" I cried out as I clutched his head in my hands and shoved my hips up. I felt instantly bad when he gagged, but when I tried to pull back, his hands grabbed my ass to urge me on. It was all the permission I needed.

I could have fucked his mouth all night, but within a matter of minutes, he was releasing my still-pulsing dick with a pop and then his mouth was on mine. I could taste my pre-cum on his tongue, and I suddenly found myself eager to return the favor so I could see how different he tasted from me.

But Dallas had other ideas because he reared up onto his knees, then flipped me over. He yanked me to my hands and knees and then shoved my pants and underwear down. I sat up long enough to work my coat all the way off, but when I went for my shirt, Dallas merely shoved me back down onto my hands and knees, then took it a step further and pressed my shoulders down against the seat. The show of dominance had my lust ratcheting up to a whole new level, and when Dallas began bumping his still-clothed crotch against my bare ass, I moaned and reached for my dick. But Dallas's hand quickly covered mine and he pulled my arm behind my back and held it there so I couldn't touch myself.

"God, Dallas, hurry," I ground out. I managed to look over my shoulder at him while maintaining the position he'd put me in. His face was twisted into a mask of fiery need and he was staring at my ass like a starving man. When his eyes met mine, I felt a zap of energy fire through my body and I wondered if I could come just from that. The pressure in my balls was saying "hell yeah" to that question.

Dallas finally released his hold on my hip and the arm he'd folded behind my back as he shrugged off his coat. The jangle of his belt had me sucking in deep breaths, because I knew I was in for a down and dirty fuck.

And I couldn't wait.

I dropped my head to the seat and tried to think of anything that would keep me from blowing as Dallas got his zipper undone. I closed my eyes when I felt his bare dick pressing against my ass. His flesh was hot and hard, and if I hadn't been so desperate to feel it filling me up, I'd have turned around and swallowed him down like he had me.

The sound of foil tearing followed, and then cold lube was being swiped over my hole by a greedy finger. The pad of Dallas's thumb massaged my opening for several seconds before a thick finger finally began to push into me. I bit my arm to keep from crying out as pain flashed through me, followed by a white-hot burning sensation. I expected Dallas to either finger-fuck me to loosen me, or add another finger, but instead, he held his finger where it was and carefully leaned over me. His mouth searched out mine over my shoulder and he began kissing me slow and deep. I got so lost in his tongue mating with mine, that I barely felt him pushing his digit the rest of the way into me. When he slid it out and then back in, I moaned into his mouth.

He never stopped kissing me.

Not as he fucked me with one finger.

Not even when he added a second.

It wasn't until his dick began pressing into me that he reared back, presumably so he could watch himself disappear into my body. I pushed my shoulders up and locked my arms so I was once again on all fours, but as tempted as I was to reach for my dick again, I didn't.

Despite my desperate need to come, I wanted Dallas with me when it happened.

Dallas was slow to work himself into my body, choosing to fuck me with shallow thrusts instead of just sinking into me all at once. The move worked because it was me who began pushing back against him hard and harder to get more of him inside of me. When he bottomed out, I let out a cry of relief.

Dallas's heavy hands closed around my hips to hold me in place as he began fucking into me with slow, deep thrusts that had me seeing stars. The pace didn't last, though, because within a minute, he was pushing into me more frantically, and his fingers pressed into my skin hard enough to likely leave bruises. I could barely hear his heavy breaths and grunts over my own, but God, did I love the sound. My orgasm was hovering just on the edge and I knew Dallas wasn't far behind me, because he began pumping into me at an unfathomable pace. The pressure, heat, and nearly unbearable friction had me calling out, "Yes, Dallas, please, yes!"

I was about to reach for my dick when Dallas's arm wrapped around my upper body and he dragged me upward so I was just on my knees. His mouth covered mine over my shoulder as he pounded into me. The new position had him hitting my prostate on every pass, which brought my orgasm closer and closer to the surface with every thrust of his dick. Skin slapped against skin as our sweat-covered bodies slid against one another. I screamed into Dallas's mouth when his calloused hand closed around my dick and began pumping me hard and fast. Between him hitting my gland and the expert hand job, I was a goner within seconds, and I bit down on the arm he had lashed across my upper chest as the orgasm ripped through me. Dallas let out a loud grunt as he slammed into me once, twice, three times and then held there as his release began filling the condom. His pulsing dick caused a violent aftershock to rock through me. I could feel his breath against the back of my neck as he clung to me, his hips involuntarily jerking against my ass as he continued to thrust into me.

The high seemed to go on forever, but when it finally did ease, Dallas's weight pushed me down onto the seat. His hand was still wrapped around my dick, but he either didn't care that it and now his seat were covered in my cum, or he didn't notice. I was too tired to really worry about it either way.

I reveled in his weight pinning me and his half-hard cock still buried deep inside of me. I couldn't say how long we lay there for, but my breathing had almost returned to normal when he finally shifted off me and carefully withdrew from my body.

As the after-effects of the orgasm waned, reality came crashing down. I managed to pull my pants up as I sat up. Dallas handed me a wad of fabric, presumably to clean the cum off my belly. Ironically, it was the bandana he typically wore around his neck – the one he'd stopped wearing around me.

I cleaned myself as best I could and then tucked myself back in my pants. My ass stung as I shifted my weight so I could pull my jeans all the way up and fasten them.

There were a million things I wanted to say to Dallas, but I could sense the distance he was already putting between us, so I kept my mouth shut. He didn't need to be able to speak for me to know what he was going to say.

It had been a mistake.

All the post-coital bliss evaporated just like that, and I quickly reached down to find my coat. "I should go," I said. "It's late."

I reached for the door handle on my side of the seat, but Dallas's hand closed over my arm. He reached forward to the console between the front seats and grabbed his phone. As badly as I wanted to escape, I couldn't just leave him without letting him have his say.

But if I'd expected his words to somehow miraculously fix the ever-widening rift between us, I was gravely mistaken.

I'm sorry.

I stared at the two words on his phone screen for a long time before I nodded. "Goodbye, Dallas," was all I managed to get out before I stumbled out of the truck. I managed not to run to my own car, despite wanting to. Once inside the car, I murmured, "Please, please," to the piece of shit car. I'd fucking die if the damn thing chose this moment to take its last breath. Fortunately, it turned over on the second try. The driveway wasn't wide enough to turn around in, so I had to back out, which was a good thing since I didn't want to risk looking at Dallas even for a second.

I had no clue if Dallas followed me home or not, nor did I really care at that point. The humiliation I'd been feeling earlier in the evening returned in full force. It was just after six, early by anyone's standards, but the second I walked in the door, I shook my head when my mother asked if I was hungry and went straight to my bathroom. I showered long enough to clean the remnants of my cum off my body and then crawled into bed. My eyes instantly fell on the stack of bills on the nightstand.

I felt tears sting my eyes as the realization hit me.

Not only had I fucked the object of my obsession, and in the back seat of his truck no less, I'd quit my job.

I'd let my pride rule my head and now I was totally fucked. The money from my first paycheck was already gone, and I'd earmarked the money I'd be earning from my second paycheck to pay the bills that were still several months overdue.

I let the tears flow because I knew what I needed to do tomorrow.

I needed to go back to Dallas and beg him to give me my job back.

So what if he thought I was weak and incapable? My pride wasn't going to pay the damn bills.

I was about to turn out the lights and try to lose myself in sleep when my phone buzzed. I didn't recognize the number for the text, but I didn't need to since the text took care of that for me.

Nolan, it's me, Dallas. Can I talk to you?

I sat up and stared at the phone. My heart clenched as I remembered how good his mouth had felt on mine. How his hot breath had washed over my skin as he'd pounded into me. He'd held me so damn tight...like he wasn't ever going to let me go.

I typed out a simple response. *Okay.*

I'm out front.

I stilled at that for all of two seconds, then jumped out of bed and went to the window overlooking the front yard. Sure enough, Dallas's darkened pickup was sitting on the curb in front of my parents' house.

I swallowed hard at the realization that, despite needing his phone to communicate with me, he'd still driven all the way to my house to actually do it.

Why?

Why did he need to be around me to talk to me?

I highly doubted he was interested in fucking me again, and certainly not on my parents' quiet, suburban street.

I typed him a message that I'd be right out and then grabbed my coat and slipped on my shoes. My parents were in the living room, so it was easy to slip out of the house unnoticed, though I wasn't sure why it mattered since I was a grown man and had the right to come and go as I pleased.

Dallas had parked his truck just short of the street lamp overhead, so it was dark in the cab. When I climbed into the vehicle, the interior lights didn't come on. I didn't like that I couldn't see him, but I didn't ask him to turn the lights on, either.

Maybe it was better that this conversation happen in the dark.

I could only think of one reason he'd come to my house to talk. He was going to make sure I knew I wasn't welcome back at the center. It was the only thing that made sense. He was giving me the kiss-off in person because he was a decent guy and he wanted to make sure little Nolan Grainger was okay after getting his pathetic ass fired.

"Look, Dallas, you don't have to-"

Dallas's hand shot out to cover my arm and I immediately fell silent. His hold on me was gentle, but firm.

He needed it to be his turn to talk.

He didn't look at me as he typed out his message. My phone

buzzed in my hand a few moments later and I felt my heart pounding frantically in my throat. I reminded myself that no matter what, I wouldn't cry in front of him.

Not again.

I turned my phone over and unlocked it.

Nolan, I'm sorry about what happened tonight. It shouldn't have.

Before I could respond, another message came through.

I'm your boss. It was a line I never should have crossed.

There was a slight pause, then came, *Did I hurt you?*

He was my boss? Present tense? Did that mean...?

I was almost too afraid to consider what it meant. If he wasn't firing me, it meant maybe I hadn't screwed up so badly that things couldn't be fixed.

Dallas tapped on my arm to get my attention. I couldn't see his face, but I could tell he was looking at me, and I remembered his last question.

"No, no, you didn't hurt me," I said quickly. To my surprise, his body sagged a bit like he was relieved. "It was...good," I said lamely. Dallas paused for a beat before returning his attention to his phone, but I stopped him with a tap on his arm. I waited until he was looking at me. "It was perfect, actually."

My eyes had adjusted to the darkness enough that I could see his lips pull into a slight smile, but he quickly dipped his head.

If you come back, I promise it won't happen again.

Come back?

"What?" I squeaked. "You want me to come back?"

Dallas nodded and then typed something else.

You've been doing an amazing job, Nolan. I'd like you to reconsider quitting. You're really good with the animals and you're one of the hardest workers I've ever met.

I couldn't believe what he was saying. I wanted to, but I just couldn't.

"Dallas, you kept checking on me, even after I'd figured out how to do everything."

I kept checking on you because I was worried about you. Not because I didn't think you weren't doing a good job, but because I was afraid you were too cold and I know how physically hard that kind of work is, even for someone who's used to doing it. I just wanted to make sure you weren't pushing yourself too hard trying to impress me or prove something to me.

I hated the flurry of warmth that went through me. "But you followed me home," I said.

Because both the cars you drive are pieces of shit. I was worried you'd break down again and who knows if anyone would have stopped. Or the wrong person stopped.

I turned my head so I was looking out the windshield. He had to be lying, he just had to.

Right?

"Why did you ignore me for the last two weeks?"

I waited for my phone to beep, but it didn't. I turned my head to look at him and saw that he, too, was staring out the windshield.

"Dallas," I said softly. He flinched and then began typing.

At first, I was hoping you'd quit because the work was too difficult. Being around you is hard, Nolan. And not just because of what happened tonight. I never saw you as weak when we were kids. Never. I wish I could have been as brave as you. I wish I'd done things differently.

I waited for another message, but Dallas stopped typing. It didn't really matter, because he'd said enough and I believed what he was telling me.

"Where do we go from here?" I asked, because I really didn't have a clue.

Come back to work, Nolan.

It was all he typed, but I knew it really was the only thing I could do. He clearly wasn't interested in pursuing anything beyond a working relationship. He'd made that clear when he'd pointed out that what had happened tonight had been a mistake. And while I didn't exactly share his feelings on the subject, I knew it was something that wouldn't have led anywhere, anyway. At best, it could have been a friends-with-benefits kind of thing, even though we weren't really friends, either.

I hid my disappointment and said, "I'll see you tomorrow, Dallas."

With that, I got out of the truck and didn't look back as I walked toward the house. We were back to exactly where we should be.

So why did I still feel like shit?

I spent a good five minutes the following morning taking stock of the light bruises on my body, including the huge hickey on my neck and the finger-shaped marks on my hips. If I hadn't seen the proof of Dallas's possession on my body, I would have passed the whole thing off as a dream.

Despite the fact that I could still feel the stinging in my ass that Dallas's generously sized cock had left behind, I still couldn't believe he played for my team. Not once in high school had I seen anything that even hinted that Dallas was attracted to men, and nothing in these past two weeks would have led me to believe it had ever been anything but women for him. I supposed it was possible he was bisexual, but it still blew my mind.

Not that I could really blame him for hiding something like that, especially when we'd been younger. Pelican Bay was, and always had been, a community steeped in its religious and family values. Since I'd been such an outcast at school, there'd been no one to officially come out to at the age of sixteen when I'd figured out I was gay. I'd been called "faggot" and "queer" often enough to figure people had come to the conclusion on their own, though I suspected they would have called me those things even if I hadn't actually been gay.

For someone like Dallas Kent, admitting to liking guys would have been equal to committing social suicide. For all I knew, it could have impacted his ability to play professional baseball. So I couldn't really begrudge him for wanting to keep the truth from people.

It did leave me wondering if he might still be hiding it, though, since he hadn't mentioned anything when I'd inadvertently outed myself the night I'd had dinner at his place.

I decided it was all irrelevant since last night had been a one-time thing. Even if Dallas hadn't been the one to say it, I should have.

Pelican Bay was a layover for me, so even if by some miracle a guy like Dallas could be interested in a guy like me outside of the bedroom, I had absolutely no desire to stay in town any longer than I absolutely had to.

Not even for Dallas Kent.

I practically saw my lips move in my reflection as I called myself a liar.

Okay, so I didn't want to be in a position where I even had to think about a choice like that. My plan was to get my parents back on their feet financially, and then I was going to find a nice big city to start over in. My career as a professional violinist was over, but it didn't mean I couldn't still use music to pay the bills.

I forced myself to push thoughts of Dallas and the night before aside and quickly got dressed. I rushed past the kitchen, not even bothering with coffee since Dallas had a small coffee pot in his office. But just as I reached the door, I heard my mother's voice.

"Nolan, is that you?"

"Yeah," I called. "I'm late for work."

"Just a minute, dear," she said, and I knew that meant I had to go to her instead of waiting for her to come to me. I hurried to the kitchen and found my mother preparing breakfast.

My mother had finally accepted the fact that I had an actual real job about a week ago and had eventually stopped insisting I be at home at certain times to watch my father, but she'd yet to figure out that said job was the only thing keeping the lights on and the bill collectors at bay.

"Sit," she said as she pointed to one of the kitchen chairs.

"I can't, I'm late," I said as I motioned to the front door.

She pinned me with her gaze and nodded toward the chair. I sat and tapped my fingers on the table. Maybe I should let Dallas know I was running late so he wouldn't think I'd changed my mind about coming back.

"What was that Kent boy's truck doing outside the house last night?"

I hated the clench in my belly as her automatic disapproval washed over me.

"He came to talk me," I hedged. *After he fucked me so good and so hard I think he might have ruined me for other men.*

"Why are you smiling, Nolan? I don't see anything amusing about the situation."

I hadn't even realized I was smiling. Since I couldn't very well tell her that getting monumentally fucked in the back of a car by your high school fantasy come to life was bound to put a smile on anyone's face, I settled for, "What situation? We were just talking."

"That boy doesn't talk," she reminded me impatiently. "What were you doing with him?"

"Talking about work stuff. Which I'm going to be late for, by the way."

"Work?" she whispered, her face pulling into a horrified expression. She actually looked out the window like she was expecting to see Dallas's truck sitting on the street, or worse, in the driveway. "You work for *him*?"

"Dallas, Mom. His name is Dallas. And yes, I work for him."

"You can't!" she said. "Your father and I will be laughingstocks!"

I couldn't stop the chuckle that came out of my mouth. "Are you kidding me?"

"Don't you laugh at me, young man," she snapped. "It's already bad enough that I have to live down the fact that my boy is a thief and a..." Her voice dropped off.

"And a fag?" I asked quietly.

For once, she actually looked embarrassed. "We don't say that word in this house."

"But you're allowed to think it, right? I guess deviant is the socially acceptable word, right?"

"That boy brought shame to this entire community when he killed his parents and started that...that zoo! Are you and he...are you...fornicating?" She whispered the last word as if someone was close enough to hear.

I climbed to my feet. "It's a wildlife center and sanctuary, Mom. It takes in animals that people fucked over and it tries to give them a better life."

"Nolan, langu-"

"And yeah, I'm a fag. I like dick. We established that when I was sixteen years old and you told me never to mention it again or I wouldn't have a family anymore. And as for that damn violin, I'm done telling you something that you should have believed without question because I'm your son."

I snatched my coat off the table. "Watch what you say about Dallas Kent. He's the only reason you still have a roof over your head," I bit out.

I was seething with a mix of rage and nerves when I arrived at the center. I met Dallas as I was rounding the corner of the office building. His arms came up to catch me before I slammed into him and his face pulled into a frown.

"Dallas, fuck, I'm sorry, but my mom, she..."

The words got caught in my throat. Dallas gently rubbed my arms up and down, then tipped my head up so I was looking at him.

"She saw your truck last night. She knows I'm gay so she assumed you were there to...you know."

There was the tiniest stiffening of his jaw as he took in my words and he dropped his hands.

But just to get his phone and type a message.

It doesn't matter.

"Yes, it does," I said. "She's a terrible gossip. It'll get all over town. I'm sorr-"

His hand came up to cover my mouth. He shook his head and then typed again.

The town hates me anyway. Just another crime to add to an already long list.

Before I could respond, he began typing another message and I remembered that we were only boss and employee. It wasn't my place to question him about stuff.

I did your morning chores already.

"Dall-"

He slapped his hand over my mouth and gave me the evil eye. Then he held up one finger, indicating I should wait.

I'm releasing the mom and baby raccoons back into the wild this morning and thought you might want to come. It will take a couple of hours, so I got up early to do your chores and mine.

I opened my mouth to answer him, but he held up his finger again and then sent me a small smirk at my look of exasperation.

And if you even think of insisting I not pay you for the time, I'll fire you, drive to your house, introduce myself to your mother, and tell her I'm there to pick you up for our three-way with Tom Hiddleston.

His eyes danced with humor after I finished reading his text, and I couldn't help but laugh. "Okay, you win. But if we ever do find ourselves face to face with Tom Hiddleston, I get to tap his ass first."

His eyes narrowed and he typed out, *You're fired.*

"Fine, you can tap his ass first."

I expected him to continue the joke, but his eyes pinned mine and then his gaze slid down my body. And just like that, the humor died and the air around us became charged with electricity. I was leaning into him before I even realized what I was doing. Thankfully, Dallas had the common sense to step back.

We should go.

I nodded because my throat felt like I'd swallowed a beach ball.

I followed Dallas to the small animal building and watched him collect a very angry mother raccoon and her babies, who'd grown considerably in the past two weeks. It took just over an hour to get to our destination – a small nature reserve in the middle of nowhere.

Dallas set the cage on the ground in a heavily wooded section of the park. There was a large stream nearby that hadn't frozen over yet. He stepped behind the cage and lifted the door, then took my hand in his and pulled me back several steps. A full minute passed before the mother raccoon and her babies emerged and then took off up a tree.

"Won't they get too cold out here?" I asked as I huddled into my coat.

Dallas shook his head and motioned to a couple of large rocks near the water's edge. I followed him and sat down. He was slower to sit down and I had to wonder if his leg was bothering him more today, since his limp had seemed a bit more pronounced. I patiently waited for him to type his response.

This stream has a strong enough current that it never completely freezes over in the winter. I've released several different kinds of animals up here, including raccoons. The mother will spend the next month or two gathering food. The babies will probably stay with her through the winter. They don't hibernate, but they spend the cold snaps mostly in their dens.

Dallas leaned into me and pointed upstream. I smiled at the sight of the mother raccoon and her babies exploring the stream. The sun was bright over our heads and helped take some of the chill away.

"How did you get into this?" I asked. "Did you always like animals?"

He nodded.

We weren't allowed to have them growing up. About eight years ago I found an orphaned deer alongside the road. I tried to find a place that could help her, but there was nothing around and none of the vets I called would take her. So I tried taking care of her myself.

"Did she make it?" I asked.

Another nod. *But I made the mistake of treating her like a pet, so when I tried to release her back into the wild, she didn't know how to take care of herself. When I came back to where I'd left her, she came running right up to me. She'd lost a lot of weight in that short time and I knew she wouldn't make it, so I took her home with me. She was the first permanent resident of the center.*

"Is that when you opened it?"

Yes. I used some of the money my parents left me and bought the farm outside of town and converted it into what it is now.

I remembered my mother's story about how his brother had tried to keep him from getting any of the money, but I didn't bring that up.

"By yourself?"

He stiffened a little, then nodded. He didn't type anything, so I took that as a silent message that it wasn't a topic he wanted to discuss.

I bumped his shoulder with mine. "Thank you for bringing me here."

Despite the cold weather and my numb ass, I found that I didn't want to leave the quiet solitude around us.

Until Dallas typed out his next message.

Tell me about the stolen violin, Nolan.

CHAPTER EIGHT

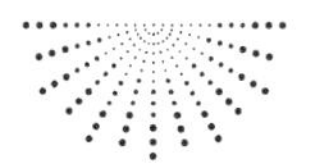

Dallas

I didn't think he would answer and he certainly didn't owe me one.

Especially considering the lengths I'd gone to the previous night to point out I was his boss and that what had happened between us had been a mistake.

A mistake I would have killed to repeat.

God, fucking Nolan Grainger had been pure heaven. And I was hopelessly addicted. But it wasn't just his body that I wanted to lose myself in.

And that was what was scaring the hell out of me.

"Um, did you know I went to Juilliard after graduation?" he asked.

I nodded. *You have an amazing talent.*

He looked up at me in surprise. "What?"

I shrugged. *I'm no expert, but whenever you played...I couldn't take my eyes off you.*

"What?" he practically squeaked.

I smiled and gave him a gentle bump. *You were saying about Juilliard,* I reminded him.

"Right. So, um, after Juilliard, I got hired to play in a couple of big name orchestras – in New York first, then Boston. But San Francisco was the crème de la crème. They hired me as First Chair three years ago."

I didn't know what First Chair meant, but I assumed it was a big deal.

"Within a matter of weeks, I was meeting really important people in the music world. Other musicians, composers, benefactors…it was really overwhelming, but it was also what I'd always dreamed of, you know? They didn't see me as 'Nerdy Nolan' or 'Grungy Grainger.' They saw me as someone who belonged among them."

You fit.

Nolan's eyes hung on my screen for a moment before he looked at me and nodded. "Exactly," he murmured. "Anyway, I met this man named Trey. He was a well-known patron of the arts – he donated tons of money to the symphony every year. He even funded a couple of scholarships for kids to go to schools like Juilliard. For whatever reason, he took a liking to me…beyond just musically speaking."

I was pretty sure I knew why the man had taken a liking to Nolan. He was gorgeous and he practically vibrated with goodness. I'd met plenty of Treys in my own climb to professional stardom, mostly in the form of sports agents who'd wanted a piece of me. I'd been offered all sorts of perks to sign with them and take a shot directly at the majors without the benefit of college, but my parents had been adamant that their kid wasn't bypassing the prestige of a degree with the Vanderbilt name on the top of it.

Nolan would have been a lamb among wolves in that kind of world.

"Trey began following my career really closely. It took me a long time to realize he was interested in me for reasons other than music. When I did figure it out, I was flattered. But I hadn't ever…you know," he said with a tilt of his head. "I mean, I almost did with this guy at Juilliard, but..."

Nolan laughed and shook his head. "Trey saw me coming from a mile away," he murmured. "It started when he bought me a violin. Have you ever heard of a Stradivarius?"

They're very expensive.

"Yes, they are. The one Trey bought was worth over a million dollars. But it wasn't a gift or anything – it was for me to play with, but it belonged to him. I think he liked the prestige of knowing a professional musician was using an instrument he'd provided. I tried to tell him no, but the second I played it, it was like...it was like an extension of my arm. I fell in love with it." He shook his head. "And that was when he had me."

Jealousy curled through my system.

You began a relationship with him? I asked.

Nolan nodded. "It happened so fast. Within a month I was moving into an apartment he was paying for. By the end of the year he was managing my money. You want to know what the kicker was?" he asked, his voice sad.

I nodded.

"He wasn't even out. And he had no intention of coming out." Nolan's eyes drifted back to the raccoons. "No one in the industry would have cared, but he kept saying his job depended on him giving off a certain impression. He was some kind of investment banker or something. It was something we fought about a lot, but he was insistent. He even had a girlfriend."

Nolan laughed, but it sounded harsh and ugly. "I actually believed him when he said the relationship with her was all for show."

He fell silent for a moment. "You know what he used to make me do?"

I knew he wasn't expecting an answer, so I didn't respond, other than to cover his hand with mine where it was clenched on his thigh. He hadn't remembered to put his gloves on, and I'd taken mine off when I'd opened the cage for the raccoons, so our skin came into direct contact.

"He used to make me do these private performances for him and his friends. Sometimes his girlfriend would be there and I'd have to play while they held hands and stuff. It was like I became a possession to him...like that damn violin."

The pain in Nolan's voice hurt my heart and I found myself putting my arm around his shoulders and tucking him up against my side. I was glad when he dropped his head on my shoulder.

"It took almost three years for me to come to my senses and end the relationship. The day after I told him I was leaving him, the violin disappeared from my apartment. Trey told the police I'd taken it to get back at him because I was obsessed with him. He told them he'd only been helping me out by paying for the apartment and stuff because I was broke. When I told them I'd given all my money to Trey to invest for me, they didn't find any proof of any investments."

I stiffened and forced Nolan to sit up so I could type out a message.

He stole your money?

Nolan nodded. "All I had left was about five thousand in my checking account. I'd given Trey access to all my accounts, so I never knew when he took the money or what he did with it, but the police couldn't link any of the transactions back to him. They believed Trey's story that I took the violin. They accused me of stealing it to both get back at Trey and because I was hoping to sell it on the black market."

What happened? Did they charge you?

Nolan shook his head and dashed at his eyes. "No, but it was close. The cops found surveillance footage of someone my size and height taking the violin from the building. But I had an alibi for when it happened. I'd flown to London to audition with the orchestra there. Trey hadn't known about it. The cops were able to see that whoever took it had some kind of tattoo on his arm. They accused me of having a friend steal it, but they didn't have any proof, so they couldn't charge me."

So it was never found?

"No. Trey told anyone who would listen that I took it. He was really powerful in the community and everyone believed him over me. He ruined my reputation – no orchestra will hire a musician who steals. The cops…they even came out here to question my parents," he whispered.

Your parents, they believed you, right?

He didn't answer, which was answer enough.

Is that why you came back to Pelican Bay? I asked.

Nolan shook his head. "Um, no. My plan was to take what little money I had left and just disappear. Maybe get a job teaching music somewhere. Then my mom called to tell me my dad had a partial stroke and told me I needed to come back to help her take care of him. I thought it would just be for a few weeks…"

The truth of the situation hit me when I remembered Nolan's sheer desperation for a job. If he'd had some money saved up, it meant he hadn't been the one with money trouble.

Which left his parents.

Jesus, had he really used his money to bail out the parents who hadn't believed their own son when he'd denied taking the violin?

"You know what the worst part is?" Nolan said softly. He looked at me briefly before turning his attention back to the raccoons. "When Trey had the locks to my apartment changed, he left my clothes in garbage bags with the doorman. But he wouldn't give me back the violin I'd been using before he gave me the Stradivarius." Nolan shook his head. "I'd saved for so long for that violin. It was worth practically nothing to a guy like him. But he knew what it meant to me…what it meant to be able to play every day, whether I was performing or not."

I fought the unholy urge to hunt Trey down and kick his ass.

After a few minutes of silence, Nolan turned to me and said, "Thanks for bringing me, Dallas. I like knowing he has a chance now." He motioned to the family of raccoons. The baby Nolan had saved was slightly smaller than its adopted sibling, but it had grown strong under its new mother's care.

I pulled Nolan's hand up to my mouth and pressed a kiss to the back of it. His skin was cold so I eased myself to my feet, ignoring the sting in my own hip, and then pulled him to a standing position. And for the life of me, I couldn't release his hand after that. So I ignored the mixed messages I was sending him and held onto his hand as I grabbed the cage with my other hand.

And I didn't release him until we'd made it all the way back to the truck.

CHAPTER NINE

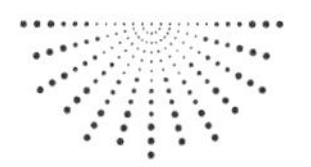

Nolan

What the hell had I been thinking?

That was the question that kept going through my mind as I stared at the aisle full of bags and bags of dog food.

Grain-free.

Large breed.

Small chunks.

Beef flavored, chicken flavored, beef and chicken...the choices were endless.

"He says just get whatever," I murmured to myself as I finally looked at the price tags and selected something halfway between the most and least expensive. After that, I picked the bag with a dog that looked most like Loki on the outside of it and began dragging the huge bags into the grocery cart.

It had been my idea to drive to town to grab the dog food after the guy who delivered all of the food and supplies for the center messed up and forgot to include the week's supply of dog food. Since there hadn't been enough left to feed the dogs their evening meal, I'd suggested to Dallas that we just buy enough to tide the dogs over until the guy brought a special shipment in a few days.

I hadn't understood why Dallas had been so hesitant at first.

And I felt pretty shitty that he'd been forced to tell me rather than me figuring it out on my own.

I don't go to town.

Those few words, along with the memory of how my mother had talked about Dallas, like he was a damn pariah, had been enough to make me realize that was exactly what he was.

It was what the town had turned him into.

And all because of a bad choice he'd made ten years ago that so many of the residents could have easily made themselves.

Dallas had been on the verge of making the forty-five-minute drive to Greenville, but when I'd offered to go to the local farm and feed store in Pelican Bay, he'd reluctantly conceded. I'd been tempted to ask him to come with me, because it bothered me more than I wanted to admit that he'd let the townspeople run him out of the place he'd been revered in as a kid, but I'd decided against it. Having had my own bout with infamy, I couldn't really fault him for it. After all, if I'd had the chance, I would have run from Pelican Bay for a second time without looking back.

As it was, I could already feel the stares and muted whispers as people began recognizing me. I'd been back for more than a month and the talk about me that had been going around while I'd been searching for a job hadn't dissipated even a bit. I suspected I had my mother's gossiping ways to thank for that. She'd ended up adding fuel to the fire by spreading the word that I was working for Dallas. I had no clue why anyone cared, since I'd never been worth noticing before my return to Pelican Bay and clearly people wanted to pretend Dallas and his animals didn't exist. But as I made my way to check out, one person after another watched me with suspicious eyes.

I half-expected someone to tackle me and accuse me of planning to steal the dog food.

All four bags that, combined, weighed more than I did.

I breathed a silent thanks when I saw that there wasn't a line at the checkout, but that thanks turned into a slew of curse words as soon as my eyes landed on the man running the register.

Jimmy Cornell.

AKA Nolan Grainger's Tormentor-in-Chief.

I didn't bother begging Fate to make it so Jimmy didn't recognize me, because his eyes lit up the second he saw me.

Like a kid who'd found his favorite toy behind the couch after months of searching for it.

"Nerdy Nolan Grainger," Jimmy said with a wide grin as his eyes raked over me. "Heard you were back in town."

The years hadn't been kind to Jimmy. He had stringy black hair that hung in a disheveled mess around his face. His once-lean frame was now carrying a decent beer belly that the store's red apron couldn't hide. His teeth were yellowed and one was actually missing. There was a certain dullness to his gaze that reminded me of many of the homeless drug addicts I'd so often seen on the streets of both San Francisco and Boston alike. I had to wonder if it was more than just too much beer that Jimmy splurged on. I'd seen enough on the news recently to know that small towns weren't immune to the vices of the big city. It wouldn't have surprised me a bit if drugs had managed to find their way to the postcard cover worthy hamlet of Pelican Bay.

"Jimmy," I said with a nod. "I'm all set," I added, hoping to speed things along. What I really needed was a customer to get in line behind me, but, of course, Fate was having too good of a time.

"You gonna ask your mama to try out some new recipes for you?" Jimmy said with a laugh as he nodded at the dog food.

I bit back the urge to lob some equally crude comment back at him since he was the son of my mother's best friend, Edith. Not only would word get back to my mother, it would get back in such a way that only reinforced her theory that I'd been corrupted by city life. I pulled in a breath and said, "I'm in a bit of a hurry, if you don't mind."

"Whatcha gotta do? Plan your next heist?" he cackled as he grabbed his scanner and began ringing up the bags.

I stayed silent as he totaled the bill and read me the amount. I handed him the credit card Dallas had given to me to pay for the food. But just before he ran it through the scanner on the register, he paused and studied the card.

"Well, looks like we got ourselves a problem. This here card ain't yours."

"It's Dallas's," I said. "The food is for his wildlife center."

"So you say," he said snidely. "How do I know you didn't steal it?"

"Fine," I said with a sigh. "I'll use my card." I dug my wallet out of my pocket and pulled out my debit card. I barely had enough left in my personal account to cover the cost of the food, but I knew Dallas would reimburse me. I handed it to Jimmy, but he ignored it and pinched Dallas's card between his fingers.

"So you're working at that reject zoo of his?" he asked. "Shoulda seen that one coming a mile away."

Ignore him, Nolan.

Ignore him.

"Seen what?" I asked, shutting out that voice in my head.

"The way you were fawning all over him in school. Couldn't stop staring at him. Guess you finally got what you wanted, huh? Wouldn't have been hard nowadays, considering things. The fag and the freak," he mused, his dull eyes shifting from the card to me.

I ground my jaw together and held out my card. "The food, Jimmy."

"So how does it work? He bends you over so your ass looks like any girl's and you get what...a good pounding? Or you in it for something else? Heard he's still sitting pretty with all the cash he got after killing his folks. That's called, what..." Jimmy mulled his words over before saying, "A mutually beneficial relationship?"

"Which part is it that riles you more?" I asked as I leaned across the counter and snatched Dallas's card from Jimmy's fingers. "The fact that even without his voice he's still more man than you'll ever be, or that it's not your ass that's getting pounded?"

Jimmy's eyes blazed with fury, but just as he was about to reach for me, a man's voice called, "Jimmy?"

We both turned to see a portly older man watching us from a doorway leading to a small office in the corner of the store near the registers. He was wearing a nametag like Jimmy's, but I could see it had the title of *Manager* underneath the name.

"Problem here?" he asked as he stepped closer to the register.

"Um, no sir, Mr. Blaine. I was just checking this gentleman out."

Thankfully, the manager hung around while Jimmy completed the transaction. I hurried out of the store, but not before I heard the manager's raised voice behind me. A part of me wanted to stay behind to watch the guy chew Jimmy out, but the other part of me was eager to get back to the center.

Funny how it had become a sanctuary of sorts for me, too, in the past few weeks.

It had been a little over a week since Dallas and I had released the raccoons, and we'd been getting along better and had even started having lunch together in Dallas's office every afternoon. I'd gotten to hear more and more about the different animals and their stories, but curiously, Dallas never talked about himself. But he did ask me a lot of questions, mostly about all the performances I'd given in different cities all over the world.

The work itself had gotten a little easier for me as my body had adjusted to the physical demands of the job. I'd been surprised when Dallas had asked me if I wanted to start helping him with other tasks that involved the wildlife. It was still just a lot of cleaning, but since I was now able to get my chores done with the domesticated animals by lunchtime, I spent the rest of the afternoon helping Dallas clean or repair various habitats. He'd let me interact with some of the wildlife that weren't considered dangerous and that weren't slated to be re-released, and I'd quickly grown as fond of them as I had of Jerry and the other animals I spent my mornings with.

The only problem with spending more time in Dallas's presence was that it made me want to spend more time in his presence.

But not just professionally speaking.

Horizontally speaking was definitely at the top of the list. I'd even had plenty of fantasies where vertically would have been extremely desirable. But I also wanted to do the stuff that came before and after.

I wanted to be able to touch him whenever I wanted.

I wanted to make him smile or laugh.

And no, he didn't actually make any sound when he laughed, but a few times I'd caught him lost in a humorous moment when he hadn't had time to be self-conscious about how he looked when he laughed without sound. Truth was, he didn't need to. His body did all the talking for him.

But it was just another case of Nerdy Nolan wanting something he couldn't have.

Because Dallas had been a perfect gentleman ever since the night he'd come to my house and told me it had been a mistake to fuck me.

We were squarely parked in the friend zone and the parking brake had been set and locked.

Stop.

Do not pass go.

My nerves from the encounter with Jimmy didn't ease until I was within a few miles of the center. The second I pulled into the driveway, Loki was there to greet me. I'd long ago lost my fear of the big animal, so as soon as I was out of the car, I dropped to my knees in the couple of inches of snow we'd gotten overnight and wrapped my arms around him. He licked my wrist and then tried to steal my glove from my pocket. Keep away was one of the few dog games that Loki liked, and it never failed to have Dallas laughing his ass off as he watched me chase the wolf hybrid around trying to get the damn thing back.

"Nope, not this time," I said as I grabbed my glove before he could pull it from my pocket. "I'm on to you." Dallas had definitely chosen well when it had come to naming the animal Loki – he was most certainly a trickster.

"Where's your daddy, huh?"

On cue, Dallas stepped around the corner of the building. He gave me the okay sign and I nodded. There was no need to tell him about Jimmy. I pulled his card from my pocket and handed it to him. "They wouldn't take it without you there so I had to pay using my money."

Dallas frowned and immediately pulled out his wallet. I covered his hand and said, "Give it to me later. Before I leave."

He nodded and then motioned to the trunk. We spent the next few minutes hauling the bags of dog food down to the dog enclosure and fed the excited animals. It was pitch dark by the time we finished, though it wasn't even five o'clock yet. Dallas and I walked side by side back up to the driveway. We stopped by my car and he gave me the money for the food. His eyes held mine for a moment and I found that I couldn't look away. I would have given anything for him to kiss me.

He pulled out his phone and typed, *Stay for dinner*?

It was the first time he'd asked me to stay since the night I'd started working for him.

"I can't," I said, disappointment seeping through me. "I promised my mother I'd be home by five-thirty. She's got plans with her friends tonight."

Dallas might have looked disappointed, but I couldn't be sure.

How is your dad?

"Struggling," I admitted. "He doesn't make it easy."

It was a huge understatement. My father had become combative with both his physical and speech therapists.

And me, of course.

Despite the assurances of his doctor and the therapists, he'd seemingly given up on whatever hope he might have had at making a complete recovery. He wasn't as aggressive toward my mother, but even she was feeling the strain of caring for him. Despite my frustration with her, I couldn't fault her for needing a break.

I thought the conversation was over, but Dallas typed me another message. *Tomorrow night?*

I went all giddy on the inside like a schoolgirl being asked out by the cutest boy in school. Sadly, it wasn't far from the truth.

"I'd like that," I said with a nod.

We said our goodbyes and I drove home. My mother was already dressed and ready to go by the time I walked in.

"He's eaten already," she said as I handed her the keys. I didn't miss the pallor of her skin beneath her carefully applied makeup or the smudges under her eyes. "He had a rough day, so he should go to bed early."

"Okay," I said. "Have fun."

My mother stood there stiffly for a moment, then nodded and put her hand on my arm and gave it a little pat before she left. The move was so uncharacteristic that I stood there in the kitchen for several long seconds after she left. I went to check on my father who was half-asleep in his chair.

"Dad," I said as I carefully touched his arm.

He slowly opened his eyes, then turned to look at me. Like my mother, he looked tired. It was scary to see how much he'd aged in the past few weeks. Fortunately, his condition hadn't worsened any.

I wasn't surprised when he pushed my hand off his arm. I sighed and said, "Do you need anything before I go take a shower?"

"Drk," he grumbled.

"A drink?" I clarified.

He gave me a jerky nod. I went to the kitchen to get him the juice my mother insisted he drink more of. I half-expected him to chuck it at me, since it wasn't the beer he probably wanted, but he accepted the glass and took a sip before setting it down on the table next to him. I hurried through my shower and then searched for something to eat. I was surprised to find that my mother had left me some of the casserole she'd made in the microwave. While she usually cooked enough for me, she often stuck it into the refrigerator, since I had a tendency to stay out until "all hours of the night."

Of course, all hours to her meant anything after five-thirty. And since I often stayed at work longer than I needed to so that I could cuddle the kittens or help Dallas with one of his rehab patients, she was right, I was technically staying out all hours.

After dinner, I watched TV with my father for a while, only taking the remote from him after he'd fallen completely asleep. By seven, I was rousing him and helping him get ready for bed. I was sitting up in my own bed going through the finances when my phone beeped.

I smiled at the sight of Loki and Dallas popping up on the screen. I'd convinced Dallas to let me take a picture of him and Loki, but he'd grumbled (yes, silently) about it the whole time. I'd been surprised (and once again, schoolgirl giddy) when he'd asked me to also pose with Loki for his phone.

Dallas: *How's your father?*

Nolan: *Good. Asleep.*

Dallas: *How are you?*

I smiled at that.

Nolan: *Better now.*

I regretted it as soon as I hit send. What if he read too much into it? Yes, it was the truth, but what if it crossed a line? I waited with bated breath for the response.

Dallas: *Me too.*

My heart damn near exploded. "Get a grip, Nolan, geez," I told myself out loud.

Dallas: *You still there?*

Nolan: *Yeah, sorry, I dropped my phone.*

"Smooth, Nolan," I murmured as I shook my head. "Now he's going to think you dropped the phone because of what he said."

It went on and on like that for a few minutes – me questioning every text I sent. But I began to relax the longer Dallas talked. We started out with our comfort zone topic of the animals and Tom Hiddleston, which then led to an in-depth discussion about which superhero universe was better – Marvel or D.C.

By the time I got the low battery warning on my phone, it was after midnight – we'd talked for four hours straight.

Nolan: *My phone is dying.*

Dallas: *Mine too. You should go to bed. You have to work in the morning and I heard your boss is a real hardass.*

Nolan: *Well, his ass is pretty hard. I mean, it's no Tom Hiddleston ass...*

Dallas: *Just for that, you're cleaning up Gentry's pen tomorrow...with a spatula.*

Since I was well aware of how large and smelly Gentry's shit was, I chuckled.

Nolan: *Okay, gotta go. Turns out I have to kiss my boss's hard ass tomorrow.*

I chuckled when a gif of Tom Hiddleston saying "That's hot" appeared on my phone.

Dallas: *Night, Nolan.*

Nolan: *Good night, Dallas.*

And just like that, I forgot about the bills and I forgot about Jimmy and I forgot about the fact that Pelican Bay and Dallas Kent were supposed to be just a temporary stop on the road to my new and better life.

My goal the next morning had been to sneak out early since Dallas had mentioned that he was going to be releasing a hawk he'd been nursing back to health that morning. Fortunately, we wouldn't have to drive anywhere to release it, so that meant we'd be able to get to work afterward.

But my plans were waylaid when I quietly walked past my parents' bedroom and saw that their door was open. My father was still asleep, but my mother's side of the bed was already made and her bathrobe and slippers weren't in their usual spot. Since I needed to get the keys from the hook near the side table in the kitchen, I had no choice but to say my good mornings and explain why I was up so early. Considering what she thought Dallas and I were actually up to, I wasn't looking forward to her look of censure when she confronted me about it.

I expected her to be standing by the stove or cleaning the counters like she was prone to do in the morning, but to my surprise, she was sitting at the kitchen table. Her back was to me, so she didn't see me. I had the chance to grab the keys and just go, but when I heard her let out a soft sniffle, I hesitated. An unexpected pang went through me when she lifted her hand to her face and wiped at her eyes.

She was crying.

"Mom?" I asked as I rounded the table so I could see her.

To my amazement, she didn't try to hide what she'd been doing.

She was a mess. Her eyes were red-rimmed and swollen behind

her glasses and her hair hadn't been brushed. Her robe was hanging open. If I hadn't known better, I would have thought something had happened to my father, but I'd seen for myself that he was fine.

"It's really true," she murmured. "I…I didn't know."

At first, I thought she was talking about the fact that I'd slept with Dallas, which didn't make sense since she'd already seemed pretty certain of that fact.

But then I saw the credit card beneath her trembling hands.

Her pained eyes lifted to meet mine. "Edith and I went with some of the ladies from the church outreach committee to dinner last night. They've all been so kind with helping me out with the cooking these past few weeks that I wanted to thank them, so I offered to treat them. The bill, it was expensive, but nothing too bad."

I already knew where she was going with this since I managed the money in my parents' accounts. They'd had even less money than I had in my own account, which was what I'd used to pay for the dog food the previous day. I'd warned my mother not to spend any more money this week until I got my paycheck, which was happening the following day.

"The waiter, he…he told me my debit card was declined, so I gave him a credit card. I thought it was a mistake."

I sighed. While I'd made enough of a dent in the credit card bill to keep the company from calling the debt collectors, they'd frozen the account.

Another fact I'd shared with my mother.

"He said the company told him to cut up my card, but he gave it back to me instead."

"Mom," I murmured. "I told you all this-"

"I know," she said with a nod. "I know you did, dear. But I thought you were just being argumentative."

I ignored the stab of pain that her comment sent through me. "I'm trying to fix it, Mom, but I need more time. Which means you need to be careful about what you spend for a while."

I was shocked when my mother reached across the table and patted my hand. She wiped at her eyes with a tissue she'd pulled from the sleeve of her robe. "I called Mr. Wilson last night when I got home – his wife's on the church outreach committee with me," she explained. "He said you paid the overdue mortgage with your own money. Is that true?"

"Yes. I paid all the bills as best I could with the money I had left in my savings."

My mother nodded and dropped her eyes. I waited for her to say something else, to thank me, at least, but she didn't. Anger burned through me, but I quelled it. It was just a reminder that I was here for one reason and one reason only. To get them back on their feet.

It wasn't to fall in love with a group of broken animals.

It wasn't to live out some fantasy with their equally broken rescuer.

It wasn't to try and fix something that was unfixable.

"I have to go," I muttered. "Don't spend any money until I can deposit my paycheck tomorrow, okay?"

I got up to leave, but my mom said, "Nolan, wait." She dabbed at her eyes and then stood, straightening her robe as she did. "I'll make you some breakfast."

"No, thanks, I need to go."

She stepped into my path and put her arms up as if to grab me. But she stopped at the last moment. "Please, Nolan, let me make you something. I can make you a sandwich with some nice ham and eggs and cheese on it...to take with you. It'll just take me a minute, I promise."

Her tone was so uncertain that I hesitated. My mother never offered to do things for me. She told me what she was doing and that was that. No argument. And while she hadn't exactly asked this time around, it was still different.

I wouldn't allow myself to read too much into it. "Fine," I said. "I'll, um, go start the car to get the heater going. Be back in a minute."

She nodded emphatically and then hurried to the refrigerator. I went out to the car and got my dad's car going, since I'd reverted to using it so my mother would have her car. It took several tries to get it going and then I cranked up the heat. When I returned to the house, my mother appeared by the door, paper bag in one hand and one of my father's thermoses in the other.

"Coffee," she said as she handed it to me. "You need something hot for your drive."

"Thanks," I said, unable to hide the suspicion in my voice. "I really have to go."

"Okay. See you tonight."

I nodded and hurried from the house. My mother's behavior was weirding me out. It was almost like she was, what...sorry?

That couldn't be right.

Could it?

CHAPTER TEN

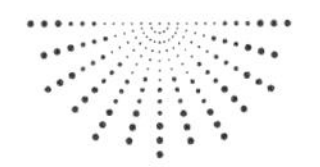

Dallas

"It was just weird, you know?" Nolan murmured as he took another sip of his wine.

Sounds like she was trying to thank you or tell you she was sorry, I typed before showing the screen to Nolan. I was using my tablet instead of my phone so it was easier for both of us.

We were sitting on my living room couch after having eaten a huge dinner that had included pot roast, mashed potatoes, and green beans. I'd opened the bottle of wine afterward in the hopes of convincing Nolan to stay a little longer. I wasn't a big wine drinker, but I'd inherited half the contents of my parents' huge wine cellar from our old house after my father had died. I had no clue about wine, but Nolan seemed to have liked whatever I'd randomly picked, because he was on his second glass. His skin was flushed with a little bit of color and his eyes were relaxed and bright. As soon as we'd sat down, he'd sunk into the soft cushions of the couch and immediately turned so he was facing me while we talked.

I liked that despite the fact that I wasn't actually speaking, he still interacted with me like I was. Most people didn't do that.

Nolan definitely wasn't "most people."

"I guess," he said. "Too little, too late," he added.

I resisted the urge to touch him. Our conversation throughout dinner had been light and easy, but when he'd mentioned needing to go home before I'd opened the bottle of wine to get him to stay, he'd gotten quiet. I hated when Nolan was quiet because he was such a vibrant personality.

"Dallas, can I ask you something? You don't have to answer if you don't want to."

I nodded. We hadn't talked much about me, so I'd been expecting him to eventually press the issue. There were still some things I never wanted to tell him, but I knew that if I wanted to keep Nolan as a friend, I needed to be willing to open up a bit more.

I watched as Nolan shifted closer to me until our knees were touching. A soft smile graced his lips and I barely hid my own smile. Nolan was definitely feeling the wine now.

"When did you know?" he asked. "That you liked guys instead of girls. Or do you like girls too?"

I shook my head. *Just guys. I knew when I was thirteen.*

"But you had a girlfriend in high school. Sarah something..."

Sarah Anders, I acknowledged. *I think she was suspicious, but she never asked me outright. She probably didn't want to know.*

I didn't add the fact that I'd had a disastrous prom night with Sarah. Thankfully, I'd been able to blame my lack of an erection on alcohol that I hadn't actually consumed but pretended that I had. I'd ended things with her shortly after that, saying I was just too busy with baseball to date anyone.

"Did anyone know?" Nolan asked, his voice sympathetic.

My older brother. I told him when I was fifteen. Right before we moved to Pelican Bay.

"Maddox. He's in the military, right?"

I managed a nod, despite the fact that pain was spreading throughout my belly.

"Hey," Nolan said, his hand settling on my arm as he shifted even closer. "We don't have to talk about it...him."

I nodded and tried to focus on how good it felt to have Nolan's fingers brushing my skin. It bothered me more than I wanted to admit that Nolan likely knew about the accident and what my brother had said to me just before he'd left to return to the army. Doc Cleary had let it slip once that Jimmy's mother, Edith, had been in the house that day and overheard Maddox telling me he'd wished I'd been the one to die in the accident instead of my mother.

Does your family know? I asked him.

"Yeah," Nolan said with a sigh. "Said I was going to go to hell and they'd pray for me and all that," he muttered with a wave of his wine glass. "On the positive side, it got me out of church for the next... forever," he added with a faint chuckle.

That explained why I hadn't seen much of Nolan at church.

Nolan settled his wine glass on the coffee table and then turned back to me. "Who was the first guy you kissed?"

That was a topic I definitely didn't want to discuss, so I pointed at him and wrote, *You tell me first.*

"His name was Anderson. Yeah, that was his first name," he said, his eyes bright. "His family was super rich and well-known – like the Kennedys or something. He was at Juilliard because he was planning on being an actor. Anyway, we met at this orientation thing and started talking while we were waiting for the tour we were on to start. About fifteen minutes into the tour, he pulls me into this room and just lays one on me. I was so surprised, I don't think I even reacted. I think he was surprised, too, because he kept telling me it was a mistake and not to tell anyone. He ran back to join the tour and never talked to me again."

I couldn't help but let my eyes drift to Nolan's mouth and think what a waste his first kiss had been.

I typed, *He was a fool.*

Nolan shot me a goofy grin. "Agreed. What about yours?"

I shook my head.

"Come on, I told you mine."

I sighed and pointed at him.

"No, I already went," he said.

I shook my head and pointed at him again. But for once, he didn't get what I was saying. I picked up the tablet.

You was all I typed.

His brow furrowed in confusion. It took him about five long seconds to finally get it.

"What?" he choked out.

You were my first kiss, Nolan.

"What?" he said, his voice going high and loud. "So that night in the truck was the first time you-"

I shook my head. God, I didn't want to do this. But I knew I didn't have a choice.

No, I've had sex with men before, I've just never kissed any of them.

Not surprisingly, Nolan was confused. "I don't understand."

I pulled in a breath. *My first time was with a guy I met in a club in the Twin Cities when I was around twenty-one or so. I fucked him in the alley behind the club, then I left. I never even knew his name. None of us were in that place for romance, if you know what I mean.*

"Oh," Nolan murmured as understanding dawned. "Do you do that a lot? Just...hook up?"

Humiliation swamped me as I nodded my head and dropped the tablet on the cushion between us. I made a move to stand, but Nolan grabbed my wrist.

"Dallas, wait, please. I'm sorry, I wasn't judging."

His hold on me was firm and I didn't want to inadvertently hurt him, so I settled back down. But I couldn't look at him.

"Dallas," Nolan whispered, and then his hands were on my face. "You're just so beautiful and kind and amazing and...it hurts to know that you've never had anyone show you..." Nolan's words dropped off. He muttered a curse word under his breath and then pressed his forehead against mine. "I'm messing this up," he said softly.

I let my hands cover his wrists where he was holding my face. We stayed like that for several beats before Nolan released me and sat back. He remained close enough that our legs were still touching.

"So how was I?" he asked, a small grin spreading across his mouth.

I rolled my eyes at him and then brought my hand up and held it flat in the air and shook it a little each way.

"So-so?" Nolan said in mock outrage. He fell silent for a moment and when he next spoke, his voice had gone heavy with seriousness. "I guess I should try to improve my score."

And just like that, the lust that had been simmering in my belly exploded. I fisted my hands to keep from reaching for him, but it was a wasted effort because Nolan was the one to lean forward. He stopped just before his mouth met mine. "Can I, Dallas?"

There was nothing on earth that could have kept me from nodding.

Nolan let out a soft breath right before he covered my mouth with his. His hand came up to gently grab my neck and I wanted to cry when I felt his thumb softly grazing over the scars on my throat. I expected him to seek entry into my mouth, but instead, he closed his lips over my lower lip, then my upper, then he just pressed one gentle kiss after another against my mouth, his lips firm but soft against mine. He kept up the pattern until I was panting against him. I'd wrapped my arms around his waist at some point and he'd ended up practically in my lap. So when he pulled back just a little, there wasn't much room for him to go since I didn't want to release him.

His eyes twinkled as he caressed my face with his other hand. "I think we may need to practice that a few more times to make sure I get it just right."

I was still reeling from the powerful kiss, so all I could manage was a nod. Nolan gently extricated himself from my grasp and returned to his spot on the couch. He reached for his wine glass and took another sip. My eyes were fastened on his mouth as he licked at his lips. When my eyes met his, I saw such warmth in them that it made my insides hurt.

Regret suddenly began clawing at my insides and I was reaching for the tablet before I could stop myself.

I'm sorry, Nolan. For everything.

He looked at me in confusion. "You have nothing to be sorry for, Dallas. You gave me a job when no one else would-"

I waved my hand impatiently.

I should have stopped it. I should have said something, but I was a coward. I knew if I defended you, everyone would turn on me.

Nolan stiffened as he finally realized what I was talking about. He set his wine glass down and then fisted his hand against his stomach. I felt tears sting my eyes for ruining this perfect moment between us. But this conversation had been a long time coming.

I'm sorry, I don't mean to upset you by bringing it all back, but you're such an amazing man, Nolan, and I'm not. I don't want you to let me off the hook for what I did back then.

"I understand," he murmured. "High school was a tough time for all of us-"

I grabbed his arm so he'd look at me and shook my head violently.

No! Don't make excuses for me or for what any of us did to you.

His armor finally began to crack. "Why are you doing this?" he whispered, his voice breaking just a bit.

Because I don't deserve you. You were always so much better than me, Nolan. Than this town. I was so glad when you got out.

"I should go," Nolan said as he tried to get to his feet.

I grabbed his arm and shook my head. I pointed at him and then my chest.

"I don't understand," he said. "I don't understand what you want from me."

I waited until I was sure he wouldn't try to run and then typed out my message.

I want you to tell me how you felt in school...how I made you feel. I want you to say the things you should have been able to say back then. I want to hear you, Nolan!

His eyes shot to mine. Tears began streaking down his face. "Hear me?" he croaked. "No one hears me, Dallas! If they had, they would have-"

He shook his head and tried to get up again. But I refused to release him. I ended up typing with one hand.

Would have what, Nolan? Tell me.

He turned away from me, but the anguish on his face was hard to miss. "Would have stopped it. Would have seen what it was doing to me..."

His eyes shifted to me and the raw emotion was like a punch to the gut. No, it was like a goddamn battering ram.

"It was worse, you know?" he said softly. "What you and everyone else did."

The tears I'd been trying to stem fell unheeded down my face. I nodded to him, but didn't pick up the tablet to respond.

It was his turn to speak.

"Jimmy, Doug, the rest of those guys – that's who they were. Throwing eggs at me or tripping me in the hallway...that was just who they were...who they probably still are. But you, the other kids, the teachers, my parents...you had to know I wasn't really that strong. That I was dying inside..."

My throat hurt so bad it was hard to breathe. I managed another nod, but it was so fucking inadequate.

Nolan wiped at his eyes. "So yeah, I had to pretend I was strong because the alternative was swallowing a bottle full of my mother's sleeping pills or sitting in my father's car in the garage with the door closed and the motor running."

I let out a harsh sob at that, though it came out sounding more like a grunt than anything else. I leaned forward and wrapped my arms around Nolan's body. I pressed my mouth to his ear and for the first time in years, began saying the words I'd wanted to for so long.

Since the first time Nolan Grainger had looked at me with that silent plea in his eyes.

Despite the fact that there was no sound to accompany my words, Nolan relaxed against me. I pulled him back against the couch cushions so that he was pressed up against my chest. His hand was resting over my heart. I waited until his body settled on mine, then pulled out the tablet and typed out the words he hadn't been able to hear.

You're my one regret, Nolan. If I could have one moment back in time, I'd pick that day with the eggs. I'd wrap myself around you so tight that you wouldn't have even known what was happening. You would have just felt safe and warm and wanted.

I held the tablet so Nolan could read the screen. He nodded against my chest, but didn't move. I could feel his tears starting up again.

I'm sorry, Nolan. I'm so very sorry. We all lost out by not hearing you, by not seeing you.

This time when Nolan read the message, he didn't react at all, so I tucked the tablet into the gap between the cushions and then wrapped both my arms around him and just held onto him. At some point, I fell asleep because when Loki woke me up the next morning, Nolan was gone.

And I had no clue if he was coming back.

CHAPTER ELEVEN

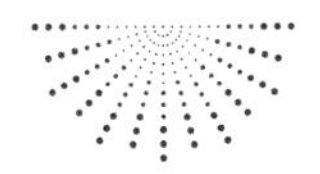

Nolan

I didn't go back to the center for two days.

And when I finally did, it wasn't because I needed the job.

It was late afternoon when I arrived, and while Loki greeted me by my car like he usually did, Dallas didn't appear, so I went in search of him.

An easy task considering Loki led me right to him.

He was sitting between the two fences surrounding Gentry's enclosure, leaning his back against the outer fence. I'd noticed early on that he had a soft spot for the bear and often spent a few extra minutes with the big animal throughout the day. Gentry was standing inside the enclosure along the fence near Dallas, scraping at the snow, probably looking for lingering berries that Dallas would feed him every day in that same exact spot.

I'd been working around Gentry's pen enough to know that I had to enter the small building that butted up against the enclosure to access the gap between the fences. Dallas had explained that bears in captivity didn't hibernate, so the building provided Gentry a place to escape the cold. There was a large door leading from the pen into the building that could be closed to secure the bear in either the enclosure or in a smaller cage within the building. The door always remained open unless Dallas was bringing in a vet to treat the bear for something. In those cases, Dallas secured Gentry in the cage by closing the door, preventing him from returning to the enclosure. There was a small walkway surrounding the bars of the cage to allow easy access to dart Gentry from any angle so he could be sedated for when the vet needed to physically examine him.

I made my way past the cage and stepped back outside. Dallas didn't notice me until Gentry did. Being around the bear, even with the heavy fence separating us, still made me nervous, but I was getting used to the way the huge animal liked to walk alongside visitors when they entered his area.

Despite seeing me, Dallas didn't move. He looked terrible, and I knew that as hard as these past couple of days had been on me, he hadn't escaped unscathed. I'd been angry at him at first for ruining what had been an amazing night.

But I knew why he'd done it.

And it hadn't been just to assuage his own guilt.

Dallas's expression was pained as he watched me approach. I wondered if he thought I was there to officially quit. It was certainly the first thing I'd thought about doing when I'd woken up in his arms two mornings earlier.

But then I'd remembered that kiss.

That amazing kiss on lips that hadn't ever touched any other man's but mine.

It couldn't have been an easy thing for him to admit. And I had my suspicions about why he'd resorted to random hookups over the years – ones that didn't include something as intimate as kissing.

Dallas started to get up, but I said, "No, stay."

He swallowed hard and sat back down. His knees were raised and there was a little room between his legs, so I slowly dropped down until I was kneeling between them and facing him. I ignored the snow seeping into the fabric of my jeans. Dallas reached for his phone, but I stayed his hand. That had a whole new level of worry drifting across his features.

"Dallas, you don't need to get your phone out because you don't owe me anything. No explanations, no apologies. I know why you did what you did the other night."

He shook his head slightly and dropped his eyes. I immediately pulled my glove off and used my fingers to tilt his chin up. His skin was really cold, leading me to wonder how long he'd been sitting there for.

"We're not the same people we were back then. I'm scared to death that you think you somehow deserved what happened to you – like it was karma or some other shit." When he lowered his eyes, I knew that was exactly what he'd been thinking.

"We're okay, Dallas. I came here to tell you that. And not because I need this job or I feel sorry for you. But because I believe what you said…that if you could go back in time, you would. And because I think that I wasn't the only one who needed to be heard."

Dallas lifted his eyes. They were swimming with tears. He shook his head and I instinctively knew what he needed from me.

I reached out to cup his cheek as I spoke. "You have nothing to be sorry for, Dallas. But if you need my forgiveness, you have it. *You have it, Dallas*."

He let out a harsh cry that sounded more like a mix between a gasp and a sob and then he was pushing into my arms. I clutched him to me as his hot tears soaked the skin of my neck and his body was racked with violent tremors. I held onto him for a long time, whispering into his ear that we were okay. When he finally quieted I gently pushed him back and wiped at his face.

"Are you finished for the day?"

He nodded.

"Will you come somewhere with me? It's guaranteed to put a smile on your face."

Another nod. When he reached for his bandana, I covered his hand with mine.

"You won't need that."

He hesitated and then put the bandana back in his pocket. His trust in me tore at my already pained heart. I reached out to take his hand and steadied him as he climbed to his feet. His limp seemed worse than normal as we made our way hand in hand out of Gentry's enclosure. Dallas let his free hand trail along the fence near Gentry's head as the bear walked alongside us.

Once outside the enclosure, Loki fell into step next to Dallas. It didn't take long for Dallas to figure out where we were going. I felt his fingers squeeze mine and he shot me a soft smile when I looked at him. Even though Dallas had already fed the kittens and they were in the process of settling down for the night, they began meowing excitedly when I flipped on the lights and led Dallas into their room. Loki followed us, and as soon as we sat down on the floor, our backs against the wall, the kittens were climbing all over us. Dallas leaned into me and when I looked over at him, he had a soft smile on his face. He held my gaze for a moment, then dipped his head and brushed his mouth over mine. The kiss was brief and chaste, but it rocked me to my core, and I wondered how I was going to be able to keep from losing a piece of myself to this man.

I shook my head as I turned my attention to the black kitten trying to climb up my chest.

Who was I kidding?

I'd already lost so much more than just a piece of my heart to Dallas Kent.

"You got me something?" I asked as I lifted my eyes from the tablet.

Dallas nodded. He looked nervous.

You can't get mad, he typed out. *Promise me you won't.*

I arched a brow at him, but since I wasn't about to spoil the mood between us, I nodded. "Promise."

He motioned for me to wait and disappeared around the corner, presumably to go to his room, since I heard his footsteps on the stairs a moment later.

It had been three days since I'd returned to the center. Things had gone back to normal, but with one big difference.

One of the walls between Dallas and me had finally come down.

It wasn't something I'd even realized until I'd arrived the morning after I'd told him I forgave him. As soon as he'd seen me, he'd smiled.

This great big, no-holds-barred smile. It hadn't been reserved or hesitant, like he was afraid of showing too much of himself.

It had been the famous Dallas Kent smile.

The one my teenage self had fallen instantly in love with so long ago.

It was the smile he'd reserved for when he'd hit a grand slam or pitched a no-hitter. It was the smile I'd seen in the picture of him and Maddox on the wall by the stairs.

Only this time it had been aimed at me.

Nerdy Nolan Grainger.

Even if the smile hadn't been enough to metaphorically send me to my knees, his touches would have been.

They were the smallest things.

His fingers brushing the outside of my hand as we walked.

His body pressed up against my back when he stood behind me to point out something he wanted me to see in one of the habitats.

His hand skimming my jawline when he went to push a stray lock of hair off my ear.

Tiny gestures with devastating impact.

But that was as far as he went. He hadn't kissed me again like he had in the kitten room. The pent-up need for more was slowly killing me, but I was helpless to do anything about it. He'd made it pretty clear that he wasn't willing to cross the employer-employee line. And truth be told, there was still a little part of me that liked to remind myself that I wasn't good enough for Dallas Kent. That I was reading into things that weren't there.

So I was pretty much a glutton for punishment by spending more and more time with the man, including having dinner at his house the past three nights. Last night we'd even watched a movie, during which I'd promptly fallen asleep. When Dallas had gently shaken me awake, I'd been lying on my side, my head resting on his muscular thigh.

And he'd been playing with my hair.

I'd practically tripped over myself as I'd rattled off an apology for falling asleep on him, but he'd just flashed that smile at me and given me the okay sign.

Surprisingly, my mother hadn't complained or questioned why I was getting home later and later each night. And she'd continued with her weird need to make me breakfast every morning. I'd finally given up trying to figure her out. I was too busy trying to make sense of my relationship with Dallas.

I straightened when I heard his footsteps on the stairs. I wasn't sure, but it sounded like his footsteps slowed as he got closer to the living room. When he finally did round the corner, his face was full of tension.

And I instantly knew why.

Because he couldn't hide what he was holding in his hand.

"Oh my God," I whispered when my eyes fell on the violin case.

Dallas was hesitant as he moved to sit down next to me on the couch. But I didn't even spare him a glance because I was too busy trying to breathe.

He'd gotten me a violin.

"What did you do?" I croaked.

Dallas eased the case onto my lap, then reached for his tablet.

It's probably not what you're used to playing, but the guy at the store said it was a really good quality one. Maybe it can tide you over till you get yours back or you get a new one.

"Dallas," I breathed in complete and utter disbelief.

He motioned to the latches on the case.

I nodded and opened it, my fingers shaking.

I knew just by looking at the violin that he'd spent quite a bit of money on it. I let my fingers slide over the wood, then the strings. The need to pick it up and play was like a living thing beneath my skin.

I couldn't accept it.

I just couldn't.

It was too much.

But one look at Dallas's hopeful expression and I was nodding my head. "Thank you, it's beautiful."

His smile made my heart stutter. He reached for his tablet and was about to type something when Loki suddenly climbed to his feet from where he'd been lying on the floor next to the couch and let out a low growl.

The three of us held there for a moment before Loki suddenly took off and darted through his doggie door. Dallas stood and went to the kitchen door that the wolf hybrid had disappeared through. He threw it open and listened. I got up and went to him, but heard nothing.

Dallas snagged his coat off the hook and motioned to me.

"I'm coming with you," I argued, and grabbed my coat. Dallas shot me a quick glance as he reached for the flashlight he kept by his coat. I was glad when he merely nodded.

It was pitch dark outside, but Dallas had installed low-level lighting along all the walkways. The motion detector lights were only on the buildings that weren't close enough to any enclosures where the animals would trip them every time they moved around at night. So we were reliant on the flashlight and the walkway lights as we made our way through the inky darkness.

We'd only gone about a hundred yards when we heard it.

A loud, rumbling roar.

There was only one animal capable of making that kind of sound at the center.

"Gentry," I breathed right before Dallas took off running. I managed to keep up, but if Gentry's enclosure had been any farther away, I would have lost Dallas for sure.

As we ran toward the building that led to Gentry's enclosure, the bear's screams – and that was the only way I could think to describe the awful sound – grew louder. As he ran, Dallas shined his light on the bear's enclosure in the hopes of locating the distressed animal. I nearly came to a stop when I saw that the door separating the outside enclosure from the inner one was closed.

I'd been with Dallas when we'd said our goodnights to the bear.

The door had been open.

Fear tripped through me when I saw that the lights in the building were on.

Loki was pacing frantically in front of the door leading to the building when we reached it. The second Dallas ripped the door open, Loki tore through it. Despite how loud Gentry's cries were, I could hear someone yelling.

"Dallas!" I shouted as fear for him took over every other thought.

But he ignored me and followed Loki into the building.

The scene I walked in on was something that had my blood running cold.

Three men surrounded Gentry's cage. They'd managed to corral the bear into the smallest part of the inner enclosure that was used only to limit the bear's movements when he needed to be darted for the vet. I knew that Gentry would have willingly walked into the cage, since Dallas gave him his favorite treat when he was in there.

It had made Gentry a sitting duck for his attackers.

And they *were* attacking Gentry as he desperately scratched at the door leading to the outside enclosure.

All three men were dressed in dark clothing, including knit caps on their heads. Two of the men were holding long black sticks in their hands.

Except they weren't sticks.

I realized that as soon as one of the men turned the stick on Loki, who had a hold of the second man's arm.

It was a fucking cattle prod.

And the second it touched Loki, he yelped and released the man.

Dallas slammed his fist into the jaw of the man who'd zapped Loki, then he tackled the man the wolf hybrid had been attacking.

I recognized the third man instantly, despite the cap. The black, stringy hair gave him away.

Jimmy Cornell.

A mix of fear and fury coiled in my belly when I saw the gun in Jimmy's hand. I was moving before he even pointed the gun at Dallas. My body slammed into Jimmy's hard and we both hit the ground. I managed to knock the gun out of his grasp and it went skittering across the floor. But I wasn't a match for the heavier Jimmy. He rolled us so that he was on top of me and punched me hard enough to have me seeing stars. As he reached back to hit me again, I reflexively threw up my arms. But the punch never came because Loki chose that moment to latch onto Jimmy's arm.

Jimmy screamed in pain and fell off of me as he fought to escape Loki's grip. My head was still spinning from the punch, but I managed to see that Dallas was still grappling with one guy. The other had stumbled to his feet and was trying to help Jimmy get free of Loki. The second he reached for one of the cattle prods, I jumped to my feet and grabbed the shovel that was hanging on the wall alongside Gentry's cage.

The shovel we used to clean up the bear's shit.

I used every ounce of strength I had to bring the shovel down on the guy's arm just as he activated the cattle prod and pointed it at Loki. The man screamed in agony and dropped the prod. He grabbed his arm and shouted a half-dozen curses.

The man Dallas had been fighting with managed to break free of his hold and he latched onto the uninjured arm of the guy I'd hit and dragged him out of the building. Loki was still grappling with Jimmy, but as soon as Dallas let out a loud whistle, the animal let go of Jimmy's arm. The man appeared startled and then he turned tail and ran.

Before he was even out the door, Dallas had already turned his attention to Gentry, who was still howling and trying to escape the cage. Tears began streaking down my face as I watched the terrified animal struggle to get away from us.

"Dallas, what do we do?" I asked.

He looked at me and then he was at my side. His fingers gently tilted my head to examine my face. "I'm okay," I said when I saw how worried he was. "We need to help Gentry."

He nodded and grabbed his phone. *Call the vet,* he typed. *Then 911.*

He pulled up a contact on his phone and handed it to me. My hands were shaking as I dialed. As I waited for someone to answer, Dallas began whistling softly as he approached the cage. The panicked animal didn't pay him any attention and I had to step away from the cage to talk to the answering service for the vet's office, since Gentry's howls were so loud. I explained the situation to the operator who said the vet was out of town, but they'd call another vet. By the time I made the call to 911, Gentry had quieted a bit. He was still jammed up against the door, his breath coming in heavy pants. There were spots of blood on the floor of the cage, but considerably more on the door.

I went to Dallas's side and linked my fingers with his as he continued to softly whistle some kind of tune to the bear. Loki, who didn't appear hurt, dropped down in front of the cage and tilted his ears back and forth as he listened to Dallas's whistling. At some point, Dallas had picked up the gun and tucked it into his waistband.

"Did they shoot him?" I asked, my voice thick with emotion as I watched Gentry.

Dallas took out his phone and typed, *It's a BB gun. The blood on the floor is probably from them shooting him with it. The blood on the door is from Gentry breaking his claws trying to get out.*

A hoarse cry escaped my throat at that, and I pressed into Dallas's side. His arm went around me. He kept up the whistling until Gentry finally lay still. The bear had curled himself into a ball, his back to us.

When Dallas's phone rang a moment later, he handed it to me. I could barely speak as I explained to the vet what had happened. He assured me he was on his way and then hung up. Sirens rang in the distance.

"I'm going to go meet the police," I said.

Dallas nodded and then took the gun from his waistband and laid it on a shelf. He reached for my hand, but I shook my head. "Stay with Gentry. He needs you."

Dallas began shaking his head, but I captured his chin gently with my fingers. "I'll take Loki with me. It's safe. They're gone."

He was clearly torn between staying with the bear and coming with me, but he finally nodded. I let my fingers skim over the gash next to Dallas's left eye. It was the only injury he'd sustained.

"Be right back, okay?" I said softly.

He nodded, then kissed my forehead.

As I left the building, Loki at my side, I spared Dallas one more glance as he knelt in front of the cage and resumed his whistling. The tears I'd finally managed to stem threatened to fall again as a terrible question popped into my head.

What if the attack had been my fault?

They were words that kept repeating on a loop as I left the building and went to meet the police.

CHAPTER TWELVE

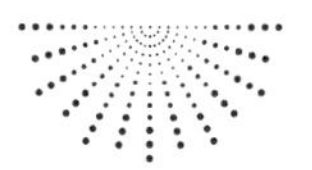

Dallas

"And you're sure it was Jimmy Cornell?" the sheriff asked for the third time. I didn't bother typing my response again. I merely nodded and returned my attention to Gentry, who was pacing back and forth in front of the door leading to the outside enclosure. I'd managed to calm him down somewhat, but the arrival of the police had gotten him worked up again. As much as I would have liked to let him outside, I knew he needed to stay in the cage so the vet could administer a sedative before examining him.

"You sure, son? You recognized him?"

"He's mute, Sheriff," Nolan groused. "Not blind."

The sheriff had wanted to hear our stories separately, so he'd questioned Nolan while his deputy had accompanied me to check on all the other animals to make sure none of them had been targeted. Fortunately, they'd all been unharmed.

Gentry had been the only casualty.

Upon our return, the sheriff had agreed to let Nolan stay inside the building while I was questioned, since it was so cold out.

On the condition that Nolan not interrupt.

A condition Nolan definitely was not happy about and that he had yet to actually follow.

Sheriff Tulley shot Nolan an irritated look and then scratched out something on his notepad.

"You didn't recognize the other two?" he asked.

I shook my head.

"Gonna need an actual answer," the man drawled.

I resisted the urge to deck the man and got my phone out. We'd been at this for an hour already, and I just wanted the man gone so I could take care of Gentry.

No, I typed and then showed him my phone.

"Fine," he said.

"I'm all done here, sir," the sheriff's deputy said as he showed the sheriff the three evidence bags holding the cattle prods and the BB gun. The younger cop's eyes met mine for a moment and I saw a flash of something in them that I couldn't pinpoint.

"Good. Take it to the office. You finished?" he asked the woman who was dusting the door for prints.

"Almost," she said. There were black smudges all over the inside and outside of the door. "Looks like the lock's been picked," she announced. The woman had already taken Nolan's and my prints to exclude ours from any she might find on the door.

The sheriff grumbled and then wrote another note on his pad.

"Any reason you know of that someone might wanna pester your..."

The man waved his hand at Gentry.

"I mouthed off to Jimmy the other day in the store he works at," Nolan said softly. When I looked at him, he refused to meet my eyes. He had his arms wrapped protectively around his body. "I got him into trouble with his boss. He knows I work for Dallas."

I could tell there was more that Nolan wasn't saying.

"What is it that you two boys were doing out here so late tonight?" the sheriff asked, his lips curling into an ugly sneer.

I could see Nolan was about to answer him, and if the jut of his chin was anything to go by, he was going to tell the man it was none of his fucking business.

A sentiment I shared.

But since I knew Nolan was doing it to try and protect my reputation, I held my hand up and Nolan remained silent.

We were having dinner when we heard Gentry.

"You were having dinner? Together?"

"Yes, together," Nolan bit out impatiently. He moved to stand at my side. "Can I ask what this has to do with anything?"

I knew Nolan was still dealing with the intense emotions the attack had caused, so, not caring that the sheriff was watching, I dropped my hand and linked my fingers with Nolan's. He squeezed them hard, then let out a little rush of air.

I wasn't surprised when the sheriff looked at us with distaste, but he kept his comments to himself.

"Fine, we're finished here," the man said.

"You're going to arrest Jimmy, right?" Nolan asked.

"I'm going to question him," he responded snidely. "Boy like that comes from good family." His eyes shifted briefly to me as he spoke and I heard the unspoken comment.

"Wouldn't surprise me if he's got better things to do than hassle your" – he nodded at Gentry – "critter."

"Sheriff," Nolan began, but I pulled him against my side in the hopes he'd get the message.

He did.

He fell silent and didn't say anything until the crusty old cop had left.

"Oh my God, what was that?" he snapped as he motioned in the direction the sheriff had gone. "It's like we were making a damn noise complaint or something." He turned to face me and said, "He'll do it, right? He'll arrest Jimmy?"

I typed a message for him.

Did you know that he's related to Jimmy? Jimmy's mother is his cousin.

"What?" Nolan said, his eyes going wide. "Then he needs to step aside, let his deputy handle the case."

Won't happen.

Nolan was clearly frustrated. "Why aren't you more upset about this?" he snapped. "Those assholes hurt Gentry, Loki...they could've hurt-"

His voice fell off. He was pacing the small room, much like Gentry was still doing.

Sheriff Tulley was my father's best friend, did you know that? I asked.

Nolan stopped long enough to read my message, then shook his head.

Short of me getting murdered, he's not likely to lift a finger to help me, not after what happened to my parents.

"My mother said you weren't arrested back then because the deputy forgot to have the hospital run your blood alcohol or something."

I wasn't surprised he'd asked his mother about me and that that was the story he'd been told.

It's complicated, I hedged. I turned around to check on Gentry, then typed out, *Kids and vandals come out here every once in a while. Luckily, none of the animals have ever been hurt, but that's because Loki usually chases people off before they can do anything major. They've slashed my tires and cut some fences, but that's been the extent of it.*

"It's not right," Nolan murmured. I held out my arm for him and he immediately walked into my embrace. I wanted to tell him that he, more than anyone, should know that things didn't always end the way they should.

I kissed the top of his head as my own adrenaline rush began to wane. I'd been so caught up in my own fight that I hadn't been able to get to Jimmy quickly enough. I'd released the one guy I'd been whaling on so I could reach Nolan and get Jimmy off him, but the other guy had tackled me. Thank God Loki had jumped back into the fray or Nolan could have been seriously hurt.

Loki jumped up from where he was lying. A second later, the door to the building opened and a man with dark hair entered, bag in hand. I didn't recognize him, but I knew who he was.

The vet.

Only, he wasn't a vet I'd ever seen before. The state had vets specializing in wildlife on retainer throughout the state. Although my center was privately owned, I serviced multiple counties in the area, so the state had set me up to use the same group of vets they did whenever I needed them.

"Dallas Kent?" the man asked as his eyes shifted back and forth between me and Nolan.

"That's him," Nolan said as he reluctantly released me.

The man held out his fingers for Loki to sniff before approaching me and extending his hand. "I'm Dr. Sawyer Brower," he said. His eyes fell briefly to my neck, but unlike the sheriff, they didn't linger on my scars. I hadn't had time to grab my bandana, and considering everything that had happened, I didn't really give a shit.

I pulled out my phone and typed a message and handed it to him. He didn't react in any way other than to take it and read what I'd typed.

Are you new, Dr. Brower?

"It's Sawyer, and yes, I am," he said. "I moved here from Alaska a few weeks ago. I was working for the federal government on a bear study, actually," he said as he nodded at Gentry. "Before that I spent most of my years after vet school at the San Diego Zoo."

He handed the phone back and moved past me, his sharp eyes settling on Gentry. "What happened?" he asked.

I glanced at Nolan and he immediately understood what I was asking. He quickly introduced himself and then told the vet the events of the evening. As Nolan spoke, Sawyer began pulling things from his bag.

His eyes never left Gentry. They blazed when Nolan got to the part about the cattle prods and BB gun.

He began asking me questions about Gentry's health and patiently waited until I typed my response out before asking the next one. I flinched when he began preparing the dart gun that would knock

Gentry out so he could get in there and examine him. To his credit, the man made sure Gentry didn't see the gun, not even when he actually fired the dart. Predictably, the whole thing set Gentry off again. Nolan immediately sought me out and wrapped his arms around my waist, but I wasn't sure if he was the one who needed comfort, or I did.

The sedative worked within a matter of minutes, and once Gentry was out, I went into the cage with Sawyer. It was painstaking work to catalogue all the injuries, but Sawyer worked quickly. He pulled at least a dozen BBs from Gentry's body and there were nearly twice as many burns from the prods. In his effort to escape, Gentry had damaged several claws and torn one toe, which the vet quickly stitched up. Gentry was just starting to come around when we finished and stepped outside the cage.

"In an ideal situation, I'd take X-rays to see if any of the BBs are lodged in any organs," Sawyer murmured as he cleaned up using the sink near the large freezer where I stored Gentry's food. "But the nearest place that could handle him is a couple of hours away, and I think the stress of traveling would do more harm than good at this point."

I nodded in agreement.

"Be sure to watch for things like labored breathing, lethargy, and limping. I'll leave you with some painkillers, but he should be okay in a few days. At least physically." He glanced at me and said, "Did you get him from a circus?"

I nodded and typed, *Roadside circus.*

"Fuckers," the man muttered. He turned around and leaned back against the counter to study the bear before glancing at me. "I'm happy to testify against whoever did this."

I nodded, then looked at Nolan. He was standing stiffly near the wall, arms crossed. The bruise on his jaw had swollen considerably and he looked wiped out. It was well after midnight and I knew we both needed to get some rest.

I went to his side, but he refused to look at me. His eyes were on Gentry.

"It's my fault," he whispered. "I pissed Jimmy off...I put you on his radar."

I gently turned him and shook my head, but he was inconsolable. Tears began coasting down his face.

"I'm so sorry, Dallas. Gentry was doing so good and he trusted you and I know how much you love him."

I was reluctant to release him long enough to get my phone out, so I just wrapped my arms around him and pressed my lips to his temple. He cried softly against my chest. I was dimly aware of Sawyer gathering his things. He was in my line of sight as he was leaving, so I saw him stop at the whiteboard I had on the wall to track Gentry's food. He wrote me a note.

I'll text you in the morning. I'll do a re-check on him later in the day.

I sent him a nod. His eyes settled on me and Nolan for a moment and I saw an unnamed emotion go through him. He was gone before I could give it too much thought.

And it didn't matter, anyway, because my sole focus was right where it needed to be.

On Nolan.

In the days following the attack, Nolan's guilt had become an all-consuming thing, and when he wasn't doing his work, he was standing outside Gentry's enclosure watching the bear suffer through the remnants of the attack. Physically, Gentry wasn't showing any signs of any additional injuries, so fortunately, it was less and less likely that he'd need to be transported somewhere for X-rays and further treatment. But that was as far as our luck had held out because Gentry had reverted to the animal he'd been when I'd first gotten him. He refused to come anywhere near me or Nolan, not even when we tried to coax him with his favorite treats, and when he wasn't pacing the length of his enclosure, he was hiding in or behind the shelter I'd built for him within the habitat. He absolutely refused to go anywhere near the building where the cage was located, so we'd had no choice but to sedate him within the enclosure so Sawyer could confirm that the stitches he'd put in were holding and to check the bear's vitals to confirm there was no additional potential damage.

As for the investigation, Sheriff Tulley had stopped by that morning to inform us that there'd been no prints on the door or weapons other than mine and Nolan's and that Jimmy had an alibi.

He'd supposedly been having dinner with his mother.

When I'd asked if he'd checked Jimmy's arm for a bite wound, the man had coldly informed me not to tell him how to do his job. The man's attitude hadn't surprised me one bit, nor had the unfettered hatred in his eyes. But Nolan had been left completely devastated.

Not only because he still believed he'd somehow instigated the attack, but also because Gentry wouldn't get any justice. I had no doubt Nolan was feeling that same level of helplessness he'd felt during his childhood when the town had turned their backs on him.

Darkness was starting to fall as I finished up in the small animal building. It was nearing mid-November and winter was starting to take hold, despite it still being officially a month away. I didn't bother looking for Nolan at the livestock barn, because I knew where he'd be. But as I neared Gentry's enclosure, I paused when I heard the sound of music drifting through the icy trees that danced above my head.

Not just any music.

Violin music.

Emotion clogged my throat as I quickened my pace. Since the night of the attack, Nolan hadn't once looked at the violin. He hadn't even bothered to take it home, since he'd been too preoccupied with everything else that had happened. In truth, I'd forgotten about the instrument myself. It had been sitting in the same spot on the couch that it had been in since I'd given it to Nolan.

As I rounded the corner, I came to a stop at the sight that greeted me. There was still enough light to see Nolan standing between the inner and outer fences of Gentry's enclosure. His back was to me and he had the violin on his shoulder. He was moving the bow effortlessly, like it was an extension of his body, and the melodic, haunting music that surrounded us left me with chills. Gentry was on the opposite end of the enclosure, pacing like normal, his food untouched. But as Nolan played, the bear slowed his pace every few steps and sniffed the air. After about ten minutes, Gentry stopped moving completely and sat down against the fence. His big head would swing Nolan's direction every few minutes, but he didn't move from his spot.

But I didn't care, because I would take even the smallest scrap of progress.

I stayed where I was, even though I really wanted to go to Nolan. I could see that his hands were chapped and red, since he couldn't play while wearing gloves. But I was reluctant to set Gentry off again with my presence, so I waited until Nolan was finished and left the enclosure. It wasn't until he was practically on top of me that he noticed me. His expression was pinched and his skin was pale.

He glanced at the violin and bow in his hand. "I thought it might help," he murmured.

My heart broke for him, because nothing I'd said about the whole thing not being his fault had made any kind of difference. I was losing him. I knew it in my heart.

He was standing right in front of me, but he might as well have been back in California.

I reached for one of his hands and rubbed it between mine, then blew on it to try and warm it up. I searched out his gloves, but before I could reach for them where they were sticking out of his pocket, he stepped back.

"I should go home," he murmured. "Here," he said as he handed me the violin.

I tried to hand it back to him, but he shook his head. "No, it's yours, it should stay here."

Frustration went through me, but before I could get my phone so I could remind him I'd given it to him, he was walking past me. "I...I think maybe I shouldn't come back for a bit," he said out of the blue.

His words chilled me to the bone and I grabbed his arm. I waved my hand impatiently.

"It's for the best," he said, then tried to pull free of my hold. My frustration turned to anger, and I grabbed his hand and began pulling him with me toward the house. I wasn't going to have this fight with him in the damn cold.

And I sure as shit wasn't going to let him leave.

He didn't fight me, which was almost worse. I'd take a pissed-off Nolan over a broken one any day.

Once I had him in the house, I stripped off his coat and boots and settled him on the couch with a blanket over his lap. I got the fireplace going and made us both some coffee. Nolan held the mug when I handed it to him, but he was too zoned out to actually take a drink. I finally took it from him and put it on the coffee table along with mine, then covered his hands with mine and began rubbing them to work some warmth into his chilled skin.

It wasn't until they'd started to pinken up that I reached for my tablet and began typing.

What's going on? You're scaring me.

I'd expected my words to evoke some kind of reaction, but I wasn't prepared for him to put some distance between us on the couch.

Like he couldn't bear to touch me.

Nolan, please, I told you what happened to Gentry wasn't your fault.

Nolan closed his eyes after reading the message. "I'm so sorry, Dallas. Everything I touch turns to shit."

Fury like nothing I'd ever known before went through me and I grabbed his arm and forced him to face me. I jabbed my fingers onto the tablet, cursing the fact that I couldn't just yell at him the way I wanted.

Don't fucking say that. Don't ever fucking say that!

"It's true," he whispered. "If I hadn't come here-"

I couldn't even take the time to tell him how his coming here had changed everything for me. There was no hesitation on my part when I slammed my mouth down on his. Nolan let out a startled gasp, but I didn't care.

I couldn't tell him what he meant to me, but I could damn well show him.

I kissed him hard and I didn't give him time to even consider not returning my kiss. I wrapped my arms around his waist and dragged him forward until he was straddling my lap. I stole into his mouth over and over again, softening the kiss until I was lazily exploring every facet of his mouth. At some point, he'd slung his arms around my neck.

When we were forced to come up for air, he let out a soft sob and buried his face in my neck. I let him hide for a minute, but then I was forcing his chin up. As soon as his eyes met mine, he shook his head. "They're going to try to take this place away from you, Dallas."

It was the last thing I'd expected to hear, but before I could even think to ask him what he meant, he barreled on.

"Jimmy's mom, Edith, came to the house this morning before I left for work. She...she was yelling at my mom about how our lies got Jimmy fired from his job. She told her she was going to sue you for defamation or something, and that the sheriff was looking into having your license pulled. I'm sorry, if I'd just stayed away from you-"

I kissed him again to silence him, then scrambled around for the tablet which had gotten knocked to the floor. Nolan tried to move off my lap, but I refused to let him, so he sat back enough so he could watch me type. He used his sleeves to wipe at his wet eyes, and every now and then, a small sob would catch in his throat.

First of all, Sheriff Tulley is welcome to try to have my license pulled. It wouldn't be the first time.

Nolan's eyes widened a bit at that and I nodded.

He might be a big fish in Pelican Bay, Nolan, but he's not even a blip on the map when it comes to the state. They know a personal vendetta when they see one.

"He's tried to shut you down before?" Nolan asked.

I nodded, then typed, *And Jimmy coming after me isn't new, either.*

"But...but he was your friend."

Was being the operative word. And friend is generous. He was a jealous son of a bitch who was waiting for me to fall. After the accident, he told anyone who would listen that I'd made it a habit of driving after I'd been drinking. I've never driven drunk. Back then, I didn't even drink.

"But the accident..."

I wasn't driving, Nolan.

He stilled and stared at the tablet. "What?" he whispered.

I pointed to the note again and then typed, *My mother was driving the car that night, not me. She was the one who'd been drinking, not me.*

"But then why does everyone believe you were?"

I sighed because the conversation had taken a turn I hadn't been planning, but I knew it was something he deserved to know the truth about. Especially if I wanted him to understand how far back my problems with the sheriff and his vengeful family went.

Because that's what my father told them.

CHAPTER THIRTEEN

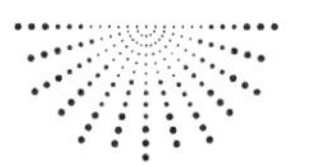

Nolan

I read Dallas's text three times before it really sunk in. "No," I whispered. "Why? Why would he do that?"

Dallas took in a breath and began typing again. I moved off his lap so I could see better and this time he let me go.

How much do you know about my parents? Dallas asked.

"Um, a little. Your dad, he was one of those preachers who do their sermons on TV. And your mom was an actress. They came to Pelican Bay after people began accusing them of..." I let my voice drop off because I couldn't bring myself to say it.

Fraud, Dallas typed. *My father was accused of stealing from his parishioners, but he was cleared when they found proof that it was the church's accountant who did it.*

I waited quietly as Dallas typed for several minutes, then handed me the tablet.

The whole thing made my father a celebrity of sorts, so he decided to parlay that into a new career. He wrote books, went on talk shows, gave motivational speeches...that sort of thing. My mother had been a B movie actress, but the scandal made her more well-known than her acting career ever had. She became one of those people who became famous for absolutely nothing. When I was a kid, we moved around a lot to accommodate my parents' ever-changing careers. Los Angeles, New York, Chicago – we lived like that for years. But then things died down and my parents couldn't get on TV or in the paper to save their lives. So, they decided to move to Pelican Bay – my father's mother had grown up here and he'd spent summers up here with his grandparents before they'd died. In such a small town, it was impossible for people like them to not be celebrities.

I nodded as I handed the tablet back to him. "My mother was so excited when they moved here," I murmured. "The famous Reverend Jeremiah Kent. She and some of the other people in town tried to get him to take over when Reverend Hill retired."

It was just another role to them, Nolan – being respected pillars of the community. They thrived on knowing how revered they were. But it was all an illusion. They both had drinking problems and my mother had been addicted to prescription pain pills for years.

"What was all that like for you growing up?"

Not easy. Maddox and I got sucked into that world, you know? We stopped being their kids and became the supporting cast. We weren't allowed to be second-best at anything. The more positive attention we brought to our parents, the better. If we failed at something or brought even a hint of shame to them, it was like we didn't exist.

"What happened the night of the accident?"

My parents had both been drinking at the Fourth of July picnic, but not heavily...or so people thought. But they'd actually consumed a lot more than they let on and by the time we were ready to go, they were both feeling it. I offered to drive, but my mother insisted. I tried three times to get her to give me the keys, but she wouldn't. There were people around, so I didn't have the guts to take them from her or make a scene. And I was too afraid to tell anyone, so I got into the back seat. She was doing okay until we got closer to home. The road leading to our house had a lot of curves and she was going really fast.

Dallas pulled in a couple of deep breaths as I read his note. I closed my fingers around his as I read the message, but was forced to release him so he could continue typing.

It happened so fast. My father hadn't been wearing a seatbelt, so he got thrown from the car. When I came to, I knew there was something really wrong with me. I could barely breathe and I could feel that there was something lodged in my neck. But I was too worried about my parents to even try to figure out what it was. I managed to get out of the car. My father was conscious, but he couldn't move. He kept screaming at me to get my mother out of the car because the engine was on fire. I managed to drag her to where my father was lying, then everything went dark. When I woke up, I was in the hospital. I'd been in a coma for nearly a month. My mother never had a chance – the crash had killed her instantly. My father was left paralyzed from the waist down.

"And you lost your voice," I murmured.

He nodded, then began typing again.

No one ever talked to me about the accident. I didn't realize why until I got home. Maddox had taken a leave from the military to care for our father while I was in the hospital. I hadn't understood why he hadn't come to see me at the hospital. When I got home, he could barely look at me. He wouldn't talk to me. One day I finally confronted him about it and he lost it. Told me he hated me because I'd killed our mother. He'd always been really close to her. I was about to ask him what he was talking about when my father told Maddox to go cool off. That's when my father told me what he'd done.

"He told everyone you'd been driving," I said quietly. I was still reeling at the betrayal this man had suffered at the hands of the people who were supposed to have loved him the most.

He begged me not to tell anyone the truth. Said my mother deserved to be remembered for all the good she'd done in the community, not for one terrible mistake. He was so upset, Nolan. He really did love her and, despite everything, they were my parents, you know?

I did. Better than anyone. Because I had a similar relationship with my own parents. "I do," I said.

My father had begged Sheriff Tulley to let the whole thing go. I didn't know he'd told the Sheriff that I'd been drinking.

"Why would he do that?" I asked. "He could have just said it had been an accident. That you'd tried to avoid a deer or something," I said, my voice rising as I considered what Jeremiah Kent's actions had meant for his son.

I don't know. I guess he was just desperate to protect his and my mother's images. They'd been drinking in the car, so maybe he'd been afraid the cops would find the bottle or something.

"My mother said Maddox said some pretty bad stuff to you before he left to go back to the army."

Dallas nodded, but didn't respond to my comment.

"Have you seen him since your dad..."

Another shake of his head. *No. After the funeral, he tried to contest the will that left me half of my parents' money. He dropped the case just before he was deployed to the Middle East.*

"Why haven't you told anyone the truth now that your parents are both gone?"

I watched as his eyes shifted to the left and followed his gaze to see him looking at a picture on a bookshelf.

A picture of his family.

Both boys were young in the picture and had big grins on their faces. It looked like the photograph had been taken at Disney World. Their parents were embracing them from behind.

They all looked...happy.

"You wanted to protect them, too," I said softly. Dallas's gaze shifted to me and he finally nodded. He typed me a quick message and handed me the tablet.

They were my parents.

"I'm sorry, Dallas. It isn't right."

I have a good life, Nolan. This place...it's saved me in so many ways.

My gut clenched at his words. What if he lost it because of me?

I felt his hands on my face. When I looked at him, he shook his head. I knew what he was trying to tell me – that I couldn't blame myself – but I couldn't get the image of Gentry clawing at that door or his cries of pain out of my head.

"I'm sorry, Dallas. I just can't stop thinking about it. I made a comment to Jimmy about him wanting you and it set him off. I didn't mean it – I was just trying to get back at him for calling you…" I stopped talking because I refused to repeat the word Jimmy had called him.

Dallas pressed his forehead to mine and let out a deep sigh. Then he grabbed the tablet.

Please don't ask me to forgive you, Nolan, because YOU DID NOTHING WRONG. I need you to believe that, but if I forgive you, a little part of you will always believe it was your fault.

I understood what he was asking, wanted to accept it, even, but I just couldn't. Dallas tapped the tablet in frustration, then began typing again.

You HEAR me, Nolan. You hear me like no one ever has before. Even when I had a voice to listen to, no one heard me. I need you to hear me now. I need you to do this one thing for me…for us.

I lifted my eyes to meet his after reading that last part.

Us?

Was there an us?

But I wasn't brave enough to ask him.

I thought back to everything he'd said and knew he was right. There was no way to know for sure if my words had somehow set Jimmy off. He'd said that Jimmy had spread lies about him after the accident. Jimmy was a bully through and through. He got off on hurting others. What if just seeing Dallas's name on that credit card had been enough to remind Jimmy that his former friend hadn't disappeared off the face of the earth?

There was just no way to be sure.

Which meant Dallas was right.

I was blaming myself for something that I couldn't have seen coming.

Jimmy had attacked me as a kid repeatedly, even though I'd never mouthed off to him. In fact, I'd done my damndest to stay off his radar altogether, yet he'd still come after me over and over again.

Dallas's hands framed my face again. When he gently forced my head up, I saw the unspoken question in them. I nodded. "You're right," I said softly. "I couldn't have known…anything could have set

Jimmy off. If it had just been me he'd been pissed at, he would have come to my house or something. It wasn't...it wasn't my fault."

I believed my own words. It didn't mean I still didn't hurt for Gentry and Dallas, but even just that little bit of weight off my shoulders made it easier to breathe.

Dallas's fingers caressed my skin, then he was pulling me forward. His lips skimmed the bruise on my jaw before he pressed a kiss to the side of my mouth. He did the same to the other side. I closed my hands around his forearms as desire sparked to life deep inside of me. I shut my eyes and allowed myself to just feel. He kept teasing me with soft kisses that never actually landed on my mouth. When I couldn't take it anymore, I opened my eyes.

"Dallas," I whispered.

That was all it took.

That one word – his name – gave him permission to seal his mouth over mine. He absorbed my cry of relief and then he was pushing me down onto my back on the couch. I heard the tablet hit the floor, but I didn't care.

We didn't need it anymore.

I'd hear him just fine without it.

CHAPTER FOURTEEN

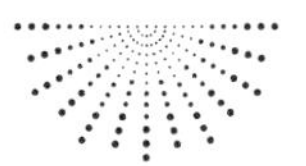

Dallas

Relief surged through me as Nolan kissed me back without any kind of hesitation. His body felt amazing beneath mine as I settled my weight on top of him. He let out a soft sigh when I trailed my mouth along his jaw and down his neck. I liked that he kept touching me, even as I began working my way down his body.

My arms.

My hair.

My shoulders.

Wherever he could reach, he touched.

Like he was afraid if he wasn't touching me, he'd lose the connection.

I could have told him that whatever this thing between us was, it wasn't going away anytime soon. But I knew it was something he'd have to figure out for himself.

I, myself, had gotten there already.

I'd been there a long time, I'd just been too afraid to admit it.

I used my right hand to push Nolan's shirt up, exposing his abdomen, then his chest. I licked over his supple skin as he worked the shirt off. The physical labor he'd been doing had given him some muscle definition that I couldn't *not* take my time exploring with first my fingers, then my mouth. Nolan's body shuddered every time I touched him, and he let out moan after breathy moan as I played with him. When I covered his nipple with my mouth and gently sucked, he practically bowed off the couch. My name kept falling from his lips, along with pleas for more.

But I took my time savoring him. The last time I'd been too desperate to be buried inside of his perfect body to take the time to appreciate what he'd been offering. It was an opportunity I wasn't going to squander a second time.

"Dallas, hurry," Nolan groaned as I worked my way up his body, instead of down it to where I knew he wanted me. I kissed him hard and shook my head. His eyes held mine and we just hung there for a moment.

Talking without speaking.

Listening without hearing.

His fingers toyed with my hair as we watched each other, then he nodded. I kissed him softly, then began making my way down his body again. Before I reached his waist, I turned him over and lavished attention on his back. He was practically mewling into the couch cushions before I flipped him onto his back again. I let my hand play with his cock through his jeans.

His damp jeans.

The knowledge that he was leaking so much that I could feel it through a couple of layers of fabric had me tearing at the button and zipper.

I needed to taste.

I practically dragged the jeans off him and he was quick to kick them off. His flushed cock bobbed against his stomach. A line of pre-cum dripped from the head and streaked across his skin. His entire cock was glistening, proof he'd been leaking from the get-go.

I shifted back on the couch to give myself some room and then lowered my head to lick up his shaft. Nolan let out a rough shout and planted his hands in my hair. He tried to force my head where he wanted it most, but I resisted and moved lower instead. I used my fingers to roll his balls around before slipping my hand even lower. When I pressed against his hole, Nolan cried out my name. I chose that moment to swallow him down.

My sweet little Nolan let out a string of filthy curse words right before he began bucking into my mouth. I settled my hand on his abdomen to hold him down and used my body to pin his legs so that he was completely at my mercy. I alternated between sucking on him and licking up and down the length of his dick, all while massaging his hole. When I reached my right hand up and placed my finger on his lips, he eagerly opened and sucked it into the hot, wet cavern of his mouth. The suction on my finger was intense and I knew he was sending me a silent message.

One I was definitely going to take him up on.

As soon as I'd driven him insane with need.

I pulled my finger free and then placed it against his hole. Just as I began breaching his body with the digit, I closed my mouth around the head of his dick and sucked hard.

"Fuck, yes!" Nolan shouted. His grip on my hair hurt in the best way.

I played with his dick long enough to work my finger inside of him, then I began finger fucking him as I gave him long, powerful drags on his cock.

"God, Dallas, I need to come. Please, I need to come."

If I hadn't been so close myself, I would have given in to his request. But I needed to be inside of him when he and I blew.

I pulled my finger free and then crawled up his body and kissed him hard. He was dragging in huge gulps of air and his eyes were bright with lust. I gently kissed him until his passion had cooled enough that I knew he wouldn't go over without me.

Because I wasn't done with him yet.

I gave him one last kiss, then sat up long enough to strip off my shirt and open my pants. I pulled my dick out and then positioned myself so that I was straddling his head. I worried that the show of dominance might frighten him, but all I saw was unadulterated need in his gaze.

I fisted my dick and gave myself a few hard strokes. Just like Nolan, I was leaking like a faucet. I waited until Nolan's eyes fell to my cock. When he lifted his eyes again, he must have seen my silent question.

"I want it," he said eagerly. "Please, Dallas, I want it."

Nolan's hands were wrapped around my thighs and his fingers were biting into my skin through my jeans. His lips were shiny and plump from my kisses and his skin was flushed a gorgeous shade of pink. I leaned forward so I was braced above him, then fed my cock into his waiting mouth. He let out a moan of satisfaction around my flesh and began sucking hard. My position meant I was in complete control, so I was careful about how much of myself I gave him. When I finally pushed to the back of his throat, he gagged briefly, but then relaxed enough to take all of me. I fucked his mouth for a few strokes before I pulled free.

I was just too damn close to blowing.

I quickly moved my body back down his and settled on him so I could kiss him. I tasted my own flavor on his tongue and marveled at how different it tasted from his.

"Need you," Nolan whispered between kisses.

I nodded because I was in the same boat. I would have liked to draw the whole thing out, but I was just too far gone. Based on Nolan's blown pupils and trembling body, I suspected he was, too.

I climbed off him long enough to shuck my pants and grab a condom and packet of lube from my wallet. As soon as I lay back down on top of him, Nolan was welcoming me with open arms and his legs were wrapping around me. Our dicks rubbed deliciously together. I somehow managed to work the condom on and added lube, but when I reached down to give Nolan some additional prep, he grabbed my arm.

"Too close," he muttered.

I kissed him as I maneuvered my hand between our bodies. I positioned my dick at his opening and slowly pushed forward. Nolan immediately bore down on me so my crown was breaching him within a matter of seconds. I kept my hand between us and closed it over Nolan's dick, spreading the lube on my hand over his skin. He gasped when I began stroking him.

I began fucking him in small increments, working my cock into his tight body a little more with each forward motion. By the time I slid completely home, we were both shaking violently. I was having trouble breathing, and a part of me began to panic because I knew what was causing it and the timing couldn't have been worse.

Nolan's fingers clasped my face. "Hey, slow your breathing for me, okay?"

I had no clue how he knew I was having problems, but I nodded and did as he said. Humiliation went through me and heat flooded my body, but not in a good way.

"Baby," Nolan whispered. "Look at me."

I did as he asked.

"Your breathing…it's part of the injury, isn't it?" he asked.

I nodded and closed my eyes.

"No, I need you to stay with me, okay?" he said as he gave me a little shake.

Embarrassment curled through me. I was lying on top of him, buried to the hilt, my hand on his dick, and I couldn't do a damn thing about any of it because I couldn't fucking breathe. I started to pull out of him, but Nolan's hand covered my ass. "Nuh-uh," he murmured. "You're not ending this. Not like this." He stroked my face. "Take a few slow, deep breaths, okay?"

I did as he said. My throat was tight, but the slower I breathed, the better it got. As air began to move through my lungs more freely, the tension in my body eased. When my breathing returned to normal, I buried my face against Nolan's neck. He cradled my head and kissed my temple, the shell of my ear, my cheek.

"You can tell me about it later, okay?" he murmured. "And if we need to stop, we can. But you don't get to pull away from me out of embarrassment, do you hear me?"

I nodded.

Nolan's hands trailed up and down my back. His inner muscles began flexing around my dick, causing me to grunt. I instinctively began moving my hips a little.

Nolan moaned at the movement. "Dallas, do you need to stop?" he asked, his voice laced with worry.

I raised my head and shook it. I knew I'd have a lot to explain, but I also knew it wouldn't scare him off. I kissed him and began gently thrusting into him. Nolan clung to me as our passion re-ignited. I could feel my orgasm right beneath the surface of my skin, so I shifted my hips enough so I could make sure Nolan went before me. The second my cock nailed his prostate, he let out a hoarse shout. His fingers dug into the skin of my back, then dropped to my ass. He gripped me hard as he urged me on. I quickened the pace until I was slinging in and out of him. Nolan's wail of satisfaction rolled over me as liquid heat hit my abdomen and then slid down my hand. I came right then and let out a loud grunting sound that would have embarrassed me if I hadn't been so far gone already.

The orgasm was violent and ongoing. Nolan's ass clamped down on my dick as I continued to spear into him. I was sure it was a high I'd never come down from, but when it did finally ease its tenacious grip on me, I collapsed on top of Nolan. We were tangled together, limbs intertwined, sweat-drenched skin slickening each other, heavy breaths melding together as we tried to find enough oxygen to kiss. Several minutes passed before I was able to find the strength to pull out of Nolan and get rid of the condom. I shifted our bodies so we were on our sides facing each other and then snagged a quilt off the back of the couch and covered our cooling bodies with it.

"That was..." Nolan began, then he just grinned.

His smile did funny things to my insides. I was still embarrassed about what had happened that had almost derailed the whole thing, but I couldn't deny how content Nolan looked. And I knew he wasn't pretending just to spare my feelings. I'd figured out a long time ago that Nolan was an open book.

You just had to know where to look to see the things he couldn't find words for.

And the things I saw just then as his eyes held mine left me reeling.

But God, what I wouldn't give to hear the words too.

CHAPTER FIFTEEN

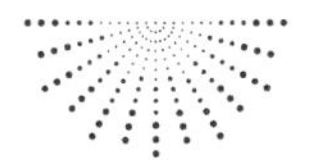

Nolan

I waited patiently for Dallas to type on the tablet. I could tell he was struggling with his words, though I wasn't sure why.

Did he really think anything he told me at this point would change anything?

It was true that I was scared that whatever he was going to tell me about his breathing wouldn't be good, but that wouldn't change anything, either. I'd already noticed some changes in his breathing in the past few weeks, especially when he was particularly stressed out. Whenever he exerted himself, his breathing took on a wheezing quality, and I hadn't missed how he'd slow down enough so that he could get himself back under control. His eating habits had changed, too. It took him considerably longer to eat and swallowing had seemed to become uncomfortable for him. I hadn't wanted to embarrass him by asking him about the changes, since they were likely tied to his injury, but I'd hoped he would tell me in his own time.

Making love, unfortunately, had forced the issue and I knew that had left him feeling embarrassed and vulnerable.

Though he shouldn't be feeling either, since being with him had been incredible. I wouldn't have thought I could have come any harder than I had the first time he'd fucked me, but oh, how very wrong I'd been.

After we'd lain on the couch for a little while, Dallas had led me upstairs to his bathroom and we'd showered together. We'd crawled into his big bed, but neither of us had even tried to sleep. I hadn't pressed Dallas to tell me what was going on, since I knew he'd tell me when he was good and ready.

He'd been ready five minutes ago when he'd grabbed his tablet off the nightstand. But ready and able weren't the same thing.

I sat up so he could type easier and while I waited for him to finish, I glanced around his room. He'd left the light in the bathroom on, but I couldn't tell much about his room other than it was spacious and minimally furnished. His bed took up most of the space and there was a small flat-screen TV on the dresser. There was a dog bed near the door for Loki, but when we'd gotten in bed, Loki had jumped up onto the foot of it, so I suspected the wolf hybrid didn't spend much time in the cushy-looking bed.

Dallas handed me the tablet.

After I woke up from the coma, I couldn't talk. But after a few months, I was able to whisper a little. My doctors had me meet with a speech therapist and I was able to make good progress. At that point, only my father knew because I'd stopped going into town. I'd drive to the next town over to get our groceries and stuff, but I didn't talk to anyone because I was too embarrassed at how bad my voice sounded. I was hard to understand.

I glanced up at Dallas and saw him watching me with trepidation. I grabbed his hand and pulled his fingers to my lips and kissed them. I kept his hand in mine as I continued reading.

After my dad died, my voice started to go again. I also started having trouble breathing and swallowing. The doctors said scar tissue was forming on my vocal cords. They performed surgery to remove it. I was able to talk again, but I was still hard to understand. Three years later, the same thing happened. The scar tissue came back and I lost my voice entirely again. I waited as long as I could because it didn't matter that I couldn't talk. But when breathing and eating started to get too hard, I had to have another surgery. That was almost four years ago.

I felt tears stinging the backs of my eyes, but managed to keep them at bay.

"So it's happening again?" I asked. "You're having trouble breathing and swallowing?"

He nodded.

"Did you go to the doctor?"

He took the tablet back. *I made an appointment, but it was for a couple of weeks ago. I didn't go.*

"Why not?" I asked in disbelief.

He glanced around the room, and I could tell he was reluctant to tell me. But he did anyway.

I liked that it didn't seem to bother you, Nolan. And I've gotten used to not talking – not being expected to. It's easier not to sometimes. But if I have my voice, it might change things. And even if I get it back, I'll lose it again. The doctors said there might come a point where removing the scar tissue won't give me my voice back at all. I didn't want you to get your hopes up, so I thought I could put it off until you left town.

I was too stunned to even speak at first.

"Get my hopes up," I whispered. "Change things?" I shook my head as the tears I'd been trying to hold back fell. "You think so little of me, Dallas?" I asked. "After everything we've said to each other…after everything we've done…"

I shook my head and clambered off the bed, my need to escape overtaking everything else. I didn't even care that I was naked. The lights came on as I headed for the bedroom door. Dallas grabbed me before I could leave the room.

He waved his hand, the confusion as clear as day on his face.

Which just made everything worse.

"I don't care about your damn voice, Dallas!" I shouted. "I fell in love with you, not whether you could fucking talk or not! How could you even think for a second that my feelings would change if you got your voice back and then lost it again? I couldn't love you any more than I already do, you asshole! If you started talking this second or never spoke a word for as long as you lived, I'd still love you."

I managed to tear free of him and dart for the stairs. I heard him hit the wall behind me, which was his way of trying to get my attention, but I ignored him.

"Narn!"

I stopped in my tracks at his garbled yell. Nothing about the word had been distinguishable, but I knew what he'd been trying to say.

My name.

I slowly turned around. He was standing a good ten feet behind me, still in the doorway leading to his room. His hand was at his throat and I wondered if the effort to call out to me had caused him pain.

"Dgnt!" he shouted, then slammed his fist into the wall next to the door. His frustration was coming off him in waves as he tried to repeat the word. But it just came out sounding like a mix between a hiss and a grunt. He kept hitting the wall and then he disappeared into the room. I jumped when I heard something crash onto the floor. Loki came rushing out of the room and dropped to the floor outside the door. A low whine emanated from his throat.

I was moving before I could even consider what I was doing.

Dallas was in a rage as he tore at the stuff on top of his dresser. Pictures went flying. The crash I'd heard earlier had been the TV hitting the floor.

"Dallas," I said softly. I knew his rage wasn't directed at me, so I wasn't scared. But the sight of him tore something open inside of me because it was finally hitting me.

What his life had become.

And it had happened long before he'd gotten locked in a world of silence.

No one had ever really loved the real Dallas Kent.

Yes, he'd been valued for many things – his good looks, his athletic talent, his charm. But he hadn't been loved.

If he had, there would have been someone left when he'd lost all those things. There would have been someone who knew how big his heart was and how badly he needed to protect others. There would have been someone who recognized how much Dallas still had to say, even when he couldn't speak the words. They would have seen that beautiful smile and twinkling eyes and done anything and everything in their power to make sure he never lost those things.

Dallas stilled when he realized I was still there. His eyes were wild as he snatched a big fat magic marker that was about to roll off the edge of the dresser. He gently grabbed my wrist and then pulled me farther into the room until we were standing in front of a large expanse of his bedroom wall. He used his teeth to rip the cap off the marker and then he began writing on the wall.

Don't go.

Please don't go, Nolan.

Love you so much.

Sorry.

Please don't go.

Love you so much.

Sorry.

He kept writing the same phrases over and over again, his hand moving frantically as he did so. I reached out to cover his hand with mine and he let out a soft keening sound in his throat.

I eased the marker from his tight grasp, then wrote on the wall next to his words.

I love you, Dallas, always and forever.

I love you, Dallas, always and forever.

I love you, Dallas, always and forever.

He let out a choked little sob every time I wrote the words. I didn't stop until there were more of my lines than his. When I lowered my hand, he turned into me and wrapped his arms around me.

As I placed kisses against his shoulder, his neck, his temple, my world righted itself again and I smiled to myself as it finally hit me.

I, Nolan Grainger, had finally come home.

"Give it back," I said with a laugh as I tried to grab my Kindle. Dallas rolled away from me and kept reading, then turned back to me and pointed at the screen. I flushed when I saw what he'd been looking at.

It was one of my favorite scenes from one of my favorite gay romance novels.

A particularly steamy scene.

"What?" I asked as I took the Kindle back. "I mostly skim the sex scenes anyway," I murmured.

He pointed to the small bookmark icon on the top of the page. I knew I was blushing when I pushed his hand away and said, "You probably did that when you grabbed it from me."

Dallas grinned and then he was pushing me flat onto the bed. He kissed one cheek, then the other, then motioned to the Kindle. Then he motioned between us.

If I'd been blushing before, I knew I was flaming now. "You...you think we should try that?" I asked, my voice sounding like I'd swallowed a frog or something.

Dallas nodded and kissed me, then pointed at me first, then himself.

When I didn't respond, he did it again. I knew very well what he was saying to me – that he thought I should do the thing in the book to him.

The very raunchy thing in the book.

My ears burned as I nodded. "Um, yeah, we can definitely talk about that."

He laughed. Whereas in the past he'd always tried to hide his expression from me when he would laugh without sound, he did no such thing this time. It was a testament to how far we'd come. Nothing was off-limits with him anymore. Any question I asked, whether it was about the scars on his body that had been a result of the accident or if I was just checking in to see how he was feeling that day, he answered without hesitation. He also hadn't hesitated to say yes when I'd asked him if I could go to his doctor's appointment the following week.

In the past week as things had settled into a quiet sort of normal for us, we hadn't really talked about the future much, but it wasn't something I needed to discuss.

I'd made my decision already.

Dallas belonged here with his beloved animals and I belonged with Dallas.

Even if it was in Pelican Bay.

And if I was being honest with myself, I had other reasons for not absolutely hating the idea of not leaving once I got my parents back on their feet. Never in a million years would I have even considered that those reasons were the same ones that had brought me back in the first place.

My parents.

Namely my mother, though things hadn't gotten any worse with my father, which I considered progress. But my mother was the one who was keeping me guessing.

It wasn't that she'd suddenly done a one-eighty and started to claim her undying love for me or anything. No, it was subtler than that. Mainly in the little things she did.

Like the breakfasts she kept making me.

And the bagged lunches for me to take to work.

Then she'd started making lunch for Dallas too because, as she'd put it, "you boys need to eat to keep the cold out."

On the nights I stayed with Dallas, there was no recrimination when I went home for a change of clothes the next day or to give my mother a break while I looked after my father.

But the biggest change had been when it came to money.

Not only had my mother asked me to show her the finances so she could start to manage the paying of the bills, she'd asked me to show her how to open her own Etsy shop so she could sell her knitting online.

I'd been so floored that she'd told me to "close your mouth, dear, or the bugs will get in," and then she'd started throwing out potential names for her new Etsy store. I'd gently explained that she might not sell much, but she'd waved me off and reminded me that every little bit helped.

I'd wisely kept my mouth shut after that.

When I'd told Dallas, he'd said that sometimes it took longer for some people to see what was right in front of them. I'd had the feeling he wasn't just talking about my mother, but I hadn't asked him about it.

It didn't matter what had or hadn't happened when we'd been kids. We were figuring it out now.

Dallas settled his weight on me and I automatically opened my legs for him. We were both wearing pajama bottoms, which he easily pushed down so he could rub his cock over mine. My Kindle and the sexy scene forgotten, I clutched him to me and lifted my hips to meet his. We'd already made love twice and my ass was pleasantly sore from the rough ride he'd given me in the shower, but I didn't care.

"Want you," I breathed against his mouth. I went to reach for the condoms and lube he kept in the nightstand drawer, but he grabbed my wrist and pinned it to the bed. He did the same with the other. Then he began slowly grinding against me. The velvety soft skin of his rock-hard dick wreaked havoc on my flesh and I struggled to get my hands free so I could grab his ass and force him to give me more.

But I had no hope of freeing myself and he knew it. He gave me little tiny kisses that were both too much and not enough and he never once let up on sliding our dicks together.

He was fucking me without actually fucking me and it was driving me crazy.

In the best way.

Heat and electricity fired throughout my body as he drove me higher and higher. I could tell he was in the same boat, because his breathing had become more labored. We'd had to be a little more careful since the night we'd made love on the couch and his breathing had become an issue, but Dallas had managed to turn the whole thing into a running joke – or tease, rather. He'd reminded me over and over again what I was in for after his surgery. He'd promised that if either of us was going to pass out, it wasn't going to be for any other reason than because he'd fucked me so well.

"God, Dallas, please, need to come."

Dallas slid his hands up so they intertwined with mine, then he picked up the pace. Within minutes, I was crying out his name as I came and he followed right behind me. He dropped his head to my chest and I automatically smiled. It was one of my favorite things to do after we made love. To have his entire body on top of mine, his arms wrapped around me and his cheek pressed against my chest. I always used the opportunity to play with his hair and the back of his neck.

I let Dallas pull me to my feet a few minutes later and lead me to the shower. After a particularly long time under the spray of hot water, we slowly jerked each other off, then rinsed one last time before getting back into bed. My interest in reading gone, I dozed on his chest while he watched TV. I was out before he turned the lights off.

I didn't wake again until early the next morning when my phone rang about half an hour before the alarm was set to go off. I fumbled for the phone, hoping I could silence it before it woke Dallas, but he shifted behind me and flipped on the lights right before my hand closed around it.

"Sorry," I said to him over my shoulder.

He flopped down behind me and wrapped an arm around my waist. I smiled at the possessive gesture and glanced at the phone, expecting it to be a wrong number.

It wasn't.

"Mom?" I said softly.

"Nolan, honey, is that you?" she asked.

I went on immediate alert because I could hear the tears in her voice. I sat up and was dimly aware of Dallas sitting up behind me.

"Mom, what's wrong?"

There was a beat of silence before she said, "Nolan, can you come home, please? Your father...your father, he's not waking up."

CHAPTER SIXTEEN

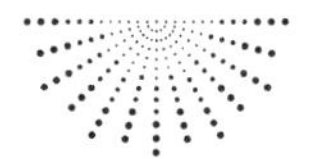

Dallas

I glanced at my watch for the umpteenth time as I straightened my tie. I hated how it felt around my neck, especially since my throat felt like a constant raw, exposed nerve and my breathing had gotten even worse over the past week. Fortunately, I wasn't in any danger yet, but I suspected I'd be under the surgeon's knife within a matter of weeks. Nolan had forced me to keep the consultation that was scheduled for a couple of days from now and continued to insist he'd be coming with me, despite my repeated attempts to tell him that his mother needed him.

The past week had been extremely hard on Nolan.

By the time we'd arrived at Nolan's house the morning his mother had called, the paramedics that Nolan had phoned right after he'd hung up with his mother had already arrived. They'd been waiting outside the house, and when Nolan had asked them why they weren't inside, they'd gently explained to him that they'd already examined his father and that he'd been gone for a while. They'd gone on to tell him that his mother had asked them to leave when they'd tried to cover Nolan's father with a sheet and remove him from the home.

We'd found Nolan's mother in her bedroom sitting on the bed next to her husband. She'd somehow managed to get him dressed in a nice pair of slacks and dress shirt and she'd been lovingly brushing his hair.

Nolan had stood frozen in the doorway for a good minute, his hand clutching mine. He'd forced himself to move into the room and go to his mother. I'd been able to tell that the sight of his father's lifeless body had been doing a number on him, but he'd managed to keep it together so he could focus on his mother. When he'd asked her what she was doing, she'd calmly explained that his father would want to look his best. Nolan had tried to get her to leave the room with him so the paramedics could attend to the body, but Nolan's mother had been insistent that his father needed his jacket. Nolan had been too immobilized with shock to help his mother work the jacket onto his father, so I'd taken over the task. I hadn't been sure if Nolan's mother had recognized me or not, but if she had, she hadn't said anything. She'd simply thanked me and then told Nolan she was ready to go.

We'd gone to the hospital so that Nolan and his mother could deal with everything that came with losing a loved one, including providing instructions on what to do with his body. The doctors had suggested that it had likely been a massive stroke that had killed Nolan's father. There'd been a small measure of comfort in knowing the man had passed quickly in his sleep.

By the time we'd gotten back to the house, Nolan and his mother had both been exhausted. Nolan's mother had tried to start cooking dinner, but Nolan had managed to get her to lie down in the guest room. I'd ushered Nolan into his bedroom to get some rest, but as soon as I'd laid down next to him and pulled him into my arms, the doorbell had started ringing.

It had gone on for hours.

The people stopping by to offer their condolences.

The food had started piling up, too.

As had the curious looks when people had seen my truck out front or when I'd answered the door myself. If the situation hadn't been so heartbreaking, I would have been amused by the looks I'd gotten. Everything from shock to disapproval.

And none of it had mattered because my sole focus had been Nolan.

To anyone who didn't really know him, it would have looked like he was handling things with a certain measure of acceptance.

The problem was, he was too accepting.

From the moment he'd seen his father's body, he hadn't shed a single tear or remarked on the fact that his father was gone. He'd thrown himself into handling all the details so his mother wouldn't have to, and when he hadn't been dealing with funeral arrangements or greeting people who'd stopped by to offer their condolences, he'd been watching over his mother who'd spent the better part of the week in the guest room. Like Nolan, she'd barely eaten or slept, and if she'd cried, I hadn't seen it.

I'd been worried enough about both of them that I'd been reluctant to leave them, but my animals were relying on me, so while Nolan and his mother had been at the hospital that first morning, I'd hurried back to the center to rush through feeding everyone. Then I'd done something I hadn't done in a really long time.

I'd asked for help.

I'd known there was no way I could manage both the center and being there for Nolan and his mother, so I'd reached out to the only person I'd known could handle the task of managing the center in my absence.

Sawyer Brower.

The vet had been back several times to check on Gentry since the attack, and my respect had grown for him with each visit. During one, I'd ended up asking him to take a look at all the other residents of the center, since it was often difficult to get a vet out there in situations when it wasn't an emergency. He'd readily agreed, and as he'd carefully examined each animal, he'd told me a little more about himself.

I'd gleaned enough about the man to know that he wasn't working a full-time job yet, since he'd only recently moved to the area. He hadn't said what his plans were, but his only obligation was as the backup on-call vet for the state.

When I'd texted him to ask if he would be able to help out at the center so I could give all my time to Nolan and his mother, he'd readily agreed and had met me that very afternoon for a quick orientation. I'd offered to pay him, but he'd waved me off. The only thing he'd taken me up on was making use of the small apartment above the detached garage next to my house so he wouldn't have to drive back and forth to his own place, which was located closer to Greenville than Pelican Bay.

The feeling of being indebted to someone was a strange thing for me, but I had no regrets. Nolan needed me. That was all that mattered.

I double-checked my appearance in the mirror. I was lucky that the suit still fit because I hadn't worn it in years. I loosened the tie enough so that it wouldn't put too much pressure on my neck. I'd fix it before the funeral started.

I checked my phone to make sure I hadn't missed a text from Nolan.

It had been a hard thing not to hear Nolan's voice this past week. Yes, he'd spoken, but he hadn't really said anything. He'd been polite to the well-wishers who'd stopped by and he'd been thorough when he'd arranged the funeral, but he hadn't actually talked.

Not to me, anyway.

I'd tried a few times to get him to tell me how he was feeling, but it was like he'd closed himself off from all the emotions that made him *him*. He also hadn't let me comfort him in any kind of meaningful way. The only time he'd let me hold him was at night when he slept.

I hadn't taken it personally, but it had left me feeling helpless.

Since there were no texts, I tucked my phone into my pocket and hurried from the bathroom. Loki was waiting for me outside the door and I gave him a quick pat. I'd been tempted to take him to Nolan's house since I knew he was missing us, but the animal wouldn't do well cooped up all day. Sawyer had sent me pictures of Loki making himself at home in the apartment Sawyer was using, so I knew the wolf hybrid was okay.

Since I'd left my truck parked by the office so I could grab the center's bills to take with me, I had to walk along the path leading from the house to the center. It gave me a chance to see some of the enclosures. Despite the cold weather, all the animals were going about their normal routine.

Except Gentry.

I didn't see him, which meant he was likely in the shelter within his enclosure.

Which I supposed was, sadly, his *new* normal routine.

The bear had been doing a little bit better since the attack and I attributed that to Nolan. In the week before his father's death, he'd been playing his violin for the stressed animal twice a day. Nolan hadn't been so sure it was helping, but I'd seen a difference in the bear. When Nolan would play, he'd pace the confines of the enclosure less and he'd eventually stop altogether and just sit and watch Nolan from afar. It wasn't much, but it was progress. When I'd first gotten Gentry, it had taken me more than a year to get the animal to even come near me, so it wouldn't surprise me if it took that long or longer to earn his trust back.

Since I had a few minutes before I had to leave, I made a quick detour so I could check on the bear. As I neared his enclosure, I saw that Sawyer was standing inside the double fence. My shoes crunching over the snow gave away my presence and he turned around.

And I instantly stopped in my tracks.

Because it wasn't Sawyer.

"Dallas," my brother said softly as his eyes met mine.

I shook my head in disbelief. If I could have talked, I probably would have said his name.

Maddox watched me for a moment, then left the enclosure area. I still hadn't moved by the time he exited the building. I watched Loki run up to my brother, but he didn't sniff him like he normally did when he met a new person.

Which meant he'd met Maddox before.

What the hell?

As he neared me, I automatically stepped back, then caught myself and forced myself to stand still. His cruel words rang in my ears as he stopped a few feet from me.

It should have been you that died, not her.

Maddox was dressed in a heavy parka and dark pants. Despite not having seen him for almost ten years, he hadn't changed much. He was a little taller than me and it looked like he'd filled out a bit more, though it was hard to tell with the type of clothes he was wearing. His hair was shorter than it had been when we were kids, though I attributed that to his life in the military. He had some laugh lines that made him look a little older than he actually was, but it was his eyes that stood out more than anything else.

The last time his dark green eyes had been focused on me, they'd been dancing with brittle anger. Now they just looked dull and tired.

"It's good to see you," Maddox murmured. His gaze settled on my throat. Most of my scars were hidden by the button-up shirt, but not all of them.

When he took a step toward me, his hand outstretched, I stepped back.

I had absolutely no interest in shaking his hand.

I wanted him to get the fuck off my property.

I was in the process of pulling out my phone to tell him that when I heard my name being called. I looked over my shoulder to see Sawyer heading toward us.

"Hey, I was hoping I'd catch you before you left," Sawyer said, seemingly unaware of the charged air that hung between me and Maddox. "Would you tell Nolan I'm thinking of him and his mother?" he asked.

I managed a nod.

"And don't worry about things around here. Maddox and I have it covered. I mean, I was doing okay on my own, but it's definitely easier with two people."

I shot Sawyer a look at that. Something in my expression must have clued him in because his smile faltered. He looked back and forth between me and Maddox.

"Um, everything okay here?" he asked.

Maddox sighed and said, "I didn't exactly tell Dallas I was coming."

Sawyer's face fell, then he looked at me. "Fuck, I'm sorry, Dallas. I thought you sent him to help me out." He shook his head.

"And I didn't correct him," Maddox admitted.

I didn't have time for this shit. I put out my hand to shake Sawyer's in the hopes he'd understand we were okay. He quickly shook it, and I pulled out my phone and motioned to it and then him to let him know I'd text him later.

"Got it," he said.

I didn't spare my brother another glance as I hurried up the path toward the parking lot.

"Dallas, please, I just need a second."

Frustration coursed through me as Maddox fell into step next to me. I shook my head violently.

He stepped in front of me on a narrow part of the path. I ground my jaw together as I was forced to stop.

"Look, Sawyer told me what happened to your friend."

I jerked my hand in a sharp motion to the right and then pulled out my phone.

I typed *Boyfriend* and stabbed my finger at the screen.

"Boyfriend," Maddox acknowledged. His eyes stayed on the phone for a moment, then drifted up to my throat. "Your voice…it never came back?" he asked softly.

I shoved him hard to get him out of my way. I needed to get to Nolan.

"I'm sorry," Maddox said as he kept pace with me. With my limp, it wasn't hard. "Look, I know you hate me and you have every right to, but I just wanted to see you and tell you-"

"Nah!" I screamed to stop him from telling me he was sorry. I didn't give a shit that he was sorry. My throat screamed in protest, but my outburst had done the trick.

It shut Maddox up.

His startled eyes followed me as I strode away from him.

I was struggling to catch my breath by the time I reached my truck, and I was forced to take a couple of minutes to will myself to relax so I could breathe easier. I focused on Nolan's voice in my head.

Baby, take deep breaths for me, okay?

Even though he wasn't there, he might as well have been because I instantly relaxed. My throat still hurt like hell, but I was able to breathe easier.

I forced all thoughts of Maddox from my mind and made the drive back to Nolan's house. I found him in his bathroom trying to put on his tie. He looked beautiful in his dark suit, but his eyes were lifeless as he looked at his reflection in the mirror.

I went to stand behind him. His eyes met mine in the reflection and I saw a little spark in them. I brushed a kiss against his temple, then began fixing his tie for him. He dropped his hands to the vanity as I worked.

We didn't talk.

When I was finished, I took his hand and led him from the room. We passed by the guest room, but it was empty. We found his mother in the bedroom she'd shared with her husband. She was sitting in the same position she'd been sitting in the morning Nolan and I had arrived to find her dressing her husband in his Sunday finest for the last time.

"Mom, you ready?" Nolan asked gently.

She nodded, then stood. "Did you boys eat something?" she asked.

"Not yet," Nolan responded. "We will after the service, okay? People are coming by to the house to say their goodbyes afterward, remember?"

"Oh yes," she murmured. "I should make a few things."

"There's plenty of food. Your friends from the church outreach committee are taking care of everything."

Nolan's mother nodded. "Yes, alright." She took in a deep breath and then reached out to place her hand on Nolan's cheek. He seemed startled by the move. She didn't say anything, just held her hand there for a moment, then moved past him.

I took Nolan's hand in mine and pulled it to my lips for a kiss. The move seemed to help pull him from his daze because he leaned into my chest and inhaled deeply. "I'm glad you're here, Dallas."

I put my hand on the back of his neck and kissed the top of his head.

I didn't want to disturb the moment to get my phone, so I sent him a silent message.

Me too.

The funeral was simple with little fanfare, but there were quite a few people in attendance. Nolan and I were sitting with his mother in the first pew in the church and I was dimly aware of the many sets of eyes on us. Part of it was likely because Nolan had grabbed my hand early on when the minister had begun speaking, but I knew a lot had to do with the fact that a perceived murderer was sitting amongst them. I ignored the need to escape their scrutiny and forced myself to focus on Nolan.

After the minister spoke, several people got up to share their memories of Edgar Grainger, but Nolan didn't.

Neither did his mother.

When the funeral ended, we returned to the house for the rest of the service. The women from the church group had left the funeral early so they could get everything set up. People began arriving within twenty minutes. Nolan kept himself busy by greeting people and accepting their condolences, many for the second time. His mother had disappeared into the kitchen to help with some of the food preparation, despite her friends telling her she didn't need to. They'd wisely fallen silent and let her help when they'd realized keeping busy was helping her keep it together. Like Nolan, she politely thanked anyone who offered their sorrow for her loss, but there was a certain emptiness to her as she listened to them.

It was like she was seeing right through them.

I'd ended up taking on the role of greeting people as they arrived and dealing with their coats. I was in the process of hanging one of the coats in the closet near the front door when I heard someone say, "So the beast has finally left the castle."

I knew that voice.

And it took everything in me not to respond with my fists.

I forced myself to turn around and saw Jimmy watching me with smug amusement from the doorway. There was little satisfaction in watching him take a step backward when I stepped forward.

"Jimmy, what are you doing?" a woman snapped from behind him. I recognized her as Jimmy's mother. She was holding onto her husband's arm as he escorted her up the steps.

Jimmy had no choice but to step into the foyer to let his parents pass. His eyes shifted from me to the very full living room.

Yeah, asshole. They're the only thing keeping me from kicking your ass.

"You," Edith Cornell said in surprise when she entered the house and spied me. Then her eyes narrowed. "You and your lies got my Jimmy fired," she bit out.

"Edith," her husband began as he tried to pull her toward the next room, but she resisted.

"My daughter works for a lawyer," she announced.

I ignored the urge to smile at the empty threat. Instead, I motioned to her coat.

"Don't you dare try to touch me," she said, her voice carrying to the next room.

"He wants your coat, dear," her husband said. He shrugged off his coat and handed it to me with a polite nod before helping his wife with hers. She huffed and muttered something under her breath about how she knew I'd been trouble from the first time she'd met me, then went to the living room to greet people. I took the coat from her husband.

"How's your bear?" Jimmy asked softly, his lips pulling into a sneer.

I barely managed not to grab him. He took off his coat and handed it to me, but right when I was about to close my fingers around it, he dropped it. Then he walked away.

Nolan needs you, I reminded myself. *Keep it together for him.*

I stuffed the coats into the closet and waited for the next group of people who were already making their way up the walkway. Another ten minutes passed before the traffic slowed. I was just in the process of putting the last of the coats in the closet when I heard a loud crash.

I rushed into the living room. My breath caught at the sight of Nolan lying on the floor. There was a silver platter on the floor next to him and deviled eggs everywhere. On the carpet, on him.

And fucking Jimmy Cornell was standing right by the doorway leading to the kitchen, his hand covering his mouth as he unsuccessfully tried to stifle a laugh.

I had my hands fisted and was striding toward Jimmy when Nolan let out a soft sob. Pain ripped through my chest as Nolan curled himself into a ball and began sobbing hysterically. The room was utterly silent as Nolan cried, and I wanted to beat the shit out of every single person there when not one of them made a move to help him.

I rushed to his side and dropped to my knees. He didn't even acknowledge me as I pulled him against my chest. His fingers curled into the lapels of my jacket as he just let go. His tears instantly soaked through the fabric of my shirt.

I wanted so badly to tell him he was okay, that I was there and I wasn't letting go, but I was helpless to do anything but hold him. I kissed the top of his head, his temple, anywhere I could reach as he clung to me. I didn't give a shit who was watching – it was just him and me. I kept brushing my lips over his head and then I made the only sound I could.

I whistled softly to him as I cradled him against my chest.

But I didn't just randomly whistle.

No, I whistled the one song I hoped he'd hear.

The song he'd been playing for Gentry over and over to show the traumatized bear that he wasn't alone.

Nolan's sobs quieted a bit, but I kept up the whistling.

"Nolan?" I heard his mother cry. "Nolan!" she said again, her voice high and wrought with concern as she dropped to her knees next to me, not caring about the mashed-up deviled eggs all over the place.

"Yep, Grungy Grainger is definitely home," I heard Jimmy say under his breath with a laugh.

If Nolan hadn't needed me more in that moment, I would have put my hands around Jimmy's throat and not let go, consequences be damned.

But it turned out that I didn't have to.

With unprecedented grace, Nolan's mother climbed to her feet. She turned around to face Jimmy and then calmly walked up to him. Jimmy had the sense to stop laughing.

About three seconds before Helen Grainger's palm cracked against his cheek.

Jimmy's head snapped to the right, but the second he straightened to look at Nolan's mother again, she slapped him again.

"You get out of my house, Jimmy Cornell. And if you ever come near my son again-"

"Helen!" I heard Edith shout, then she was rushing into the fray, her husband at her back. "What are you doing?" she cried as she examined her son's face. "Are you crazy?"

"You haven't seen crazy yet, Edith, if you don't get him out of my house."

"Nolan tripped, Helen! Jimmy was just minding his own business. It's not his fault your son is a-"

"Edith, the Good Lord himself won't be able to help you if you say even one more word about my boy."

Edith's mouth snapped shut and she grabbed Jimmy's arm. "Let's go," she bit out.

Helen dropped back down next to me and Nolan. He'd quieted in my arms, but I wasn't sure if he'd seen the altercation.

"Nolan, honey," Helen whispered.

Nolan turned his head enough so he could see her. Tears were still streaking down his face. "He's really gone, Mom."

"I know he is," she said as she opened her arms to him. He straightened and then slowly wrapped his arms around her waist. She whispered things to him as he continued to cry.

"Old bastard probably couldn't wait to get away from this freak show," Jimmy muttered as he pushed off the wall and began to follow his parents.

He didn't get two feet before I straightened and then knocked him on his ass with one punch. The room let out a collective gasp and I heard Edith scream, but I didn't care. As soon as Jimmy got up again, I decked him again. I was going for a third punch when someone got between me and Jimmy.

It was Doc Cleary.

"It's enough, son," the man said as he pushed against my chest. Physically, he was no match for me and I could have easily moved past him, but he played on my weakness and said, "Nolan needs you."

I managed a nod and stepped back, tearing my eyes away from the blood pouring from Jimmy's nose. Edith was shouting for someone to call the cops, but I didn't care. I settled my hand on Nolan's back and rubbed large circles against it as he cried in his mother's arms. I was dimly aware of Doc Cleary talking to Edith in a low voice, but I had no clue what he said. People began cleaning up the mess around us as I helped Nolan and his mother to their feet. Helen continued to speak softly to Nolan as she led him down the hallway toward his room.

I felt a hand on my back and turned to see Doc Cleary watching me with sympathetic eyes. "Come on, son. Let's get these folks cleared out of here."

I nodded because I needed something to do to keep me from going to Nolan.

Because I wasn't the person he needed right now.

CHAPTER SEVENTEEN

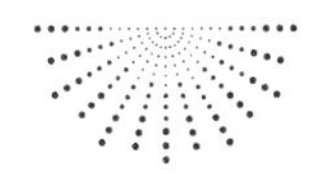

Nolan

I smiled to myself when Dallas's arm automatically wrapped more tightly around my waist when I tried to move away from him. Even in sleep, he was reluctant to let me go. It made my stomach do funny things.

I glanced at the clock and decided to give myself a few more minutes to just enjoy the warmth that was permeating my skin wherever Dallas was touching me. It wasn't that I'd exactly felt cold this past week, it was more like I'd been numb. I honestly didn't recall much of what I'd said or done after I'd walked into my parents' bedroom and seen my father's body. What I did remember included doctors explaining that there was no way to have seen his death coming, people coming by almost nonstop to bring food and extend their sympathies, and the minister and several others standing in front of a packed church telling everyone what a good man my father had been.

I'd wanted to ask them how they knew he was a good man. I

wanted to ask them if he was so good, why hadn't he loved me? I wanted to know why I hadn't been able to find even one memory of him that I could share.

By the time the service at the house had started, I'd accepted that I'd never have the answers to any of those questions.

Then Jimmy Cornell had tripped me as I'd been bringing a tray of deviled eggs into the living room for guests.

And my world had finally shattered.

There'd been no reason to get up anymore. No reason to show that I hadn't been broken.

My father was gone, taking my last chance to tell him I was sorry for never being good enough along with him.

Then Dallas had happened.

Dallas and his amazing ability to reach me without words.

I'd clung to him like he'd been my lifeline, because that was exactly what he was. What he'd always be.

I felt Dallas shift behind me and then his lips pressed against the back of my neck. I slowly turned over so I was facing him. As soon as I did, his arms went around me and he tugged me forward until our bodies were touching practically everywhere. I tucked my arms under his and held on for a while, absorbing his strength.

As out of it as I'd been this past week, I'd never lost sight of the fact that Dallas had stayed with me. He'd been there at every turn, and even when I'd mentally and physically pushed him away, he'd stayed.

"Who's watching the animals?" I asked.

He held me for a moment longer, then shifted so he could get his phone off the nightstand.

Sawyer Brower.

"The vet?" I asked in surprise.

He nodded, then his jaw tightened.

"What?" I asked as I brushed my fingers over his cheek. "Did something happen?"

I'll tell you later.

I leaned back enough so he could see me. "I'm okay now, Dallas. Because of you. I'm back."

He nodded, then typed, *Maddox was helping him.*

"He was helping Sawyer?"

Another nod.

"Did you know he was back in town?"

He shook his head. *Don't know why he's back. Don't care.*

I suspected he knew more than he was saying, but it was something I'd talk to him about later when things had settled down a bit. I snuggled against his chest. "Dallas, is it just me, or did my mother bitch-slap Jimmy Cornell yesterday during my father's wake?"

I felt a slight rumble in Dallas's chest, then he nodded against me.

"Good," I murmured. "It would have sucked if that had just been a dream."

I felt him laugh again, then he pulled me in tighter. I felt his mouth moving against my ear. I knew what he was telling me.

"I love you too," I said softly, and I held onto him until the alarm reminded us it was time to face another day.

My body was still tingling in satisfaction when I walked into the kitchen half an hour later. After getting out of bed and telling Dallas to sleep for a few more minutes, I'd gotten into the shower. I'd barely managed to even get my hair wet before Dallas had been opening the door and climbing into the small stall with me. Things had started off with him just washing my hair, then my body, but it hadn't taken long for the near-constant desire simmering between us to explode into a white-hot inferno of need.

By the time Dallas had snagged a condom and lube from his shaving bag, I'd been begging him for relief. He'd given me only the minimal prep necessary before he'd pinned me face-first against the wall and worked himself deep inside of me. He'd fucked me hard and fast, a sign that we'd gone way too long without one another. As I'd come, Dallas had been forced to cover my mouth with his hand to muffle my cries of relief. My knees had been so weak, he'd had to hold me up for several minutes. When we'd started to clean each other up, our bodies had begun to respond to one another again and Dallas had promptly pushed me out of the shower stall with a shake of his head. I doubted he would have had the same response if we hadn't had his doctor's appointment to go to this morning.

I was surprised to see my mother sitting at the kitchen table. Over the past week, she hadn't left her room much – the guest room. I wasn't sure when she'd return to her own room, if she ever did.

"Morning," I said. Awkwardness washed over me as I remembered how I'd clung to her the day before. Even after we'd gotten to my room, I hadn't been able to let her go. It was like the dam that Jimmy's act of cruelty had burst open had refused to be stemmed until every drop of water had found its way through. I still had no clue how long I'd cried on her shoulder for, or at what point she'd left the room. All I remembered was her soft words in my ear telling me it was going to be okay and then waking up in Dallas's arms.

"Morning, dear," she said softly. I felt her eyes on me as I went to get some coffee. "How are you feeling?" she asked.

"Um, good," I murmured. "I'm, um, going with Dallas to his doctor's appointment this morning. Will you be all right by yourself for a little while?"

"Of course."

She sounded like her old self and part of me was actually disappointed by that, but I refused to dwell on the reason why.

I grabbed a second cup of coffee to take back to the room with me for Dallas, but when I turned, my eyes fell on the photo album my mom was slowly flipping through.

And on one picture in particular.

Of my father holding a baby.

Me.

Of him holding me.

I could only classify his expression in the picture as one of...awe.

"You've never seen these pictures before, have you?" I heard my mother ask.

I shook my head. I knew I should get moving, but I was stuck in place. I watched as my mother removed the picture and slid it across the table toward me.

"He was so happy that day."

I swallowed hard and lifted my eyes to meet hers. But I couldn't give voice to the question I wanted to ask.

What did I do to make him hate me so much?

My mother slid another picture across the table. It was of a family I didn't recognize. There was a stern-looking older man, a petite woman, and three small children. No one in the picture was smiling.

"He didn't know I kept this picture," she murmured.

"Who are they?" I asked as I let my eyes fall over the three young children.

"That's your father's family," she explained. "He's in the middle, his sister Jeannette is on the left, and his brother Andrew is on the right."

I slowly sank into the chair in front of me and set the coffee mugs down. I let my fingers skim over my father's image. "I have an aunt and an uncle?"

"No."

I looked up at her in surprise. "Andrew died when he was ten. His father...your grandfather...beat him to death."

I felt tears sting the backs of my eyes.

"Jeannette killed herself a couple of years later."

"What?" I whispered.

"Your father was a hard man, Nolan. But he did love you."

I shook my head, but found it impossible to speak.

"It's true that neither of us were expecting you. We...we never wanted kids."

I nodded because I'd figured as much.

"Life for your father was very hard growing up. His father hurt him almost every day of his life, Nolan. For no other reason than he was a bad man. Your father was convinced that whatever it was that made his father hurt him was also in his blood. One of the first things he told me when we met was that he didn't want kids...he didn't want to risk becoming like his father and hurting his child."

"What happened to him? His father, I mean."

"He went to prison for killing Andrew. Died a few years later of cancer. Jeannette became involved with someone just like him when she was eighteen. She jumped off a bridge a year later when she found out she was pregnant."

I choked back my tears as I turned the picture over so I wouldn't have to look at the doomed family.

"What about you?" I asked. "Why didn't you want to have kids?"

"I grew up in a completely different kind of household. It was just me, my mother, and my father. They believed kids should be seen, not heard. Emotions were frowned upon, obedience was rewarded. There were no hugs or tears or laughter growing up. I didn't want to bring a child into the world that I couldn't share those things with."

"But you kept me."

"We did. We knew you were a gift from God and we loved you from the moment you were born, Nolan. You have to believe that," she said sadly. "We tried, we really did. But for us, we were fighting so much more than just the normal fear that comes with being new parents. Your father was obsessed he might end up hurting you, and I had no idea how to be a mother. Yes, I fed you and changed your diaper, but I didn't know how to do any of the rest of it. I'm not saying this to excuse anything," she said, then shook her head. "He wasn't a bad person, your father. He just didn't know how to relate to you. As you got older, you started to like some of the things Andrew liked when he was a little boy. The reading, the music…it just scared your father, and it was easier for him to pull away."

I hated the tear that managed to escape my eye. "You had to know what people were saying about me…what they were doing to me. Jimmy, his friends," I whispered. "You never tried to stop it."

It was my mother's turn to stifle a sob. "I know," she nodded. "We thought it would force you to act differently."

"You mean more like a real boy," I murmured.

"We were wrong, Nolan. Just like we were wrong not to encourage you to pursue your music."

"Why are you telling me this?" I asked, unable to keep the bitterness from my voice.

"Because none of it was your fault, Nolan. You didn't do anything wrong. You didn't do anything that made us not love you. You were a kind-hearted, sweet, beautiful little boy who deserved so much more than you got."

I could feel myself shutting down as the emotions became too much. "It doesn't matter," I murmured.

I was about to get up when she slid another picture across the table. I swallowed hard when I recognized it. It was from two years earlier when I'd played at the Kennedy Center. Another picture followed, this one of me performing in London.

More photos appeared in my vision.

New York.

Berlin.

Paris.

San Francisco.

"What are these?" I asked.

"We...we couldn't afford the really close seats," she said softly.

I lifted my eyes. "You were there?" I whispered.

"The first time we heard you play was in Minneapolis. We didn't have the camera with us, though. You were amazing, Nolan. You just blew us away. We began watching for when your orchestra was scheduled to perform in Minneapolis again, but then you joined the one in San Francisco and they weren't coming to Minneapolis. So we went to you."

I shook my head in disbelief. "That must have cost you a fortune-" My words dropped off and I looked down at the pictures again. "Oh my God."

"We knew it wasn't the most responsible thing to do, but we knew it was the only chance we'd get to see you again. We had enough money saved up for the trips, but then some stuff started happening with the house. The furnace blew last year. Then the roof needed to be replaced. We just...we got in over our heads."

"Why didn't you just call me?" I asked.

"And what, Nolan? Ask you to come home? After all we'd done to drive you away? We didn't have the right. You'd found this amazing new life – the life you always deserved. Pelican Bay was always going to be too small for you. If I hadn't needed help with your father…"

I didn't need her to finish the statement. I wasn't sure how I felt about knowing they'd been forced to call me. I wanted to believe what she was saying was true – that she'd known how hard it would be for me to come back here, but I just couldn't make it work in my mind.

"These past few weeks after Dad…after his stroke. You had a chance to try and fix things. But you couldn't even…" My voice cracked and I had to pull in a deep breath. "You couldn't even be bothered to treat me any better than when I'd been a kid."

I saw my mother's eyes fill with tears as she nodded. "Wanting to change isn't the same thing as being able to change," she said softly. "I know that doesn't make it right-"

"The violin," I interjected, not wanting to hear the rest of her statement. Maybe because I might be tempted to accept it. "You believed what the police told you about me taking that damn violin."

"They were very convincing," was all she said.

Pain unlike anything I'd ever known ripped through me. It felt like my entire life had been a lie.

"I need to go," I bit out as I staggered to my feet. I was heading for the doorway to leave the kitchen when my mother called my name. I stumbled to a stop, but didn't turn.

"The Kent boy, Dallas, he loves you."

I wasn't sure if she was telling me or asking me, so I just said, "He does."

"Good," she whispered. "Good."

My head felt like it was going to explode. I rounded the corner, intent on going to find Dallas so we could get out of there, and nearly ran right into him. I could tell by the pained expression on his face that he'd heard everything. When he opened his arms, I walked right into them. He held onto me for several long minutes as I tried to get control of myself.

"Can we get out of here?" I croaked. I felt like I couldn't fucking breathe.

I felt him nod, then he was taking my hand in his and leading me from the house. I didn't spare my mother a glance as we walked past the kitchen.

I couldn't.

I didn't want to go home after Dallas's doctor's appointment, but he convinced me that we needed to spend one more night with my mother to make sure she was okay. As angry as I was at her for all the shit she'd dumped on me this morning, I knew he was right. I'd been too preoccupied with what the doctor had been explaining about the surgery he wanted to schedule for Dallas within the next week to really dwell on what my mother had said. But as we made our way back to her house, I couldn't *not* think about it.

The things she'd told me about my father's childhood and his fears made sense, and I held a certain amount of pity for both him and my mother. But I couldn't just dismiss their ineptitude as parents completely. They'd had too many opportunities to get at least some of it right. The fact that they'd come to some of my performances was like salt in an already gaping wound. If they'd just fucking told me they were proud of me...

"Dallas," I said softly before looking at him.

He glanced over at me from behind the wheel. He must have seen something in my eyes because a moment later, he was pulling the truck over to the curb. He held out his hand to me. The console was between us, so I couldn't move against him the way I wanted, but the contact was enough.

"Would you forgive them?" I asked. "Your parents? Would you forgive them if you had the chance to talk to them again?"

He grabbed his phone and released my hand long enough so he could type.

I think I already have.

"How is that possible?" I asked. "After everything they did to you... how does any of it become okay?"

Not okay. But hating them won't undo any of what happened. Neither will forgiving them.

"So why do it?"

Because I think carrying that anger around is harder than just accepting that people make mistakes. No one's guaranteed perfect parents, just like no one's guaranteed the perfect life, no matter how much they plan for it.

"I'm angry, Dallas. I'm so very angry," I admitted.

Be angry, Nolan. Just don't let it change who you are. If you do, they win.

I nodded and mulled over his words as I sat back in the seat and stared out the windshield. Dallas got the truck moving, but didn't release my hand until we arrived back at the house. As soon as we were out of the vehicle, Dallas snatched up my hand again, then pulled me to his side. I loved that even though we were in public, he wasn't hiding what we were to one another. Our relationship may have been forced out into the open by circumstances, but the people of Pelican Bay were just going to have to deal with it.

As we reached the door leading to the kitchen, I steeled myself for the next encounter with my mother, since her car was sitting in the driveway. She was once again sitting at the kitchen table, but she wasn't alone.

The man sitting opposite her turned to face me when my mother said, "Nolan, you have a visitor."

I recognized him as one of the police officers who'd questioned me in San Francisco repeatedly after the Stradivarius had gone missing. Fear went through me and I automatically sought out Dallas's hand.

"Officer Cohen," I said with a nod.

I felt Dallas pull me to his side as soon as I said the name. I'd told him about how I'd been questioned by the cops and the threats they'd thrown my way, even after they'd admitted they couldn't press charges against me.

Had he found something he could use to arrest me?

"Mr. Grainger," he said. "I'm sorry to just stop by like this, but I wanted to tell you in person rather than over the phone."

"Tell me what?" I asked, finding it incredibly difficult to swallow.

"We found the violin."

"You did? Where?"

"In Mr. Lancaster's possession."

"What? Trey had it?" I asked, completely confused.

"We found it at his house in Pacific Heights after receiving an anonymous tip to look there. We also received a digital file of a recording between Mr. Lancaster and another person outlining his plan to frame you for stealing the violin. He was going to sell it on the black market *after* collecting the insurance policy on it. He also admits on the tape to stealing the money he was supposed to have invested for you."

"What...what does this mean?" I asked. I could feel Dallas's heat at my back as his fingers massaged up and down my spine, probably to try and soothe me.

It was working.

"It means he'll face charges. He's already hired an attorney and it's doubtful he'll face much prison time, but he won't get away scot-free. Whoever sent us the tape also leaked it online. The truth has already started to hit the papers. You should be completely vindicated by dinner time, Mr. Grainger. And I would recommend you hire an attorney. Even if Mr. Lancaster's attorneys manage to plead him down to a lesser criminal charge, he's got no case in civil court. The district attorney said the punitive damages alone could be worth ten times what that violin is valued at."

I glanced at my mother who sent me a small smile, but she didn't comment otherwise.

Which I was glad for.

It was just all too much as it was.

The man grabbed his jacket off the back of the chair he'd been sitting in. "I wanted to fly out here myself, Mr. Grainger, because I owe you an apology. All the people involved with your case do. Sometimes we get it wrong. This time, we got it really wrong."

I managed a nod, but nothing else. But then Dallas's words about anger and forgiveness rang in my ear.

Don't let it change who you are.

"I understand, Officer Cohen. Thank you for coming all the way out here to tell me."

The man nodded, but didn't try to shake my hand.

Something else I was glad for.

I was just too damn raw.

"I'll show myself out," the officer said and then he nodded at my mother, then Dallas, before he left the house.

The silence in the room grew awkward, but before I could say anything, my mother reached behind her and grabbed a plastic container full of cookies. She placed it on the kitchen table. "You boys should run on along now. I'm sure you've got work you need to get back to."

Her voice cracked a little bit and her eyes were bright as she pasted a too-big smile on her face. "I'm going to go visit at the church a bit. Lorraine mentioned needing some help getting ready for the clothing drive this weekend." She paused, then grabbed the cookies and handed the container to Dallas. "Dallas, you take as good care of my boy at home as you did when you were here, you hear me?" she said. I didn't see Dallas's response, but I had no doubt he'd nodded.

My mother went to grab her purse. She started to walk past me, but then stopped. Her eyes were wet with tears, but none fell. "You drive real safe, okay? Snow's just starting to fall."

I nodded and watched her walk to the coat rack to grab her coat.

Don't let it change who you are.

"Mom…" I waited until she turned to look at me. "You too."

She smiled tremulously. "I will, honey. See you soon." She held my gaze for a moment before she left the house.

I knew it hadn't been much, but it was all I'd had left in me. And when Dallas's arms wrapped around me from behind and he pressed a kiss against my cheek, I knew it had been enough.

CHAPTER EIGHTEEN

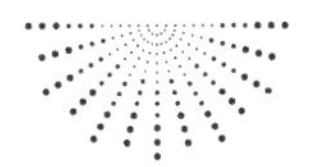

Dallas

"Baby, wake up, we're here," Nolan murmured. His lips skimmed my temple and then his fingers closed around mine. My brain felt fuzzy as I forced my eyes open. I sat up and automatically reached for the bandage on my throat, but Nolan gently grabbed my free hand. "It needs to stay on for a few more days, remember?" he said.

I nodded, though the move made my already pained head hurt more.

"Why don't you stay in here and I'll run into the office to get the papers?"

I shook my head, then straightened and tried to clear the cobwebs in my brain. I knew it was just the lingering effects of the pain pills, but I was tired of feeling so out of it. I'd had my surgery five days earlier, and while it had been deemed a success in that my breathing had improved and I was able to swallow the soft foods I was allowed to eat with no problem, it would be several weeks before I'd learn if my voice would return.

Nolan had been at my side both before and after the surgery, making me wonder how I'd ever managed it on my own the last couple of times. I'd also been fortunate to have Sawyer offer to continue handling the center while I was laid up and Nolan was taking care of me. I hadn't seen my brother again since the day of Nolan's father's funeral, and I'd been relieved.

Mostly.

I hadn't allowed myself to think about the other emotions I'd been feeling.

I took my phone out and typed, *It will be faster if I get them.*

"Okay," Nolan said. Not surprisingly, he got out of the truck and came around to my side to help me. I didn't really need the help since I'd regained most of my strength, and I'd cut the dosage of pain medication in half so I wouldn't be as off-balance, but I certainly wasn't going to begrudge Nolan putting his hands on me.

Especially since I wasn't sure how much longer I'd get the opportunity.

After news of who'd really stolen the violin had been made public, Nolan had been inundated with calls, both from reporters and from former colleagues and friends. After a while, he'd stopped answering the phone. We hadn't really talked about what Nolan's plans were, since he was still trying to cope with his father's death and the things his mother had told him, but I'd inadvertently overheard one of the messages Nolan had gotten on his voicemail when he'd left the phone on the speakerphone setting as he'd played it and I'd been in the bathroom getting dressed.

It had been from someone with the orchestra in London that Nolan had been auditioning for when the theft of the Stradivarius had occurred. They'd wanted the opportunity to talk to Nolan about him joining their orchestra.

The call had come the day before my surgery, so I had no idea if Nolan had called them back, and I was too afraid to ask. In my heart, I knew he needed to go – there was just no choosing between cleaning up after animals in a wildlife sanctuary with a broken man and playing in one of the most renowned orchestras in the world.

But that didn't make it any easier to know my time with him was running down at a fast clip. I suspected he was waiting until I was fully recovered before he broke the news to me. As hard as it would be to let him go, I couldn't be the person that held him back. I couldn't be the reason he didn't follow his dream.

Nolan put his arm around my waist to steady me as I got out of the truck. As soon as he closed the door behind me, Loki appeared. I knelt down and greeted my friend. He licked my hands, then turned and took off around the corner. As I rose, he reappeared.

But he wasn't alone.

My gut clenched at the sight of Maddox.

I shook my head angrily and pointed at the driveway. When he didn't move, I began looking for my phone.

"Hang on, it's in the car," Nolan said as he put his hand on my arm. I met his worried eyes. I had no doubt he recognized Maddox and even if he hadn't, he would have figured it out from my reaction. I'd told him about my encounter with Maddox in more detail just before my surgery, but I'd been too angry to talk about it and Nolan hadn't pressed the issue. I saw Nolan's silent message and nodded.

I did need to calm down.

This man might share my blood, but he was nothing to me anymore, and I wasn't going to give him that kind of power over me.

Maddox kept his eyes on me as Nolan went to get my phone. He handed it to me and I began typing.

"Maddox, I'm Nolan," Nolan said, but he made no move to shake Maddox's hand.

"It's nice to meet you, Nolan. I'm glad my brother has someone looking out for him."

Maddox's words only served to piss me off even more. I finished typing, then realized I'd have to get closer to him to show him the screen. Nolan seemed to understand my dilemma because he took the phone from me and began reading the message.

"What are you doing here? I don't want you here."

Maddox's eyes stayed on me as Nolan read.

"Sawyer called me and asked me to help out today. He got an emergency call over in Callas County. He'll be gone for hours and he didn't want you guys to have to worry about anything when you got back from your appointment."

I knew I should have been at least a little grateful, but I couldn't get there. Not while I had his words about wishing I'd died in place of our mother still in my head.

Nolan handed me my phone. I was about to start typing, but then waved my hand. I just couldn't do it. I was too damn tired.

And any apology Maddox had for me was just too damn late.

Ten years too late.

I started to head toward the office, but Maddox stepped in my path. "Dallas, please, just let me say this and then I'll go. You'll never have to see me again."

My body ached and my head was starting to hurt, probably from the pain meds. But I knew Maddox wouldn't leave until he'd said what he needed to say. His stubbornness matched that of my ornery zebra.

"Baby, let's go inside the office," Nolan said as he came to my side. I suspected he knew I was struggling, but I shook my head and pointed to the ground in front of me. I didn't want Maddox comfortable – I wanted him gone.

"Dallas, when I got that call that night, I was just so damn scared. They wouldn't tell me anything over the phone…just that there'd been an accident and I needed to come home. I spent hours praying to a God I didn't believe in that you guys were all okay. But deep down, I knew you weren't. When I got to the hospital and they told me you and Dad were alive, I was so happy. I vowed that no matter how badly you were hurt, I'd take care of you. I didn't care what it took."

Maddox's voice was uneven, but I tried to ignore that fact.

"Then they told me about Mom and I just…"

He shook his head and fell silent for a moment. "For a whole month you were touch and go. I went to the hospital every day and sat with you. The nurses said you could hear me so if I wanted to talk to you, I could." He let out a rough chuckle. "The things I said to you, Dallas. I begged, I threatened, I bribed...anything to get you to open your eyes. And then you did and I knew you'd be okay. Our family wouldn't be the same, but we'd still be a family."

I hated the pressure that was building in my chest.

"It was hard to hold it together," he said softly. "But I knew I needed to be the strong one. I didn't give myself time to think about Mom or the accident. I planned the funeral, I worked on the house so it could accommodate Dad's wheelchair, I dealt with all the people who kept coming by...there were reporters who kept rehashing the scandal...it was just too much. I wasn't sleeping, I was emotionally drained from dealing with Dad's mood swings..."

I knew what he was talking about. Between the loss of his wife and the prospect of being confined to a wheelchair for the rest of his life, our father had been volatile to say the least. There'd be days where he would be swimming in grief and other days where he'd be cursing me, God, and anyone who would listen. He'd lashed out physically at me on more than one occasion.

"So when Dad told me right after you woke up that you'd been drinking that night and that you'd refused to hand over the keys when he'd told you to..."

"What?" Nolan interjected. My head snapped up at the same time and my brother's voice dropped off.

"He told you he tried to stop Dallas from driving that night?" Nolan asked.

Maddox looked confused. "Yeah, he said he and mom only got into the car because they were afraid for your safety. He said he kept begging you to pull the car over."

Pain exploded in my chest and I bent over at the waist to try to quell the intense pressure.

"And you believed him?" I heard Nolan snap. To me, Nolan said, "Baby, let me take you home."

I nodded because I was done.

I was more than done.

"Wait, what do you mean?" Maddox asked. "Why wouldn't I have believed him?"

"He was your brother, Maddox," Nolan bit out. "Did you think to even ask him what really happened that night? Did any of what your father said even make sense? Dallas never drank. He never went against your parents!"

I settled my hand on Nolan's arm to try to settle him down. He shifted his eyes to me and took a deep breath. "Sorry," he murmured, then put his arm around my waist.

He was in the midst of helping me back to the passenger seat of my truck when the sound of an engine broke the silence around us. A mustard-colored, late model sedan was making its way up the driveway, though it was struggling a bit in the heavy snow. The car pulled next to my truck. I couldn't make out much about the driver other than a mop of black hair, but the car was filled to the brim with garbage bags, loose clothes, and a couple of sleeping bags.

There was also a kid in the back.

The driver said something over his shoulder to the kid, then got out of the car. I was taken aback by his appearance. He was young – late teens or early twenties at best. His raven-black hair fell in waves across his forehead and his dark blue eyes were surrounded by heavy eyeliner. There was a hoop piercing of some kind on his lower lip and large gauges in his ears. His fingernails were painted several different bright colors. He was wearing skinny jeans and a long-sleeved purple shirt with some kind of band logo on it. His feet were buried in the snow, but I saw nothing to indicate he was wearing boots.

"Shit, it's cold," he muttered as he tucked his hands up under his armpits. He grinned and then looked around at the three of us. His smile faded as he seemed to pick up on the tension in the air. His eyes lingered briefly on Maddox. My brother was staring at the guy like he had no clue what to make of him.

I was in the same boat.

"Holy fuck, is that a wolf?" the guy said as Loki came around the car and began sniffing him.

"Can I see?" a small voice said as the back door opened.

"Hey, no, stay in the car," the guy said. "It's too cold out here for you."

"No, it's not," the voice said, and the guy had no choice but to hold the door for the little boy as he staggered out of the car. I estimated him to be four or five years old. He, at least, was dressed for the elements. His parka had characters from the Disney movie *Cars* on it, and he was wearing rain boots which, though not ideal, at least kept the snow at bay. A red knit cap covered hair that was the same dark shade as the guy's. Loki immediately went to investigate the little boy. The guy kept a close watch, but he didn't panic as animal and boy checked each other out.

"What's his name?" the boy asked.

"Loki," Nolan said. "What's your name?"

"Newton," the kid said without looking up. He was clearly fascinated with Loki because he laughed when Loki licked his face, then began gathering up handfuls of snow and throwing them in the air to see if Loki tried to catch them.

"Can we help you?" Nolan asked the guy.

"Um, yeah, you're Nolan Grainger, right?" he said as he shifted his eyes to Maddox once more. I couldn't blame him – my brother looked ready to kill someone. If I hadn't been pissed at him, I would have told him to stand the fuck down.

"I am," Nolan said. "Have we met?"

"Um, no, my name's Blaze."

"No, it's not," the kid piped in. "It's Isaac."

"Newt," Isaac said in exasperation. "Remember what I told you? You're the only one who gets to call me Isaac."

"Sorry," Newt said, though he didn't seem all that sorry.

"Yeah, um, so Blaze is kind of a stage name," Isaac murmured. "I guess you can call me Isaac," he offered. "Anyway, I have something that belongs to you."

Isaac stepped around Newt and Loki and went to the trunk of his car. Nolan let out a soft gasp when he spied the violin case in Isaac's hand.

"It's my violin," he said softly as Isaac handed him the case. "What are you doing with it?"

Color flooded Isaac's face and he dropped his eyes.

"It's you," Nolan said in disbelief. "You're the one the cops saw on my apartment building's surveillance video. You stole the Stradivarius."

CHAPTER NINETEEN

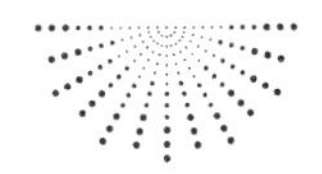

Nolan

"Yes and no," Isaac said. His eyes shifted to Dallas who'd tensed next to me when I'd thrown out my accusation.

"Stealing's bad," Newt piped in. "Isaac says so." The little boy sat down in the snow and Loki immediately dropped down in front of him.

"It is," Isaac said to Newt. "Stand up, buddy. Your pants will get wet."

"You said I could play in the snow."

Isaac sighed. "I know I did, but we have to get you some snow pants first, okay?"

"Okay," Newt responded, but he didn't get up.

"Look," Isaac said to me. "I took it, but only because Trey said you wouldn't give it back to him. Then I saw the news about you being accused of stealing it."

"You're friends with Trey?" I asked.

"Friends, sure," Isaac murmured as he glanced at Newt. "Let's go with that."

My stomach sank as I realized what he was saying. So not only had Trey been cheating on me with a woman, he'd been fucking another guy behind my back, too.

"I shouldn't have taken it, but Trey was pretty convincing and he paid me a lot to get it back for him. When I realized it was a scam, I thought about going to the cops, but I…I just couldn't," he said as he glanced at Newt.

I saw Dallas type something into his phone and hand it to Isaac.

"Um, yeah, I sent those recordings to the cops. I started taping Trey when I realized he'd lied to me. I didn't want to go down for that shi…stuff, you know?"

I didn't get a chance to respond to Isaac because a couple more cars chose that moment to pull into the parking lot. I glanced at Dallas, who just shrugged. The center could easily go weeks without a single visitor, but for whatever reason, today it was Grand Central Station. If Dallas hadn't looked so worn out, I would have laughed.

But any thought of humor died out the second I saw the two vehicles that pulled directly behind Dallas's truck and Isaac's car.

The sheriff.

And animal control.

Dallas tensed next to me, then straightened from where he'd been leaning against the car door. Isaac reached down to pick Newt up and took several steps back so that he was closer to the front of his car… and Maddox. He seemed panicked and I saw him whisper something in Newt's ear, causing the little boy to nod his head. I wanted to reassure him the police weren't there for him, but I didn't want the sheriff to overhear me.

Sheriff Tulley took his time striding over to us. The smug look on his face was a really bad sign.

"Mr. Grainger, Mr. Kent," he said with a nod. His eyes shifted to Maddox and widened slightly. "Didn't know you were back in town, son," he said.

"I'm not," was all Maddox said. When the sheriff's gaze moved to

Isaac, I saw Maddox subtly move closer to the pair. Fortunately, the sheriff didn't linger on the younger man and little boy.

"Mr. Kent, we've received several complaints about your," – he waved his hand around – "business. This serves as notice that a public forum has been scheduled for tomorrow night to address those concerns and what steps will be taken to shut you down, since this place is clearly a threat to the residents of Pelican Bay." The man handed Dallas a folded-up piece of paper.

Dallas angrily ripped the paper open and scanned it, then started typing on his phone. But the sheriff didn't even wait to hear what Dallas had to say before continuing.

"We've also received a complaint that your wolf viciously attacked a resident who was in the area recently."

"That's a lie," I interjected.

The sheriff shot me a hard look, then handed Dallas a second piece of paper. "This is an order authorizing me to remove the animal from the premises for quarantine purposes and to determine what action should be taken to make sure he can't hurt anyone else."

My heart leapt into my throat as the animal control officer suddenly stepped forward with a snare and looped it around Loki's neck. The wolf hybrid, who'd been standing quietly nearby, jumped when the snare tightened around his neck, then tried to jerk back.

Dallas let out a strangled shout and then he was striding toward the sheriff. I tried to stop him, but he was too strong. Luckily, Maddox stepped in front of Dallas and grabbed him by the arms. "Don't," he told his brother. Dallas fought him as the sheriff watched, his hand resting on the butt of his gun. Panic tore through me.

"Dallas," I said as I grabbed his face so he would look at me. "Please don't. We'll get Loki back, but not like this, okay?"

"Dallas," Maddox said so softly that only Dallas and I could hear him. "It's what he wants."

Dallas's eyes shifted to the sheriff, then Loki who was being dragged to the animal control vehicle. The animal was struggling violently. Dallas nodded to Maddox and stopped trying to get past him. As soon as Maddox released him, Dallas motioned to Loki, then himself, followed by the animal control truck.

"He wants to put Loki in the truck himself, Sheriff," I quickly said. "Please," I added, though it nearly killed me to beg the man for anything. "It will go easier on everyone if Dallas does it."

The asshole was clearly enjoying his victory, because he studied Dallas, me, and then Loki for a long time – much longer than was necessary – before he finally nodded. Dallas quickly moved past me and the sheriff and hurried to Loki's side. The animal instantly calmed at his presence. Dallas let his hands stroke over the wolf hybrid's coat, then carefully gathered him in his arms. He put him in the truck, then removed the snare. I felt tears sting the backs of my eyes as he hugged his pet.

"Let's go," the sheriff snapped impatiently and walked toward his car as the animal control officer gently forced Dallas to step back. Dallas didn't move as the cars left. I hurried toward him when he suddenly swayed.

I didn't manage to reach him until after he'd fallen to his knees in the snow.

I waited until long after the pain pills had taken effect to release my hold on Dallas. He was pressed up against my chest, but the drugs had knocked him out enough that when I untangled my body from his, he didn't wake up.

It had taken quite a while to convince Dallas to take the pills once we'd reached the house. His silence had worried me, and my hope was that it was just the lingering pain and the medication he was on that was keeping him from reacting to the loss of Loki. He'd been so out of it that he'd even let Maddox help me get him to the house and then up to his room. Dallas had tried to refuse the pain pills I'd handed him, but he'd given in when I'd promised I would be there when he woke up and that we'd figure out how to get Loki back. Neither of us had any doubt that the sheriff had been lying about someone getting attacked. We also knew he held no jurisdiction when it came to trying to close down the center, since it wasn't technically located in Pelican Bay. But that didn't mean he couldn't get enough support from residents to have them flooding the state with calls demanding the center be shut down. There was no question as to the sheriff's motives, since he'd made it clear that he hated Dallas for the accident he still believed had been Dallas's fault. Not to mention the way Dallas had embarrassed Jimmy at my father's wake.

I brushed a soft kiss over Dallas's temple, then went downstairs to check on Isaac and Newt. The young man had been worried when Dallas had collapsed and had asked if there was anything he could do. Since Maddox had been there to help me with Dallas, I'd told him we were okay, but when he'd suggested he and Newt should leave, I'd asked him to come with us to the house. Not only did I still have questions about his involvement with Trey and the Stradivarius, I was also worried about him and Newt. I hadn't missed how scared both of them had been when the sheriff had shown up. The reaction could have been attributed to the violin, but it could have been something else, too.

My instincts were telling me it was the latter.

I found him in the kitchen doing the breakfast dishes I hadn't had time to get to before Dallas and I had made the trip to Minneapolis for the follow-up appointment with his surgeon.

"You don't have to do that," I said as I searched the area for Newt. I finally spotted the little boy asleep on the couch in the living room.

Isaac practically jumped out of his skin. "What? Oh, um, I don't mind. Keeps me busy. How's your friend?"

"Asleep," I murmured.

"That shit out there was real," Isaac muttered. "Fucking cops," he added under his breath.

Yep, he was definitely running from something.

I went to the island in the kitchen and trailed my fingers over the violin case sitting on it. I flipped the latches on the case and studied the instrument. I'd paid a small fortune for the instrument when I'd gotten my first job performing with an orchestra in New York. Losing it had been like losing a part of me, but strangely enough, its return wasn't doing much for me. My gaze automatically shifted to the violin on the coffee table in the living room.

The one Dallas had gotten for me.

The one I played for Gentry every day, the one I played for Dallas every night.

It was a lower-quality instrument compared to the one Isaac had returned, but somehow, I played better on it than I had on any other violin I'd ever used. I had no doubt it was less about the instrument and more about the audience.

I felt Isaac's gaze on me and turned to find him watching me. He dropped his eyes and then reached for a plastic container I hadn't noticed on the counter. "Um, your mom asked me to bring this with me. It's lasagna, I guess. Said you and your man would be hungry after such a long day."

"You talked to my mom?" I asked, lifting a brow as I accepted the container.

"Um, yeah, I went to your house first and she said you'd be here. She told me how to get here."

The container was heavy in my hand, indicating it was likely filled to the brim with food. I'd only seen my mother a few times since Dallas and I had returned to the center, but on the occasions I'd gone to the house to check on her, she hadn't let me leave until my arms were laden down with plastic containers full of everything from full meals to cookies to soup. At first, I'd thought she'd just ended up making too much for herself because she hadn't gotten used to cooking for one, but then I'd realized that there was way too much food for even two people.

Meaning she'd purposely cooked the food for me *and* Dallas.

"Thanks," I said. "Are you hungry?" I asked, holding up the container.

The guy was super skinny so I figured even if he wasn't hungry, he should eat anyway.

"No, that's okay. Newt and I should go," he said as he wiped his hands on his pants and then started heading toward the living room.

"Isaac, please, I'd like you to stay," I said. "I have some questions for you."

He stilled, then nodded. "Yeah, okay."

I went and grabbed some plates and silverware and then motioned to the couch. Isaac grabbed the plastic container and followed me. He sat down to next to Newt and put his hand on the boy's head. "Newt, are you hungry, buddy?"

Newt sighed and stretched a bit, then opened his eyes. He shook his head and then sat up and pressed against Isaac's side so his head was on his chest. He promptly fell back asleep. Isaac lovingly ruffled the boy's hair and then dropped a kiss to the top of his head.

"Is he your son?" I asked as I handed Isaac a plate full of lasagna.

"Um, no, he's my brother."

I nodded, though, in truth, the age gap surprised me. But I didn't comment on it. I was in the process of scooping some lasagna on my own plate when it hit me.

"Isaac...Newton," I said with a smile. "Seriously?"

Isaac smiled and rolled his eyes. "I'd like to say our mother had a weird sense of humor, but the truth is, she was just plain weird."

The comment was made with a smile, leaving me to guess he hadn't meant it as a criticism.

I let Isaac eat for a few minutes, but found it hard to get more than a few bites of the lasagna down myself. It tasted fine, but I was just too worried about Dallas and everything that had happened tonight to even think about something as simple as eating.

"Tell me how you ended up with my violin, Isaac," I said softly.

He paused his chewing, then swallowed hard and set the nearly empty plate down on the couch cushion next to him, careful not to disturb Newt in the process. "Um, Trey, he gave it to me...as payment."

"Payment? I don't understand. Payment for what?"

Isaac refused to look at me. He glanced down to check that Newt was still out. "He had his kinks, you know? There's only one sure way to find a guy who will agree to that shit and keep his mouth shut about it, especially for a guy like Trey."

It took me a full fifteen seconds to understand what he was trying to tell me. Before I could even think about what I was saying, I breathed, "You're a prost-"

"Escort," Isaac cut in. His chin lifted just a little, like he was daring me to say anything else. When I didn't, he said, "Trey said I could pawn the violin – it wasn't expensive enough to set off any alarm bells like the one I took from your apartment for him."

"Why didn't you do it?"

"Because I'm not a thief." He tilted his head and said, "Yeah, okay, I guess I stole that really fancy violin, but I already told you-"

"I believe you," I interjected. "Trey *is* a very convincing guy. I should know that better than anyone."

"Hey," Isaac said, and I looked up, not even realizing I'd dropped my eyes. "I make a living off being able to read guys and what they want. He had me snowed almost from the start."

I nodded. "Thank you," I murmured. "For sending that tape to the cops…for making it in the first place. For bringing my violin back."

Isaac shrugged and let his fingers card through Newt's hair. "Guys like that shouldn't always get to win, you know?"

At that, we both fell into a contemplative silence for a moment.

"Do you want any more?" I asked as I nodded at the lasagna.

He shook his head. "So, um, the guy upstairs, he's your boyfriend?"

I nodded. "This is his place."

"The whole thing? Like all the animals and stuff?"

"Yeah, he rescues and rehabilitates them."

"And his" – Isaac motioned to his own throat – "is that…is he okay?"

"He had surgery a few days back to deal with some complications from a car accident, but he'll be okay."

Isaac nodded. "What about the brick wall that was with you guys?"

"The what?" I asked.

"The guy who looked like he'd run out of villagers to crush."

I smiled when I realized he was talking about Maddox. "Maddox, Dallas's brother," I said.

"Did his mama name him Mad 'cause that's what he is?" Newt

asked tiredly. His eyes had opened at some point and he was watching me, but he hadn't moved from his brother's side.

"It's Maddox, buddy," Isaac corrected.

"He was mean. He kept looking at you funny," Newt murmured.

Isaac's hand settled on his brother's back. "Remember what I said about what other people think about us?"

Newt nodded. "They're just scared 'cause they don't like themselves much."

"Right," Isaac said. "Buddy, do you want to eat something before we get going?"

Newt shook his head. Isaac carefully lifted him and climbed to his feet.

"Can I ask where you're headed?" I asked as I stood.

"New York."

"Do you have family there or something?"

"We're gonna get lost again," Newt whispered.

Isaac's eyes darted to meet mine, but he just shook his head. "He's tired," he mumbled. "I'm really sorry about what happened to your wolf – I hope you get him back."

"Loki was nice," Newt said softly, then his head lolled on Isaac's shoulder and I knew the little boy was out again. I stepped in Isaac's path to stop him.

"Isaac, do you guys need a place to stay for a couple of days? Or even just the night?"

"What? No," Isaac said quickly.

Too quickly.

"It's late and the roads are sure to be covered in a few inches of snow by now. The plows don't get to the back roads sometimes for a couple of days. The closest hotel is in Pelican Bay and it's too cold to sleep in your car."

Isaac hesitated for a moment, then murmured, "We'll be fine."

"Please, Isaac, I'll worry about both of you if I know you're out there. Just stay for the night. The weather should clear by tomorrow."

The young man shifted back and forth on his feet, clearly torn. It wasn't until Newt snuggled closer against him that he finally nodded. "Okay, yeah. Thanks."

I nodded, but didn't make a big deal out of him agreeing. I could tell he was already on edge about the whole thing. I led Isaac upstairs and showed him one of the guest rooms. There weren't any sheets on the mattress, but I quickly found some in the closet near the guest bathroom and got the bed fixed up. The room smelled a little stale, but it wasn't too bad.

"Let me know if you need anything, okay?"

"Yeah. I, uh, need to go grab our stuff from the car."

I nodded. "I can stay with Newt if you want."

Isaac hesitated, then nodded. "I'll just be a couple minutes."

It ended up being closer to ten, and I was about to go outside and look for the young man after an unreasonable fear settled in my belly that he'd ditched his little brother. But I'd just as quickly dismissed the thought since I could tell how much Isaac loved the boy.

"Everything okay?" I asked when Isaac reappeared, a small duffle bag in hand. He looked flushed and he was breathing hard.

"Fine," he bit out.

"Did something happen-"

"No," he said sharply. "Yes. Maybe. I don't know."

I could tell he was off-balance and I briefly wondered if I'd done the right thing in asking him to stay.

"You should tell your boyfriend's brother to just back the fuck off."

"My boyfriend's…Maddox? You saw Maddox out there?"

"Prick," Isaac muttered. "Sorry," he murmured, then he began searching through the duffle bag. I decided to leave him be when I saw that his hands were shaking.

"Goodnight, Isaac," I said as I began to pull the door shut.

"Nolan."

"Yeah?"

Isaac kept his back to me. "Thanks." He motioned to the room with a jerk of his head. "For this."

"You're welcome. See you in the morning."

I closed the door and went to check on Dallas, who was still soundly sleeping. I returned downstairs with the intent of cleaning and locking up the house, but nearly jumped out of my skin at the sight of Maddox standing in the kitchen, arms crossed.

God, Isaac was right, the man did look like a brick wall with his broad chest, bulging biceps, and perpetual frown. Hell, Newt had nailed it – Mad did fit the guy.

"Sorry," he had the decency to say. "You shouldn't let him leave. He's in trouble."

I could only assume he was talking about Isaac. "Did he tell you that?"

"Didn't need to."

I wondered exactly what had happened between the two, but before I could ask, Maddox said, "Dallas gave up on believing our parents would change, but I guess I never did. That's why I didn't even think to question our father when he said Dallas was driving. Dallas never even denied it."

Maddox paused before saying, "I didn't think our father was capable of a betrayal like that. But I guess I never thought I was capable of saying what I said to my own brother. I didn't mean it, but it doesn't matter. I said it and I let the shame of what I did afterward keep me from telling him how wrong I was."

"You tried to keep him from getting his half of the inheritance. You let him face this vindictive town by himself for years. The one person he should have been able to count on and you weren't there."

"Yes," was all he said. He turned to leave, then stopped and said, "Will you tell him something for me?"

I didn't respond because I wasn't sure I could give him the answer he wanted. My only concern was protecting Dallas. Even if I felt a certain measure of pity for Maddox and how badly he'd fucked up his relationship with his brother, Dallas did and always would come first.

"Tell him…tell him I have his back."

That was all he said before he walked out the door.

CHAPTER TWENTY

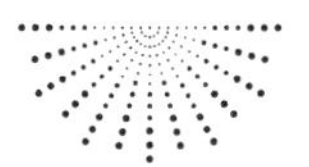

Dallas

I wasn't sure what I'd been expecting to find when I'd walked downstairs after carefully extricating myself from Nolan's hold so he could sleep a bit longer.

It certainly hadn't been to see a little kid sitting on the floor of my living room playing with a whole bunch of little Matchbox cars. And I most definitely had no clue how to react when Newt smiled up at me and said, "You wanna play?"

I'd already known Nolan had invited Isaac to spend the night, because he'd sent a text to my phone at some point the night before, presumably in case I'd ended up waking before him. Even in his text, I could tell Nolan had been nervous, because he'd gone on and on explaining how Isaac and Newt were brothers and he thought they were on the run from something and that something had also happened between Isaac and Maddox. There'd been a second message about needing to give me a message from Maddox, but that he'd do it in the morning.

It had been information overload, but luckily, I'd been feeling clearheaded enough to process it. I'd been tempted to stay in bed with Nolan until he woke up, but I was too on edge about what had happened the night before. My concern for Loki was ruling most of my thoughts. I knew the claim that he'd attacked someone was bogus, but it wouldn't take much for people to believe whatever story the sheriff and his dickish relatives had concocted. I was less concerned about the future of the center, because I had quite a few things on my side.

Money, for one.

Which meant I could afford to hire a kick-ass attorney.

And I had connections that the sheriff and his small-town mind couldn't fathom. I'd call on every single one of them if that was what it took.

I gave Newt a quick nod, then held up my finger to indicate I'd just be a minute.

"'Kay," he said brightly. He was wearing pajamas with cars all over them.

I grabbed myself a cup of coffee and then went to sit down next to the little boy. He began lining the cars up in front of me. "Which ones do you want?"

There were more than a dozen faded cars to choose from. I pointed at him, then me. The sharp little boy quickly picked up on what I was saying. "Sure, I'll pick for you." He told me things about each car that he picked for me, then did the same for the cars he kept for himself. I almost missed it when he said, "You can't talk, huh?"

I shook my head.

"Is that 'cause you got hurt?" he asked, pointing to my bandaged throat.

I nodded.

"That's okay, I can make the sounds for you," he said as he motioned toward the cars. "Let's race, 'kay?"

I stifled a smile and nodded. As we began moving the cars around an imaginary racetrack, Newt made all sorts of sputtering sounds. I'd lost track of how many times we went around the "track" when Newt suddenly threw his hands in the air and his eyes went wide. "You won!" he exclaimed. "You won!"

I laughed, even though it made my throat hurt. I was so preoccupied that it wasn't until arms wrapped around my shoulders from behind that I realized we weren't alone anymore.

"Morning," Nolan said softly as he kissed my cheek.

I turned to look at him and felt that familiar sensation deep in my belly. God, how I loved this man. I kissed him chastely on the mouth.

"Morning, Newt."

"Good morning. Wanna play?"

Nolan laughed. "Maybe in a minute. Where's your brother?"

"Fixin' the car. We gotta hit the road," Newt said absently.

"Something's wrong with your car?" Nolan asked.

Newt nodded. "Isaac says it's a piece of sh-junk."

I smiled at Newt's combining of the swear word Isaac had clearly caught himself saying before correcting himself with the more kid-friendly term.

"Son of a biscuit-eater!" came a shout from behind us just as the kitchen door opened and a burst of cold wind and snow flew into the house before Isaac jammed the door shut. I noticed he wasn't wearing a coat again. It made me wonder if he had one. I was reminded of when Nolan had first started working at the center.

"Problem?" Nolan asked, smiling at Isaac's quasi-swear word.

Isaac seemed surprised to see us both. "Um, sorry. Yeah, my car won't start."

I climbed to my feet and motioned to myself, then outside. "Thanks," Isaac said. I pulled on my coat and boots, but when he made a move to follow me, I motioned for him to stay put. Bitter cold greeted me as I stepped outside. I hurried to the sedan and made quick work of examining the engine. It took less than a minute to diagnose the problem. What I was seeing didn't make sense, so I hurried into the house to ask Isaac about it. It was just Nolan in the kitchen when I got inside.

"Isaac took Newt upstairs to get him changed," Nolan said before I even asked. "Hey," he said. "What is this?" he asked as he held out his hand. I furrowed my brow and took out my phone.

Sparkplugs.

"Sparkplugs?" Nolan asked, clearly confused.

Yeah. They're probably from Isaac's car since he's missing two. Where did you find them?

"Um, that's the thing. They were in the fridge. In the butter dish," Nolan responded as he motioned to the now-empty butter dish.

I shook my head and then typed one word.

Maddox.

"Maddox? You think he put them there?"

I know he did. It was something we used to do when we were teenagers. When our parents were too drunk to drive, we'd remove the sparkplugs from their cars and hide them in the butter dish, since we figured they'd never look there. We'd put them back in the cars as soon as they sobered up. I just don't understand why he removed them from Isaac's car.

Even as I typed the words, my thoughts drifted to Maddox. We'd always had to work so hard to keep our parents from endangering themselves and others when they'd been intoxicated, that we'd sworn to each other that we'd never drink and drive. As much as I hated to admit it, his anger made sense. I couldn't say I wouldn't have been just as enraged if the situation had been reversed. It would have felt like a personal betrayal of epic proportions if I'd learned he'd ever driven drunk. And if he'd killed a loved one while doing it...

"He mentioned something last night about how we shouldn't let Isaac leave – that he was in trouble."

Do you think that's true? I asked.

Nolan nodded. "He's definitely running from something."

I wasn't sure what to say to that. Before I could dwell on it too much, Nolan said, "Maddox asked me to give you a message."

I nodded as I remembered Nolan saying that in his text.

"He said...he said he has your back."

I stiffened at that.

"It means something, doesn't it?" Nolan asked.

I nodded, then typed, *Growing up with our parents was tough. The pressure sometimes got to be too much and I'd have these moments where I'd just want to give up. Not play ball anymore, not go back to school...it got so bad at times that I talked about running away. I just needed a break from it all, you know?*

Nolan nodded as he read my message.

Maddox would always talk me down. But he didn't tell me not to do something. He'd always say he had my back no matter what I decided to do. If I wanted to quit ball, he said he'd fix it with my parents so they were okay with it. Even when I said I wanted to run away, he told me that if I really meant it, he'd come with me. He'd buy the bus tickets, he'd sneak us out of the house, he'd do whatever it took to make it happen. To fix it.

My throat felt tight, but I knew this time, it had nothing to do with my condition.

I don't know why he said it now.

Nolan rubbed my arms, then he was hugging me. "We're going to figure it all out, okay, Dallas? We're going to get Loki back and we're going to get the town off our backs once and for all."

I nodded, but he must have seen something in my face. "And we're going to talk about what's going on in that head of yours every time you look at me. Like you're surprised I'm still here."

I sighed because I should have known better than to think I could hide anything from him. I nodded again.

I have some calls to make about the meeting tonight.

"Okay, I'm going to go feed the animals. What do we do about this?" he asked as he held out the sparkplugs.

I looked at them for a moment, then grabbed them and put them back in the butter dish. I returned the dish to the fridge and stuck it all the way in back where it wasn't visible.

I might have still been pissed at Maddox, but I also knew he was onto something with Isaac and Newt. But if there was any chance at figuring out what it was, we needed them to stick around for a bit.

Nolan smiled, brushed his mouth over mine, told me he loved me and then went upstairs to get dressed.

The small conference room in Pelican Bay's town hall was packed with people when Nolan and I entered. I ignored the hushed whispers that followed us as we made our way down the narrow aisle. We'd purposely waited outside the room until our case had been called, so we wouldn't have to deal with all the stares. But it wouldn't have mattered. There was no reason to suspect the majority of the people were there for any other reason than to watch Pelican Bay's former-golden-boy-turned-freak and the town-reject-turned-famous-and-very-much-vindicated-violinist fight to save a group of animals not one of them gave two shits about. The fact that we were holding hands just caused the audience to titter even louder as we made our way to the small podium in front of a long table with five people sitting on the other side. Sheriff Tulley stood off to one side. Of the town council members, I only recognized Doc Cleary.

I glanced over my shoulder to make sure Isaac and Newt had found a place to stand off to the side of the room. Surprisingly, they'd ended up along the wall near where Nolan's mother was sitting on one of the many folding chairs that took up most of the small space. Nolan and I had told Isaac he didn't need to come, but Newt had actually been the one to take the decision away from his brother. He hadn't thrown a temper tantrum or anything when Isaac had said they'd be staying at the house. He'd merely looked his brother in the eye and said that Loki needed him because he could tell the mean people who'd taken Loki what a nice dog he was. I'd seen a spark of pride go through Isaac as he'd studied his little brother, then he'd nodded and told Newt he was absolutely right – that Loki did need Newt to tell the truth about him.

"The room will come to order," the man in the middle of the table said as he used a small gavel to get everyone's attention. The crowd immediately fell silent. "We're here to discuss the matter of the Lake Hills County Wildlife Rescue and Sanctuary owned and operated by Dallas Kent. We've received a petition to ascertain whether or not this business continues to serve the best interests of our community. Mr.

Kent, do you have something you'd like to say before we open the discussion to the floor?"

I'd already typed my remarks out on my computer at home so I nodded to Nolan so he could read them, but before he could speak, Doc Cleary said, "Just a minute, son." He turned his attention to the head of the committee. "Jeb, if I'm not mistaken, Mr. Kent's business doesn't reside within the city limits of Pelican Bay, so even if what that petition is alleging is true, this committee and the town of Pelican Bay have no jurisdiction."

"Well," the man began, but Doc Cleary held up his hand. "Furthermore, I'm greatly bothered by the fact that Sheriff Tulley has not provided the names of the actual complainant or complainants that inspired this so-called order."

"As I've said, my office is still pulling together that paperwork," Sheriff Tulley interjected.

"Of course you are," Doc Cleary said. "Just like you're supposedly still investigating the attack on Mr. Kent's property. Need I remind you that while this town has no jurisdiction in civil matters, our reciprocity agreement with our sister towns means you work for the residents of all of those communities, including Mr. Kent? I also find it interesting that you didn't think it prudent to recuse yourself from the case when a member of your own family was identified as one of the assailants in the attack on Mr. Kent, Mr. Grainger, and two of the animals that call the center home."

The crowd behind us broke into hushed whispers. Sheriff Tulley's face went red. "How I do my job is none of your concern," he muttered.

"It is when you cover up crimes."

The entire crowd went silent and there was a collective shifting as everyone turned in their chair to see who the voice belonged to.

I didn't need to check, because I knew that voice.

Had known it all my life.

Tears stung my eyes as I realized what was happening.

Maddox had come…and he was having my back.

I felt Nolan's fingers squeeze my hand. He nodded at me and sent me an encouraging smile.

"Lieutenant Kent," the committee head said in surprise. "This is a surprise and an honor."

I forced myself to turn around so I could see my brother. He was standing just inside the doorway. He looked stern and forbidding, but I was surprised to see a line of sweat dotting his brow.

Was he nervous?

Maddox didn't get nervous.

He had nerves of steel.

"Wish I could say the same," Maddox said. Then he reached behind him and opened the door. He gave someone outside a brief nod, then all of a sudden Loki came trotting into the room. People gasped and several people along the aisle pulled back a bit when Loki padded toward me.

"What the hell?" the sheriff shouted, but I only had eyes for my pet.

"Don't even think about it, Sheriff," I heard another voice say. I glanced over my shoulder and saw that the sheriff had his hand on the butt of his gun. The new voice belonged to the sheriff's own deputy who was standing next to my brother.

"What is going on here?" the committee head yelled.

I dropped to my knees and wrapped my arms around Loki. He licked my face, then he was moving to Nolan to greet him.

"I think you want to hear this, Jeb," the deputy said. His eyes shifted to the sheriff. "All of it."

"Fine, come forward," he said with a wave of his hand.

I watched my brother approach, followed by the deputy. Right behind them was Sawyer.

What the hell was happening?

As my brother stepped past me, he patted my shoulder. He sent me a small smile, but I didn't miss how tense he actually was. He was definitely sweating and I could see that he was struggling to regulate his breathing.

"Floor's yours, Lieutenant," Jeb said. Maddox nodded, then called Loki's name. The wolf hybrid trotted right over to him and sat in front of him. Maddox's eyes scanned the room before settling on Newt.

"Newt, do you think you can help me with something?"

All eyes turned to Newt and his brother. Isaac flinched at the scrutiny, but Newt didn't seem to even notice."

"Are you still mad, Mad?" he asked as he eyed my brother.

Several people laughed as Maddox stood stock-still for a moment before his lips pulled into a slight smile. "No, I'm not."

Newt nodded, then turned to his brother. "I gotta go help Loki, 'kay?"

Isaac smiled and ruffled his brother's hair. "'Go get 'em, kiddo."

Despite all the eyes watching him, Newt walked without hesitation to my brother, then proceeded to throw his arms around Loki. A few people in the audience tittered, but otherwise the room was silent.

"Deputy Miller, can you explain why this animal was removed from my brother's property last night?" Maddox asked.

"Sheriff Tulley received a complaint that he bit someone who was walking past your brother's property."

"Do you think Loki bit this person?"

"Yes, I do."

More gasps filtered through the crowd. I felt my stomach drop out at the deputy's words. Nolan's fingers bit into mine.

"Three weeks ago when the man helped Jimmy Cornell and another man break into the center and attack a bear that lives on the property."

"That's a lie," the sheriff snapped. "Deputy Miller, I expect your resignation on my desk in the morning. Now leave this room before I have you arrested."

"Deputy Miller, you will ignore that order," Jeb said. "I think we'd all like to hear this. Do you have proof of what you're claiming?"

"Yes, the suspect confessed this morning. He said he was pressured into filing the complaint and submitting to having pictures of the bite marks on his arm taken."

"Pressured by whom?" Doc Cleary asked, though it was clear he already knew the answer.

"Sheriff Tulley and Jimmy Cornell."

"That's a lie!" Sheriff Tulley shouted again.

"Sheriff, if you interrupt one more time, I'll direct Deputy Miller to arrest you and have you forcibly removed from the room," Jeb warned.

Maddox motioned to Sawyer to step forward. "Can you tell everyone who you are, please?"

"My name is Sawyer Brower. I'm a vet specializing in the care of large animals and wildlife. I treated Gentry, the bear who lives on Dallas's property, after he was shot repeatedly with a BB gun and burned with cattle prods."

Another round of hushed gasps went through the crowd.

"You've been working around Loki, right?"

"I have. For a couple of weeks now."

By this time, Loki was lying on the floor and Newt was playing with his ears.

"Is Loki pure wolf?" my brother asked.

"No, he's a wolf hybrid. That means he's a mix between a wolf and a domesticated dog. You can tell by the shape of his muzzle and his larger build."

Maddox looked at Doc Cleary. "Do you agree, Doc?"

The vet nodded. "I do."

"Sawyer, you've worked around wolves before, right?" Maddox continued.

"I have. I've participated in studies on them in Canada and in several national parks in the Rockies."

"The behavior Loki exhibits, would you say he leans more toward wolf or dog?"

"Dog."

"Is there any way to prove he isn't dangerous?"

Sawyer chuckled. "A Chihuahua can technically be considered dangerous if they aren't raised right. Their bite might not hurt as bad, but they can still cause damage, especially to a small child. In Loki's case, he's attacked someone only under circumstances that any family dog would – that they'd be expected to, actually. He was protecting the members of his pack like many domesticated dogs do. Human, dog, bear – doesn't matter. Loki went after people who were harming his family."

"Wolves have a high prey drive, don't they?" Maddox asked. "They'll pursue things that are smaller or weaker than them and kill them, correct?"

"Correct."

To me, Maddox asked, "Dallas, do you trust Loki? Do you trust him with this boy's life?"

I nodded without hesitation, even as I began to guess what Maddox had planned.

To Isaac he said, "Do you trust me not to let anything happen to your brother?"

The tension in the room grew to astronomical proportions at the question. I could see Isaac hesitating and I knew it was a lot to ask. He'd known us less than twenty-four hours and for whatever reason, he and my brother had gotten off to a rocky start. Isaac finally nodded.

Maddox knelt down and let his fingers settle in Loki's fur as he spoke to Newt. "Newt, can you do me a favor and run as fast as you can to your brother? Loki's going to go with you, okay, so don't be scared."

"I'm not scared," the little boy declared. "Loki likes me."

With that, he got up to run to Isaac. Loki jumped to his feet and darted after Newt, easily overtaking him. There was a collective gasp and someone let out a cry of distress, but everyone fell silent when Newt made it to his brother untouched.

"Come on back, Newt," Maddox called

Loki again ran next to Newt. It wasn't until the pair reached my brother that he pressed his big body up against Newt's expectantly. The little boy patted Loki several times.

Maddox looked over his shoulder at Jeb. "I'd like to ask that my brother be allowed to take his pet home tonight while Deputy Miller works to have the false complaint removed."

"Agreed," Jeb said as he glanced at the other committee members who were all nodding. "Deputy Miller, I trust you'll go through the appropriate channels to discuss your concerns about Sheriff Tulley's conduct?"

"Yes, sir, I will," he said.

"Good luck with that," the sheriff barked. "I've been protecting this community for years."

"You've also been lying to them for years," the deputy retorted. "Like after a certain accident where you forced me to tell everyone I'd forgotten to ask the hospital staff to run blood alcohol tests on Dallas Kent."

The sheriff paled, but the deputy ignored him, then turned his attention to me. "I'm sorry, Dallas. The sheriff told me your father said you were driving that car and that you'd been drinking. But I knew he was lying because I saw the results of the blood alcohol tests myself. I'd just started in the job and didn't want to lose it, so I never said anything."

"What is he talking about?" Doc Cleary asked as he rose to his feet.

Maddox was the one to answer. "Our father asked the sheriff to cover up the fact that our mother was the one who'd been driving that night and that both she and our father were drunk. When he realized our father had lied to him, instead of telling the truth about what really happened that night, Sheriff Tulley covered up his role in the lie by getting rid of the evidence that proved Dallas hadn't been drinking. What really happened the night of the accident was that Dallas tried to stop our parents, but couldn't. He also hadn't had a single drop of alcohol that night. After the car rolled down the ravine, he managed to pull our mother from the car before he lost consciousness. When he woke up, he found out what my father had done, but he never said anything."

Maddox's eyes shifted to me. "Because he wanted to protect our mother, despite the fact that she was gone. That's what he does," he said softly.

"He protects those he loves."

CHAPTER TWENTY-ONE

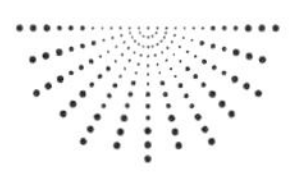

Nolan

Dallas's fingers squeezed mine at his brother's words. I was barely holding it together as every single word spoken finally revealed the truth to the world about what an amazing man I'd fallen in love with and who somehow had come to love me back.

I ignored the whispers of the crowd behind me and turned to look at Dallas. I could see he was fighting back tears. I pushed into his arms as the voices around us grew louder and louder. I tuned out Sheriff Tulley's voice as he began yelling at his deputy, then the council members. The room got louder and louder until poor Newt was forced to cover his ears with his hands.

"It's over, baby," I whispered in Dallas's ear.

He nodded against me, then, not caring who was watching, kissed me softly. We became lost in our own little world until the sound of the gavel pulled us back to reality. Jeb hammered the block of wood in front of him repeatedly as he called out to the room to settle down. People were still talking above him, though, so he kept at it.

That was when I finally noticed Maddox.

He was practically dripping sweat and he'd shut his eyes. His hands were clenched at his sides and his body jumped every time the gavel hit the wooden block. No one else seemed to notice the behavior, but when Dallas tensed next to me, I realized he'd seen it too. He was pushing past me when Isaac suddenly appeared in front of Maddox, stepping over Loki and Newt in the process. His hands went up to grab Maddox's face and I could hear him calling the man's name. Maddox opened his eyes, but he seemed to struggle to focus them on Isaac.

"Dallas," I said, but before either of us could move forward, people began appearing in front of us, blocking our view. I was dimly aware of several of them telling Dallas they were sorry, but my focus was on Isaac and Maddox. The younger man had managed to get ahold of one of Maddox's clenched fists and began pulling him from the room. Loki and Newt quickly followed.

Before Dallas and I could turn to go after them, Jeb shouted again for the room to come to order. Once he added in the threat that he'd clear the room if people didn't comply, everyone shut up, and those that had gotten up scrambled to get back to their seats. Jeb spoke only long enough to announce that the town council's business with Dallas was concluded and no further action would be taken against him or the center. He spouted a blanket apology to Dallas, but like me, I suspected Dallas wasn't really listening, because his eyes were on the door Isaac had led his brother through.

"Dallas."

Dallas and I both turned at Doc Cleary's voice. "Is there anything you want to say, son?"

I knew what Doc Cleary was offering with the question. A chance for Dallas to have his "I told you so" moment. He had free rein to call every single person out in that room for what they'd done to him. He took out his phone and typed something, then handed it to me. I steeled myself for whatever it was he wanted me to say to the now-silent room, but when I saw his words, I smiled.

"I have lots of amazing animals that need to find their forever homes...plus one crabby zebra. Any takers?"

The crowd erupted into laughter. As Dallas threaded his fingers through mine and led me from the room, my eyes connected with my mother's and she sent me a smile and a nod. Warmth spread through me at the expression on her face – one I could only classify as pride.

I held up my hand to my ear to mimic a phone and she smiled wide and nodded.

And in that moment I knew what it was that had made that spark of warmth flare to life inside of me.

My mother was finally starting to hear me.

We never found Maddox that night - only Isaac, Newt, and Loki where they'd been waiting by Dallas's truck for us. Isaac hadn't said much other than to explain that Maddox had left on foot shortly after Isaac had gotten him outside. Sawyer had joined us outside and had mentioned that Maddox had gotten a ride to the meeting with the deputy. Dallas and I hadn't realized it, but Maddox had become friends with Deputy Miller years earlier just before Maddox had left for West Point. When he'd gone to the deputy to ask for his help in getting Loki so he could prove to the community the wolf hybrid wasn't dangerous, the deputy had come clean about the accident and his role in it.

We'd hoped to find Maddox back at the center, but he hadn't been there, either. We'd managed to convince Isaac to spend another night with us, though we hadn't yet told him about his car.

"How are you feeling?" I asked Dallas as I closed the bedroom door behind me. I'd already locked up for the night. Loki had decided to sleep with Newt and Isaac, which hadn't surprised me since the little boy and the big animal were practically attached at the hip at this point.

Dallas was in the midst of changing into his sleep pants, giving me a scrumptious view of his backside. In the week between my father's funeral and Dallas's surgery, I'd gotten to feel just how perfect Dallas's ass was because we'd changed things up when we'd made love one night. Since I'd never topped and Dallas had never bottomed, it had been awkward and nerve-racking at first, but once I'd been buried deep inside his body, none of that had mattered.

It had been perfect.

And while I would always likely crave to be filled just a little bit more, I knew it was something we'd definitely do again.

Dallas nodded, then pointed to his throat and gave me a thumbs up. I knew he probably wasn't feeling a hundred percent yet, but the fact that he hadn't taken a pain pill and still seemed relatively comfortable was a good sign.

I went to him and wrapped my arms around him. His strong arms surrounded me, making me feel safe and wanted. But it was the little kisses he pressed against my temple, my cheek, my jaw, that had me feeling so grateful for the twist of fate that had brought us back together.

Dallas kissed me, but before he deepened the kiss, I pulled back and said, "We need to talk about something."

His eyes immediately filled with concern, but he managed a nod. I knew exactly what he was worried about, but I couldn't blame him. I'd suspected as soon as my name had been cleared in the theft of the Stradivarius what would go through his head. There just hadn't been time to deal with it.

I took his hand and led him to the bed. I had him sit on the edge of the bed, but instead of sitting next to him, I crawled onto his lap so I was straddling him. I twined my arms around his neck. He motioned toward his phone on the nightstand.

"You don't need it yet," I said. "Because you're going to listen while I talk, because I want you to really hear me, okay?"

He sighed and nodded.

"I'm not leaving you."

I didn't expect the words to miraculously ease his worry because I knew that wasn't the crux of the argument.

"Look at the words on the wall behind me, Dallas. Really look at them."

His eyes shifted to where we'd written on the wall several weeks earlier when we'd told each other that we loved each other for the first time. Dallas had painted over his words, but he'd left mine.

"Always and forever doesn't mean until a good job offer comes along or you get your voice back and then lose it again or the shit from our pasts tries to rear its ugly head. It means nothing will ever change how I feel about you. Even if you told me you didn't want me anymore, it wouldn't change how much I love you. So, unless you tell me to go-"

He didn't even let me finish my sentence before he was shaking his head. He kissed me hard, then shook his head some more.

"Nvr," he suddenly whispered, his voice so low I barely heard it.

But it was there.

And it was fucking beautiful.

"Ov you Non."

I let out a watery cry and covered my mouth with my hand. I dropped my head to his shoulder and cried. He kept repeating that he loved me in the same broken whisper until I gently covered his mouth with my hand. "Stop, the doctor said you weren't supposed to try talking for two more weeks." I brushed my mouth over his. "Thank you. That was so beautiful, Dallas."

He kissed me again, then motioned to his phone. I started to get up so I could get it for him, but instead of letting me go, he wrapped his arm around me and lifted me so he could grab it himself. I chuckled when he settled me back on his lap.

Don't want you to give up your music, Nolan.

"I won't. I was so focused on music getting me out of this town that I forgot why I fell in love with it in the first place. But playing it for you, for Gentry, it just…it's better than any performance I've ever given and worth more than any paycheck I've ever earned."

Dallas began typing again and I quickly covered his phone with my hand. "But I did want to talk to you about something."

He lowered the phone and nodded. "The orchestra in London travels all over Europe every spring doing performances. This year they want to do something new. They want to showcase a couple of performers who would do solo performances in each city. They've asked me to be one of the performers."

I expected him to tense up, but he smiled broadly and quickly nodded.

"Wait," I said with a laugh. "I'm not finished."

His chest rumbled and there was the tiniest bit of sound to accompany his laugh.

"I was wondering if you might consider coming with me."

He did tense a little then, and I knew why, so I quickly said, "I know it would be hard for you to leave the center, but I have some thoughts on that."

He nodded for me to continue.

"While you were checking on Gentry tonight, I asked Sawyer if there was any chance he'd be interested in helping out, since he doesn't plan on opening up his practice until next summer. I also thought we could see if Isaac was interested in working here for a while. If not, we can hire a couple of really good people. You work too hard as it is, Dallas-"

It was his turn to cover my mouth with his hand as he typed one-handed on his phone.

Yes.

The simple word had my heart surging with joy. "That's it?" I asked. "Just like that?"

I never left Pelican Bay because there was no place to go. But my place is with you now, Nolan. Where you go, I go - whether it's for a few weeks or for the rest of our lives.

"Really?"

"Illy."

"Love you so much, Dallas," I whispered, then I kissed him. His phone hit the floor right before his hands came up to cover my back, then he was rolling me onto the bed beneath him. Within minutes, he had us both naked and he was reaching for the lube. He grabbed a condom too and held it up for me, but I shook my head. Dallas had gotten tested as part of his pre-operative bloodwork and I'd taken advantage of the walk-in clinic at the hospital to do the same. And while we hadn't actually talked about when we'd lose the condoms, I knew it was something we were both ready for.

Dallas tossed the condom away and then he began working me over until I was writhing beneath him. He kissed me as he began pushing into me, likely to swallow my cries of pleasure since we had houseguests. He made love to me slowly, driving me to the edge over and over again before backing off. By the time he began fucking me past the point of no return, I could barely breathe. Neither could Dallas, but luckily for a whole other reason than a problem with his throat. I clung to Dallas as I came, and moments later when his release scorched my insides, he whispered his love in my ear and I didn't admonish him for it.

Because I would never get tired of him saying the words to me, whether he did it with his voice or his body.

I'd hear him either way.

Always.

CHAPTER TWENTY-TWO

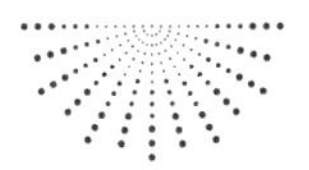

Dallas

It took me two days to figure out where Maddox had gone and I'd cursed myself for my stupidity more than once that it had taken me that long to begin with.

The drive to the house by the lake was hard for me, since I hadn't been up the winding road even once after my father had died.

There'd been no need to return to the house I'd shared with my parents and my brother because Maddox had inherited it. I'd just assumed he'd sold it, but when my family's former neighbor, Mr. Zimmer, had stopped by the center in search of a new cat to keep his other cat company, he'd let it slip that he'd seen Maddox at the house a few times in the past couple of weeks.

In the two days since Maddox had done what he'd promised and fixed everything, I'd been inundated with visitors at the center. Most had been there merely to gawk or extend their apologies for having assumed the worst about me. Others had taken me up on my comment about having many animals in search of their forever homes. After years of solitude, I was, admittedly, not handling the sudden change well. Fortunately, Nolan had known what it would do to me and he'd often rescued me from visitors by slipping in the fact that I was still recovering from surgery and needed to rest. He'd also managed to talk Isaac into helping deal with all the people who were interested in adopting a new pet. Nolan had played it smart and framed the request so that it seemed less about us helping Isaac and more about him helping us.

Which he had been.

He'd balked at the idea of being paid to help out, especially since he and Newt were still staying in the house, but Nolan had managed to convince Isaac that he'd be earning every penny.

Much like I'd said to Nolan so long ago.

Newt, for his part, had been put to work too. His job was to help anyone who was interested in adopting a kitten, since he'd become as obsessed with them as he was with Loki. He'd named all the kittens and would tell anyone who would listen all about each kitten, from what toys they liked to play with to which ones were the best cuddlers.

Nolan and I had talked to Sawyer about whether or not he was interested in starting at the center as a paid employee now, versus waiting until the spring when Nolan and I went to Europe. He'd accepted the offer with the caveat that he had obligations as the on-call vet for the area, which I'd readily agreed to. I'd also asked him if he'd become the center's regular vet, even after he opened up his own practice. He'd been more than happy to accept that offer as well.

Having a little extra help meant Nolan and I weren't killing ourselves trying to do it all. It also meant I could potentially take in more animals. I had the space and money to build more habitats; there'd just never been enough of me to go around when I'd been doing it on my own.

We'd also gotten word from Deputy Miller this morning that Sheriff Tulley had been fired and that he was facing obstruction charges. Jimmy and his two buddies had already been arrested for the attack on Gentry.

As I made my way up the small bluff, I slowed when I got to the curve where my mother had missed the turn and we'd gone over the embankment. I couldn't see down into the ravine where the car had ultimately landed, but I didn't need to. It would be etched into my brain forever. Despite what I'd told Nolan about not carrying anger around, it was admittedly more difficult to find the forgiveness for my father a second time around. I could only figure that he hadn't been in his right mind when he'd told Maddox I'd insisted on driving that night *and* that I'd refused to give him the keys when he'd asked for them. I knew I'd get to the point that I'd be able to let go of the anger, but it would definitely take some time.

It took just a few more minutes to reach the old Victorian mansion overlooking the water. It was incredibly run-down and I suspected once the snow melted, it would reveal that the surrounding land that had once been acres of pristinely landscaped grass and gardens was an overgrown mess. I didn't see any cars in the wrap-around driveway, but that didn't mean anything since Sawyer had mentioned that he'd never actually seen Maddox drive to and from the center.

There was no answer when I knocked on the door, but when I tested the knob and found it unlocked, I didn't hesitate to enter.

The house was freezing cold, so it wasn't a shock to find Maddox sitting in front of a roaring fireplace in what had once been the den. He'd moved the cloth-draped furniture aside and rolled a sleeping bag out on the floor. My brother sat unmoving in the single armchair in front of the fireplace, a bottle of liquor at his feet.

"Took you long enough to figure it out, little brother," Maddox murmured.

I walked around the chair so I was facing Maddox. He looked tired, but not drunk.

I held out my phone to him to show him the message I'd typed for him even before I'd left my house.

"Don't thank me," he said as he leaned back in the chair. "All I did was tell the truth. It was long overdue."

I typed, *What do you want from me, Maddox?*

"I want you to have the life you should have had ten years ago. I want to go back to that moment and do what I should have done."

What should you have done?

"Told you how fucking glad I was that I hadn't lost you too."

I hated how lackluster his voice sounded. Maddox had always been the more intense of the two of us, but this was different.

"Did the kid and his brother leave?"

At twenty years old, Isaac wasn't exactly a kid, but to my thirty-two-year-old brother, I supposed he did seem quite young.

No, he's working at the center for a little while. Nice trick with his car.

Maddox waved his hand impatiently. "Little fool doesn't know what's good for him," he growled. It was the first bit of life I'd actually seen in him.

What happened to you the night of the meeting, Maddox?

"I would have thought it would be obvious to you."

I paused before typing.

PTSD?

Maddox downed the rest of the alcohol in his glass.

"Textbook case," he said as he stared into the fire. "Roadside bomb in Mosul. Overturned Humvee, heavy fire, six of my men killed instantly. Three more didn't last long enough to be evac'd. One guy got out besides me. I'm fucked up in the head, he's got no legs. Purple Heart medals for both of us. Textbook," he muttered.

Is that why you don't drive?

He looked at me in surprise. His first real reaction besides his comment about Isaac.

"How did you know?"

Just a guess, I said, not wanting to get into the details. *What are your plans?*

When he didn't answer, I carefully lowered myself to the floor. My hip hadn't been hurting as much as it had earlier in the winter. It was another reason that taking it easier around the center and splitting the workload with more people would be a good thing.

I'd like to tell you about my plans. But I want to start by telling you something that someone I love very much and who I once hurt very badly told me not long ago.

Maddox read the message and nodded. I felt his eyes on me as I typed.

We're not the same people we were back then, Maddox. And I believe that if you could change things, you would. I would, too. I would have told you the truth then and there and I would have made sure you believed me instead of letting you walk away. Because you were the most important person in my life. But I chose to let you believe a lie because inside I was still that little kid who wanted to please his parents. It was a lot easier to live that lie than accept the truth. My hope is that you don't do what I did and start to believe that you deserved what happened to you. My hope is that you don't relive that day and wonder if there was something you could have or should have done differently. My hope is that you will accept that I forgive you for the things you said and did back then. My hope is that we can one day be brothers again. My hope is that you forgive yourself because I really want back the person who's always had my back.

As Maddox began reading my message, he nodded a few times. But then his mouth fell and I saw him swallow hard. At one point, he reached up to wipe at his eyes, but when he handed back the phone, he didn't say anything. Disappointment flared, but just as I started to get to my feet, he reached out to grab my arm. His voice was heavy when he said, "You said you wanted to tell me about your plans."

Relief went through me and I settled back on the floor. I smiled to myself as I typed an almost identical message to one I'd typed just six short weeks ago.

A message that had changed my life forever.

In the best way.

Do you need a job?

EPILOGUE

Nolan

Six months later

Exhilaration swept through me as I cleared the last note and the theater broke out into applause. The audience quickly climbed to their feet as several people called out "Bravo!" and "Encore!"

My heart was racing as I bowed to each section of the audience. I tried to spy Dallas through the crowd, but there were too many moving bodies to manage it. I caught a glimpse of my mother in the balcony, but no Dallas. It wasn't until a good two minutes later as everyone sat back down that I could finally see that Dallas wasn't sitting next to my mother. My mother sent me a small wave and even from where I was standing, I could see she was beaming. I blew her a kiss and saw her wipe at her eyes.

I still couldn't get over the fact that she was here.

Not because I didn't think she wanted to be, but because she'd made such a fuss about not attending any more of my performances if she couldn't pay for the trip herself. And since her knitting and part-time work at the library were barely covering her regular bills, I'd accepted that the only performance she'd see of mine this year was the first one I'd given in London six weeks earlier.

She'd cried when I'd asked her if she'd wanted to come to that one. Then, like this last time, she'd fought with me about my insistence that Dallas and I would pay for the trip for her. Dallas had been the one to talk her into letting us treat her by turning up the Dallas Kent charm to full wattage. But she'd been a goner when he'd laid the Dallas Kent smile on her.

I still had no clue how she'd managed this trip with her limited means, but I didn't care. She'd made it and that was what mattered.

My relationship with her had steadily improved over the last six months. We'd taken it really slow by starting with a couple of phone calls here and there. Our first big test had come at Thanksgiving time and we'd both passed with flying colors. My mother had, not surprisingly, been missing my father, but cooking for so many people had been a good distraction. Christmas had been a quieter affair, and Dallas and I had ended up inviting her to come to our house.

Our house.

I wasn't even sure when I'd officially moved in with Dallas. It had just happened after my father's funeral. I hadn't even noticed until my mother had stopped by one day with the boxes she'd been storing at the house. She'd decided to put the house up for sale shortly after Christmas so she could move into a senior living community. When she'd brought me the boxes, I'd stupidly asked her what I was supposed to do with them. She'd patted me on the cheek and said, "You've got that great big house, Nolan. I'm sure you can find some room in it somewhere." When Dallas had appeared a few minutes later, I'd still been standing in the driveway, boxes in hand, staring in the direction my mother had driven off in. When I'd asked Dallas if we were living together, he'd merely chuckled, taken one of the boxes from me, and dropped a kiss on my nose.

And that had been that.

"A big thank you to Mr. Nolan Grainger for that incredible performance of Paganini's *Caprice No. 4 in C minor"* the conductor said into a microphone as he walked on stage. The audience began applauding again, so I quickly did another round of bowing and then nodded my thanks to the audience, then the conductor. Just as I was about to walk past the man, he grabbed my arm.

"For those of you who've been following Mr. Grainger's story, you'll know how fortunate we are that he decided to continue to share his gift with us. I'm extremely pleased that he let the London Symphony Orchestra be a part of his return to our little world. But I'm even more pleased that we have the opportunity to be a small part of his next journey."

I glanced at the man in confusion, since I had no clue what he was talking about. I looked up in the balcony to see if Dallas had returned, but his seat was still empty. Worry went through me. What if he wasn't feeling well? He'd completely recovered from the surgery six months earlier, but what if something else was troubling him?

I didn't even notice the audience had stopped applauding until I heard a few hushed whispers drift up onto the stage. I saw that most everyone was looking to my right, so I glanced that way and completely froze at the sight of Dallas walking across the stage. The conductor moved aside as Dallas reached me. I shook my head as I looked from him to the audience. He looked nervous.

I was completely clueless.

"Dallas, what...what?" was all I managed to get out.

"Hi, baby," he said. His speech had improved dramatically over the past several months, especially since he'd been working so hard with his speech therapist. But to the average person, it still sounded like a harsh whisper and I knew it still tended to embarrass him.

"Hi," I croaked as he leaned in to kiss my cheek.

He stepped back, only to reach for the conductor's microphone, which the man promptly handed over.

What?

"Nolan, I have something I want to ask you."

As soon as he said the words, I began to cry. I nearly dropped my violin – the violin Dallas had given me – but the conductor thankfully grabbed it and my bow before stepping away again.

"Yes," I said, and the audience laughed. Dallas did too. I clapped my hand over my mouth. I lifted it long enough to say, "Sorry."

Dallas took my hand and pulled it to his lips for a kiss. The audience was dead silent as he began speaking. "Nolan, the last few times I got my voice back, I didn't care if I lost it again because no one was listening anyway. There was no one to hear me. Not until the cute, skinny boy who played a mean violin and that I couldn't keep my eyes off of returned to me as a beautiful, kind-hearted man who gave more than he was given. Who loved more than he was loved. Who listened more than he spoke. As much as I love being able to speak to you, I don't fear the day when my voice may once again start to fade. Because I know you'll hear me, Nolan. I know you'll hear me no matter what. Just like I will always hear you and I will always love you. Always and forever. I know you said yes already, but I need to hear it again. Will you marry me, Nolan?"

I had no clue how I managed it, but I somehow got the word "yes" out a second time, though it probably sounded like a frog croaking more than anything else. Then I was in his arms, crying like a baby as he whispered in my ear that he loved me.

"Love you," I said with a nod as he gently pushed me back. He wiped at my tears and then reached into his pocket. At some point the audience had burst into applause, but I hadn't even heard it because I'd been so focused on Dallas. My hands were shaking like crazy as he slipped a beautiful white gold ring on my finger, then he was pulling me into his arms again. I managed a glance at my mother who was wiping at her face with a handkerchief. And I knew in that moment that Dallas had brought her to this final performance so she could share this moment with us.

That knowledge brought a fresh round of happy tears. He held me tight as he whispered, "Let's go home, Nolan."

I nodded because for the first time in the history of ever, I, Nolan Grainger, was actually looking forward to going home.

The End

ABOUT THE AUTHOR

Dear Reader,

I hope you enjoyed the start of what I hope will be an intensely emotional new series. And don't worry, Dallas and Nolan will be back in Maddox's story as he tries to resist the enigma that is Isaac.

As an independent author, I am always grateful for feedback so if you have the time and desire, please leave a review, good or bad, so I can continue to find out what my readers like and don't like. You can also send me feedback via email at sloane@sloanekennedy.com

Join my Facebook Fan Group: Sloane's Secret Sinners

Connect with me:

www.sloanekennedy.com
sloane@sloanekennedy.com

ALSO BY SLOANE KENNEDY

(Note: Not all titles will be available on all retail sites)

The Escort Series

Gabriel's Rule (M/F)

Shane's Fall (M/F)

Logan's Need (M/M)

Barretti Security Series

Loving Vin (M/F)

Redeeming Rafe (M/M)

Saving Ren (M/M/M)

Freeing Zane (M/M)

Finding Series

Finding Home (M/M/M)

Finding Trust (M/M)

Finding Peace (M/M)

Finding Forgiveness (M/M)

Finding Hope (M/M/M)

The Protectors

Absolution (M/M/M)

Salvation (M/M)

Retribution (M/M)

Forsaken (M/M)

Vengeance (M/M/M)

A Protectors Family Christmas

Atonement (M/M)

Revelation (M/M)

Redemption (M/M)

Defiance (M/M)

Non-Series

Letting Go (M/F)

Printed in Germany
by Amazon Distribution
GmbH, Leipzig